T0114830

Praise for Terry Pratchett and
A BLINK OF THE SCREEN

"In the history of comic fantasy, Mr. Pratchett has no equals for invention or for range." —*The Wall Street Journal*

"Clever . . . insightful. . . . [Pratchett's] wry wit is as good as gold." —*The Boston Globe*

"One of the giants in the world of fantasy literature." —*New York Daily News*

"You can't call what Pratchett does satire—it's far too good-natured for that—but he has a satirist's instinct for the absurd and a cartoonist's eye for the telling detail." —*The Daily Telegraph* (London)

"A short story collection covering the entire career of one of our most prolific, and beloved, fantasy writers. . . . One of the main draws of [*A Blink of the Screen*] for serious fans, or aspiring writers, will be the chance to trace the evolution of Pratchett's craft—but there's plenty here for readers who have never heard of him to enjoy." —*Kirkus Reviews*

Terry Pratchett

A Blink of the Screen

Terry Pratchett is the acclaimed creator of the globally best-selling Discworld series, the first of which, *The Color of Magic*, was published in 1983. In all, he is the author of more than seventy books. His novels have been widely adapted for stage and screen, and he was awarded multiple prizes over the course of his career, including the Carnegie Medal, as well as a knighthood for services to literature. Worldwide sales of his books now stand at more than 85 million (but who's counting?), and they have been published in thirty-eight languages. He died in 2015.

www.terrypratchettbooks.com

A BLINK OF
THE SCREEN

BOOKS BY TERRY PRATCHETT

The Discworld® Series

Other Books About Discworld

TURTLE RECALL: THE NEW
DISCWORLD COMPANION . . . SO FAR
(with Stephen Briggs)

NANNY OGG'S COOKBOOK
(with Stephen Briggs, Tina
Hannan, and Paul Kidby)

THE PRATCHETT PORTFOLIO
(with Paul Kidby)

THE DISCWORLD ALMANAK
(with Bernard Pearson)

THE UNSEEN UNIVERSITY
CUT-OUT BOOK
(with Alan Batley and Bernard Pearson)

WHERE'S MY COW?
(illustrated by Melvyn Grant)

THE ART OF DISCWORLD
(with Paul Kidby)

THE WIT AND WISDOM OF
DISCWORLD
(compiled by Stephen Briggs)

THE FOLKLORE OF DISCWORLD
(with Jacqueline Simpson)

THE WORLD OF POO
(with the Discworld Emporium)

THE COMPLEAT ANKH-MORPORK

THE STREETS OF ANKH-MORPORK
(with Stephen Briggs, painted
by Stephen Player)

THE DISCWORLD MAPP
(with Stephen Briggs, painted
by Stephen Player)

A TOURIST GUIDE TO LANCRE—
A DISCWORLD MAPP
(with Stephen Briggs,
illustrated by Paul Kidby)

DEATH'S DOMAIN
(with Paul Kidby)

MRS. BRADSHAW'S HANDBOOK
(with the Discworld Emporium)

Shorter Writing

A BLINK OF THE SCREEN

A SLIP OF THE KEYBOARD

Non-Discworld Books

THE DARK SIDE OF THE SUN

STRATA

THE UNADULTERATED CAT
(illustrated by Gray Jolliffe)

GOOD OMENS (with Neil Gaiman)

THE LONG EARTH
(with Stephen Baxter)

THE LONG WAR (with Stephen Baxter)

THE LONG MARS (with Stephen Baxter)

Non-Discworld Novels for Younger Readers

THE CARPET PEOPLE

TRUCKERS

DIGGERS

WINGS

ONLY YOU CAN SAVE MANKIND

JOHNNY AND THE DEAD

JOHNNY AND THE BOMB

NATION

DODGER

DRAGONS AT CRUMBLING CASTLE

A BLINK OF THE SCREEN

Collected Shorter Fiction

Terry Pratchett

Foreword by A. S. Byatt

ANCHOR BOOKS
A Division of Penguin Random House LLC
New York

FIRST ANCHOR BOOKS EDITION, FEBRUARY 2016

The Library of Congress has cataloged the Doubleday edition as follows:
Pratchett, Terry.
[Short stories. Selections]
A blink of the screen : collected shorter fiction / Terry Pratchett ;
foreword by A. S. Byatt.—First United States edition.
pages cm
I. Title.
PR6066.R34 A6 2015   823'.914—dc23   2014034843

Anchor Books Trade Paperback ISBN: 978-0-8041-6921-9
eBook ISBN: 978-0-385-53831-2

Book design by Michael Collica

www.anchorbooks.com

147429898

My thanks to my old friend and agent Colin Smythe, who spent a lot of time sieving through a lot of dusty old newspapers to find my tracks. Amazingly, he really likes doing this kind of thing . . .

Contents

Contents

Discworld Shorter Writings

Appendix

Foreword by A. S. Byatt

I remember buying my first Pratchett—it was *Men at Arms*—in a bookshop in Sloane Square. I badly needed to be psychologically elsewhere and the bright heap of Discworld novels looked like a possible retreat. I turned them over. At first glance Josh Kirby's covers with pink and bosomy cartoon women as well as energetic dragons did not seem to be my kind of thing. I think what persuaded me was the word *Ankh-Morpork*. Anyone who could think that up was a real writer. And a discworld had been part of my childhood—there was an illustration in the book of Norse myths I had, of an Indian myth of a world balanced on four elephants on a giant turtle surrounded by a snake.

I took the book home, read it without stopping, and was hooked. I bought all the books and read them in order. Every summer, whilst thinking out my writing, I read them again. There is always a joke I hadn't quite got. There is always the quite extraordinary narrative pull of a great storyteller. Later I came to appreciate Josh Kirby's art too. His creatures have a gleeful wild energy and intricacy—both brash and sophisticated—which is exactly right for these tales.

Terry Pratchett says his readers are people who work with computers. But my literary friends are often addicted as I am—I once had a very polite tug-of-war over a new book (I think it was *Thief of Time*) with my scholarly and brilliant editor in a bookshop where I was giving a reading. Last week I had a good talk with a philosopher at a high table about imaginary worlds in general and Pratchett in particular. Also, people who don't read, read Pratchett. Boys of twelve who hate books. I hope he is never taught in schools—his biography on the back of the books used once to claim that "some people had accused him of literature," and of course he is literature, but best enjoyed in solitude and retreat.

J. R. R. Tolkien used the term "secondary worlds" to describe fictive, invented worlds with their own creatures, geography, history, people. Human beings have always needed the existence of the other, the unreal—imaginary people and things that are other than ourselves—from fairy tales to myths to urban legends. A maker of secondary worlds needs great resources of inventiveness—both on the large scale and in the fine detail. Pratchett's world is wonderful because he has the sheer energy of the great storyteller: you think you know all it is possible to know about a dragon, or a policeman, or a plot or a landscape, and he tells you more, a lot more than you had any right to expect, and this is exhilarating.

From book to book he gets better and his world gets more intricate. He gets more and more attached to his own characters, who become more complicated—consider the way in which Captain Vimes grows from being a drunk in charge of a dysfunctional Night Watch to a commander who can arrest two armies for a breach of the peace. He finds it hard to go on disliking characters. He can invent irritating minor forms of life: an imp that operates a Gooseberry—or Disorganizer—belonging to Vimes, which is redeemed by the discovery that it can do the office accounts; an accountant called A. E. Pessimal, sent to inspect the Watchmen, who turns out to be a hero. (Wikipedia constantly illuminates Pratchett. I didn't know that the word *pessimal* means "bad to a maximal extent" or "most wanting in quality or value.") But he can do real evil too: take Mr. Pin, the villain in *The Truth*, or the Chief Quisitor, Vorbis, in *Small Gods*—both with the ferocious single-mindedness, true cruelty, and narrow vision which can't change.

As Tolkien says, secondary worlds must be coherent. There is a risk of the creator being romantic, or being seen to have designs—didactic or sentimental—on the reader. I reread Tolkien for the landscape and the persistent sense of danger. I have problems with stories of real children who find themselves in secondary worlds—rather as though their reading had engulfed them. J. K. Rowling is a brilliant inventor of details of magic, but her world has its origin in a boarding school, a place to which I do not want to return. I never enjoyed C. S. Lewis, because I felt he was morally manipulating me as well as his characters. Philip Pullman writes beautifully and dramatically but he is writing against Lewis, and again runs the risk of becoming didactic and controlling. Pratchett, despite the slapstick, the terrible jokes, and the very clever complicated jokes, is somehow wise and grown-up. As a reader I trust him.

I was once asked by a television interviewer, "Isn't all this simply really about us?" and I indignantly replied, "No," because I needed my secondary world to be other, separate, and coherent. But he is of course writing about us. He is good at policemen, businessmen, fraudsters, murderers, banks and shares, and at music with rocks in it besides, as well as at goblins, witches, dragons, trolls, and dwarfs. And of course, computers. But he writes neither satire nor allegory. What gets into his world is *in* his world, with its own energy and logic.

The shorter stories collected in *A Blink of the Screen* often consist of incursions from the secondary world into our world. A fantasy writer kills off his barbarian hero only to find him on his doorstep, come to "meet his maker." Death dances in a disco. The first story, "The Hades Business," was written when Pratchett was thirteen. It concerns the irruption of the Devil into an advertiser's flat. Pratchett is apologetic about it but it has a gleeful pace and a very satisfactory ending. All his stories have satisfactory endings. I particularly like the one based on a real incident in 1973 when a lorry overturned in Hollywood let out some crates of chickens, who settled in a shrubbed verge. I like the weird one in which desperate travelers are trapped inside the world of Victorian Christmas cards, with snow covered with "tiny tinselly shards," monstrous robins, and a "dreadful oblong slot." There are tales about computers, including one, written in 1990, which is told by "an amiable repairman, not very bright but good with machines" who works on machines inside which people create their own reality. (Again with a good ending.)

There is also a collection of stories from the Discworld—including a long and wicked one about Granny Weatherwax and a hilarious version of the national anthem of Ankh-Morpork.

And there is a grim little poem about how

They don't teach you the facts of death,
Your mum and dad. They give you pets.

Pratchett comments, "I tried to write this as though I was thirteen years old, with that earnest brand of serious amateurishness. This is possibly not a long way from how I write at the best of times . . ." I can see what he means. What his teacher understood when he was thirteen, and what we all, thirteen-year-olds, nerds and geeks, reading writers and university teachers, recognize with glee is that he is a born writer, a maker, inimitable.

Non-Discworld

Shorter Writings

The Hades Business

Science Fantasy magazine, ed. John Carnell, no. 60, vol. 20, August 1963. An earlier version was published in the *Technical Cygnet,* the High Wycombe Technical High School magazine.

Argh, argh, argh . . . if I put my fingers in my ears and go "lalalala" loudly I won't hear you read this story.

It's juvenile. Mind you, so was I, being thirteen at the time. It's the first thing I ever wrote that got published. In fact it's the first thing I ever wrote with the feeling that I was writing a real story.

It began as a piece of homework. The English teacher gave me twenty marks out of twenty for it, and put it in the school magazine. The kids liked it. I was a writer.

And this was a big deal, because I hadn't really been anything up until then. I was good at English. At everything else I was middling, one of those kids that don't catch the teacher's eye and are very glad of it. I was even bad at sports, except for the one wonderful term when they let us play hockey, when I was bad and very dangerous.

But the other kids had liked it. I'd sniffed blood.

There were three, yes, three professional sf and fantasy magazines published in the UK in those days. Unbelievable, but true. I persuaded my aunt, who had a typewriter, to type it out for me, and I sent it to John Carnell, who edited all three. The nerve of the kid.

He accepted it.

Oh boy.

The £14 he paid was enough to buy a secondhand Imperial 58 typewriter from my typing teacher (my mother had decided that I ought to be able to do my own typing, what with being a writer and everything) and, as I write, it seems to me that it was a very good machine for fourteen quid and I just wonder if Mum and Dad didn't make up the difference on the quiet.

Fortunately, before I could do too much damage with the thing, study and exams swept me up and threw me out into a job on the local paper, where I learned to write properly or, at least, journalistically.

I've reread the story and my fingers have itched to strip it down, give it some pacing, scramble those clichés, and, in short, rewrite it from the bottom up. But that would be silly, so I'm going to grit my teeth instead.

Go ahead, read.

I can't hear you! Lalalalalalala!

Crucible opened his front door and stood rooted to the doormat.

Imagine the interior of a storm cloud. Sprinkle liberally with ash and garnish with sulphur to taste. You now have a rough idea as to what Crucible's front hall resembled.

The smoke was coming from under the study door. Dimly remembering a film he had once seen, Crucible clapped a handkerchief to his nose and staggered to the kitchen. One bucket of water later, he returned. The door would not budge. The phone was in the study, so as to be handy in an emergency. Putting down the pail, Crucible applied his shoulder to the door, which remained closed. He retreated to the opposite wall of the hall, his eyes streaming. Gritting his teeth, he charged.

The door opened of its own accord. Crucible described a graceful arc across the room, ending in the fireplace, then everything went black, literally and figuratively, and he knew no more.

A herd of elephants were doing the square dance, in clogs, on Crucible's head. He could see a hazy figure kneeling over him.

"Here, drink this."

Ah, health-giving joy-juice! Ah, invigorating stagger-soup! Those elephants, having changed into slippers, were now dancing a sedate waltz: the whiskey was having the desired effect. Crucible opened his eyes again and regarded the visitor.

"Who the devil are you?"

"That's right!"

Crucible's head hit the grate with a hollow clang!

The Devil picked him up and sat him in an armchair. Crucible opened one eye.

The Devil was wearing a sober black suit, with a red carnation in the buttonhole. His thin waxed moustachios, combined with the minute beard, gave him a dignified air. A cloak and collapsible top hat were on the table.

Crucible had known it would happen. After ten years of prising cash from the unsuspecting businessman, one was bound to be caught by Nemesis. He rose to his feet, brushing the soot from his clothes.

"Shall we be going?" he asked mournfully.

"Going? Where to?"

"The Other Place, I suppose."

"The Other Pl—? Oh, you mean home! Good Heav— oops! pardon me—Hell! no! No one's come Down There for nearly two thousand years. Can't think why. No, I have come to you because I need some help Down There; the Hell business is just not paying—no more lost souls. Only chap that's come Down There for the last two thousand years was a raving nit called Dante; went away with quite the wrong impression. You ought to have heard what he said about me!"

"I did read something about it somewhere."

"Indeed? Bad publicity for me, that. That's where you come in."

"Oh?" Crucible pricked up his ears.

"Yes, I want you to advertise Hell. Clumsy! You've spilt your drink all over the carpet."

"W-why me?" croaked Crucible.

"You are the owner of the Square Deal Advertising Company, are you not? We want you to make the public conscious, Hell-wise. Not for eternal damnation, of course. Just day trips, etcetera, Grand Tour of Hell, and all that."

"And if I refuse?"

"What would you say to ten thousand pounds?"

"Good-bye."

"Twenty thousand?"

"Hmm. Aren't I supposed to give you some tasks; sand ropes and all that?"

The Devil looked angry.

"Forty thousand and that's my last offer. Besides"—the Devil pressed the tips of his fingers together and smiled at the ceiling—"there are some rather incriminating facts about the Payne-Smith Products case, which we could make public?"

"Now you're speaking my language. Forty thousand pounds and hush about the P and S case?"

"Yes."

"Done."

"I'm so glad you see it my way," said the Devil. Crucible seated himself behind his mahogany desk and took out a pad. He indicated a polished silver box.

"Cigarette?"

"Thanks."

Crucible took a cigarette himself and felt for his lighter. Suddenly, a thought struck him.

"How do I know you are Old Nick?"

The Devil shuddered. "Please! Nicholas Lucifer to you. Well, I know about the P and S case, don't I?"

Crucible's eyes gleamed.

"You may be some smart-aleck Dick. Convince me. Go on, convince me!"

"Okay, you asked for it. By the way, that gun in your left-hand pocket would be useless against me." The Devil leaned nonchalantly, extending a finger towards Crucible.

"See? You're a phoney, a low do—"

Crack!

A bolt of lightning shot across the room. The end of Crucible's cigarette glowed.

"I—I—I'm convinced!"

"So glad."

Crucible became his old self.

"Let's get down to business. I take it you want Hell to be exploited in every possible way?"

"Yes."

"Well, I'm afraid I can't do much until I have seen the place—from the living point of view, you understand."

"Quite. Well, I could take you back with me, but that might be a hair-raising experience for you. Tell you what, if you wait at the corner of this street, at—shall we say, eight o'clock this evening?—I could pick you up and we could walk there. Okay?"

"Right."

"I'll be seeing you, then. Cheerio!"

Poomf!

He was gone. The room was again filled with sulphurous smoke. Crucible opened the windows and then closed them again. If some busybody saw the smoke, he would have a hard time explaining to the Fire Brigade just why there was no fire. He strolled into the kitchen and sat down thoughtfully; he wished he had read more fantasy.

In wishing the Devil would mind his own business, Crucible was thinking along the same lines as certain other beings. Where they differed was the reason. Crucible opened the fridge and took out a can of beer.

Having someone running around loose, who knows about things one would prefer to keep to oneself, is dangerous. Crucible's love of money warred with his love of freedom. He wanted that forty thousand pounds, but he did not want Lucifer running around loose.

Suddenly, the perfect solution struck him. Of course! Why not! He grabbed his hat, and hurried out to the local church.

Crucible stood in the pouring rain at the corner of the street. A small stream of water was coursing down his back and flooding his suedes. He looked at his watch. One minute to eight o'clock. He shivered.

"Psst!"

Crucible looked round.

"Down here."

He saw that a manhole in the middle of the pavement was raised. The Devil poked his head out.

"Come on!"

"Through there?"

"Yes."

He edged himself through the narrow hole.

Splash!

He would have to put his shoes on "Expenses."

"Well, let's be off," said the Devil.

"I didn't know one could get to Down There along the sewers!"

"Easiest thing there is, old man. Left here."

There was no sound but the echoes of their footsteps: Crucible's suedes and the Devil's hooves.

"How much further?"

They had been walking for several hours. Crucible's feet were damp and he was sneezing.

"We're there, old man."

They had come to the end of the tunnel. Before them stretched a dark valley. In the distance, Crucible could see a giant wall, with a tiny door. Across the valley ran a black river; the air was tainted with sulphur.

The Devil removed a tarpaulin from a hump by the tunnel mouth.

"May I present Geryon II!"

Crucible blinked. Geryon II was a Model T Ford crossed with an Austin 7, tastefully decorated in sulphurous yellow.

The Devil wrenched at the offside door, which fell off.

They climbed in. Surprisingly, the car started after only a few swings of the starting handle.

They chugged across the sulphur plain.

"Nice car."

"Isn't it! Forty dragon-power. Built her myself from a few bits and pieces from Earth. Trouble with springing out of the floor near a junkyard," said the Devil, gritting his fangs as they cornered at speed in a cloud of sulphur, "is the fact one often surfaces under a pile of old iron." He rubbed his head. Crucible noticed that one of his horns was bandaged.

They skidded to a halt by the river. The car emitted clouds of steam.

A battered punt was moored by the river. The Devil helped Crucible in and picked up the skulls—pardon me—sculls.

"What happened to what's his name—Charon?"

"We don't like to talk about it."

"Oh."

Silence, except for the creaking of the oars.

"Of course, you'll have to replace this by a bridge."

"Oh, yes."

Crucible looked thoughtful.

"A ha'penny for them."

"I am thinking," said Crucible, "about the water that is lapping about my ankles."

The Devil did not look up.

"Here."

He handed Crucible a battered mug, on which the initials "B. R." were just discernible. And so they continued.

They stood in front of the gate. Crucible looked up and read the inscription:

ALL HOPE ABANDON, YE WHO ENTER HERE.

"No good."

"No?"

"Neon lights."

"Oh, yes?"

"Red ones."

"Oh, yes?"

"Flashing."

"Oh, yes?"

They entered.

"Down, boy; get off Crucible."

Three tongues licked Crucible simultaneously.

"Back to your kennel, boy."

Whining, Cerberus slunk off.

"You must excuse him," said the Devil, as he picked Crucible up and dusted him down. "He has never been the same since he took a lump out of Orpheus's leg."

"It didn't say that in the story."

"I know. Pity, because the real story was much more—er, interesting. But that's neither here nor there."

Crucible took stock of his surroundings. They appeared to be standing in a hotel lobby. In one wall was a small alcove containing a desk, on which a huge Residents' book, covered in dust, lay open.

The Devil opened a small wooden door.

"This way."

"What?"

"My office."

Crucible followed him up the narrow stairway, the boards creaking under his feet.

The Devil's office, perched precariously on the walls of Hell, was rather dilapidated. There was a patch of damp in one corner, where the Styx had overflowed, and the paper was peeling off the wooden walls. A rusty stove in the corner glowed red-hot. Crucible noticed that the floor seemed to be covered with old newspapers, bills, and recipes for various spells.

The Devil dropped into a commodious armchair while Crucible sat down in a tortuous cane chair, which all but collapsed under his weight.

"Drink?" said the Devil.

"Don't mind if I do," said Crucible.

"Very nice drink, this," said Crucible. "Your own recipe?"

"Yes. Quite simple—two pints bats' blood, one— I say! You've gone a funny colour! Feel all right?"

"Ulp! Ghack! Um—quite all right, thanks. Er—shall we get down to business?"

"Okay."

"Well, as I see it, our main difficulty will be to make the public take Hell—and you for that matter—seriously. I mean, the generally accepted theory of Hell is a sort of fiery furnace, with you prodding lost souls with a pitchfork and hordes of demons and whatnot running around yelling— Hey, that reminds me, where is everybody—er, soul?"

"Who?"

"Lost souls and demons and banshees and whatnot?"

"Oh, them. Well, like I said, no one has been down here for two thousand years, except that nit, Dante. And all the souls down here gradually worked their way up to Purgatory, and thence to—yes, well, the demons all got jobs elsewhere."

"Tax collectors," murmured Crucible.

"Quite so. As for fiery furnaces, the only one still in working order is the Mark IV, over there in the corner. Very useful for my culinary efforts but not for much else."

"Hm. I see. Have you a map of Hell handy?"

"I think so." The Devil rummaged in an old oak desk behind him and produced a roll of yellow parchment.

"This is the newest map I have."

"It'll do. Now let me see. Hum. I take it this is where we came in."

"Yes! That shading is the Sulphur Plain."

"That's good. I'm sure the Acme Mining Company would give a lot to have the mining rights—"

"Oh, yes?"

"Of course, we would have to build a proper road over it for the increased transport—"

"Oh, yes?"

"Get a large tunnel dug down from Earth—"

"Coffee bar here. Dance hall there. Racetrack at the far end. Bowling alley over—"

"We could put a funfair here—"

"Leaving room for a restaurant there—"

"Put some ice cream stalls here and here, and here—"

"All-night jazz band there. Get in touch with your demons and offer them higher wages to come back to help run the place—"

"Get Orpheus to organize a jazz band—I'm sure Apollo would oblige—"

And so it continued. Soon the map was covered in symbols representing everything from a dance hall to a cycle track. Then they sat back and discussed Stage One: putting Hell in the public eye.

Of course, there were difficulties at first. The time when the Devil materialized in the middle of the pitch on Cup Final day springs to mind. Still, he got a front page splash in all the popular newspapers. A famous brewery sued him for loss of custom, since most of the Cup Final spectators signed the pledge after seeing him.

Telephone lines all over the world smouldered, melted, and slowly fused together as Crucible was plagued with offers from the big financial magnates. Advertising firms fought for the Devil's patronage. Work on the London–Hell tunnel was progressing fast under Crucible's supervision. The Devil moved in with him, saying that all the cranes and bulldozers and whatnot were making Hell hell.

"See how Cerberus loves his Yummy-Doggy! Your dog can have that glossy coat, those glistening fangs, those three heads, if you feed him Yummy-Doggy! Yummy-Doggy in the handy two-ounce tin! Cerberus says Yummy-Doggy is scr-r-rumptious! Ask for Yummy-Doggy!!"

"Men of distinction smoke Coffin-Nales!"

"Tell me, Lucifer, why do you smoke Coffin-Nales?"

"I like that cool, fresh feeling; the flavour of the superb tobacco; the fifty pounds your firm's paying me for these corny adverts—"

"Tell me, sir, what are your views on the colour bar?"

"Well, I—er—I mean to say—um—er, well—er, that is—"

"What do you think of the younger generation?"

"Well—er—um—ah—yes! Definitely!"

"Do you agree that violence on television is responsible for the deplorable increase in the nation's crime statistics?"

"Well, ah—um—no. That is to say, er—yes. I mean, er—no—ah—um."

"Thank you very much, sir, for coming here tonight and giving us your views on topics of immediate concern. Thank you. Well, ladies and gentlemen, tune in next week for another—"

Crucible surveyed the company dispassionately. There was the usual bevy of disgruntled backbenchers, would-be starlets, bored reporters, and of course, the usual fatigue party of guards, all sipping themselves horizontal on third-rate champagne. A motley and mottled crowd. Crucible, who was becoming quite an expert on crowded atmospheres of late, diagnosed this one as a particularly fruity blend of stale smoke, fleurs du mal, and methane, not to mention the occasional waft of carbon monoxide. He turned to the Devil, who was performing wonders with the cocktail shaker.

"This, my friend, is what is laughingly called a party; a ritual still found in the better parts of Belgravia. It seems to consist of a—"

"Oh, lay off it, Cru. This is the besteshed jag I've hadsh in five hundred yearsh, and I'm gonna make the besht of itsh—"

A muffled *crump!* indicated that the Devil had "made the besht of itsh," to the best of his ability.

It was a crisp November morning, and in the secluded thoroughfare that was Cranberry Avenue the birds were singing, the leaves were falling, and Crucible was having his breakfast. Between mouthfuls of bacon and mushrooms, he gave the newspapers the swift port-to-starboard. The gossip column caught his eye and he remembered the Devil.

Throwing the paper in the wastebin, he wiped his mouth on his napkin and padded into the spare bedroom.

Chaotic was the scene that met his eye. Paper hats, balloons, and streamers were lying around the room and there were of bottles not a few. The Devil himself, still clad in Crucible's second-best dress suit, was sprawled across the bed, snoring loudly.

"Wakey-Wakey!" shouted Crucible heartlessly. The effect was impressive. The Devil shot a clear two feet in the air and came down clutching his head; the language he used turned Crucible's ears bright red.

Crucible busied himself in the kitchen, and returned with a cup of black coffee.

"Here."

"Ouch! Not so loud." *Slurp!* "Oh, that's better. What happened last night?"

"You tried the effect of vodka and green Chartreuse."

"Ouch!"

"Quite. Now, best foot—er, hoof—forward. Hell's opening ceremony is at twelve."

"I can't go like this—ouch!"

"Sorry. You'll just have to drink gallons of black coffee and bear it. Now, come on."

Jazz resounded around the walls of Hell. Pop music echoed along the dark corridors, mingling with the click of slot machines. Espresso coffee flowed in rivers. The scream of hotted-up motorcycles mingled with the screams of banshees both ghostly and human (guitar strumming, for the use of). The growth of Hell's popularity only equalled the growth of the Devil's bank account.

Up high in his balcony, on the wall of Hell, the Devil poured himself a drink of water and took three tranquilizer pills.

The storm raged. For the last month the Northern Hemisphere had been beset by thunderstorms unequalled in the records of mankind. The weathermen spent all their working days testing their corns, seaweed, and other oracles but had to confess themselves at a loss.

In the large study of his new country house, Crucible threw another log on the fire and settled himself deeper into his armchair. The storm continued.

His conscience, perforce the most robust and untroubled in Europe, was troubling him. Something was wrong with this Hades business. Certainly not on the monetary side, for his commission over the last three weeks had been exceedingly generous, as his country house, two cars, five racehorses, and one yacht plainly stated.

Hell had been a great success. The top people were going to flock there and it had had the approval of the Establishment.

But something was wrong. Something to do with those heavy storms.

Somewhere in his mind, the inner Crucible, equipped with wings, halo, and harp, was bouncing up and down on Crucible's conscience. The thunder murmured.

Poomb!

The Devil appeared, looking very agitated, and ran to Crucible's cocktail cabinet. He poured himself a Belladonna, and whirled round to Crucible.

"I can't stand any more of it!" he screamed. His hand was shaking.

"More of what?"

"Your lot! They've turned my home into bedlam! Noise! Noise! Noise! I can't get a good night's rest! Do you realize I haven't slept for over two weeks? Nothing but yelling teen—!"

"One moment. You say they disturb you?"

"Very funny!"

"Why not close Hell for a while and take a holiday?"

"I've tried. Heaven knows—!"

Rumble!

"I've tried! Will they leave? No! A bunch of thugs threatened to 'get' me if I tried to close their noisy, blaring paradise—"

RUMBLE!

"I can't move without being mobbed by savage hordes of autograph hunters! I'm famous! I can't get a bit of peace! It's hell down there!" The Devil was now kneeling on the floor, tears streaming down his face. "You've got to help me! Hide me! Do something! Oh God, I wish—"

The thunder split the heavens in twain. The sky echoed and re-echoed with the sound. Crucible slumped in his chair, his hands clapped over his bursting eardrums.

Then there was silence.

The Devil lay in the middle of the floor, surrounded by light. Then the thunder spoke.

"DO YOU WISH TO RETURN?"

"Oh, yes, sir! Please! I'm sorry! I apologize for everything! I'm sorry about that apple, truly I am!"

On the bookshelf, a bust of Charles Darwin shattered to fragments.

"I'm sorry! Please take me back, please—"

"COME."

The Devil vanished. Outside, the storm subsided.

Crucible rose, shaken, from the chair. Staggering over to the window, he looked into the fast-clearing evening sky.

Then out of the sunset came a Hand and Arm of light, raised in salute.

Crucible smiled.

"Don't mention it, sir. It was a pleasure."

He closed the window.

SOLUTION

Technical Cygnet, July 1964

I really can't remember this one. There was a period, a long, long time ago, when I was dashing out ideas and concepts and half-baked bits of dialogue to see if, magically, they would catch fire and become a decent short story or novel. Those that didn't make it were dumped in the bit bucket, and if you can remember what that means, then you have been around computers for as long as me. I must have written it and then danced away to try something else.

"Gold? Or is it diamonds this time?"

Pyecraft swung round. "What the—!"

The inspector stepped through the tiny hatchway into the cockpit, and pointed vaguely towards the small rear cabin.

"There is a very large parachute compartment back there. I had to throw out your parachute though, so it's in your own interest that you watch the controls."

Pyecraft eased the joystick back. "I'll have your hide for this," he muttered. "After the indignity of a search at Lemay, you stow away on my private plane—!"

"Why don't you shut up?" suggested the inspector sweetly. "There are just the two of us here, so we'll have less of the 'outraged citizen' act. It doesn't suit you." He lit a cigarette and carefully refrained from offering one to Pyecraft. "Johan Pyecraft, I arrest you in—"

"What for? You can't prove a thing."

"Smuggling."

"Smuggling what? His arm slid slowly down between the seats to the small brass fire extinguisher.

"I don't know yet. However, you have made fifteen trips over the mountains, in these battered old aircraft, in the past three weeks; you suddenly have a lot of money; and you are a known smuggler. So I say to myself, Gustave, I say, where is he getting all this money? And I answer myself, Gustave, *mon ami,* he is back in his old trade."

"You found nothing at Lemay." Pyecraft grasped the extinguisher.

"Exactly. And so you must have brought it on to the plane since. Therefore you will please to turn the machine around and—"

He sidestepped neatly as the heavy extinguisher flew past him; Pyecraft, caught off-balance, finished the swing in the centre of the instrument panel.

High on the frosty mountainside two small figures huddled round a feebly glowing fire.

The inspector looked again at the remains of the aeroplane.

"That was good flying."

"We might as well have crashed; if the cold doesn't get us, the wolves will."

They both gazed at the fire for a few moments.

"Come on," coaxed the inspector. "You might as well tell me now. Just what was it that you were smuggling?"

Pyecraft looked at him sadly.

"Aircraft," he said.

THE PICTURE

Technical Cygnet, May 1965

Good grief! That was a long time ago! I'm quite glad I never tried to sell this one, but once again I was playing with the words to see what happens. It's a thing that authors do sometimes.

It wasn't really a superb work of art.

The artist had painted the sky the wrong colour and covered it with blotches in an attempt, seemingly, to hide his mistake; the perspective, what there was of it, was wrong; and the vegetation would not have been found in the wildest nightmare. The whole thing was a surrealistic portrait of hell.

Even the frame barely held together.

Jon kept it on the wall—one of the padded walls—of his cell. Strange and horrific though it was, it was some connection with the Outside, some reminder that there were other things besides eating, sleeping, and the occasional visit of the doctors. Sometimes they would watch him through the grille in the padded door, and shake their heads.

"No cure," said one.

"Unless we take away that—that picture," said the other.

"You will kill him if you do."

"He will kill himself if we don't; you know that it was the cause of his—his—"

"His madness."

"There is no other word for it. That picture is the centre of his life now; I believe it is the only thing that he does not doubt. Yesterday he told me that it portrays the only true world, and that this one is really false. We can do nothing against such stubbornness."

"Then it is either kill or cure?"

"Yes. I will tell him when I examine him. Perhaps the shock of having his world removed will cure him."

It didn't seem to. Jon still sat hunched and brooding in the corner of his cell, staring at the picture, trying to remember . . .

He heard the soft tread in the passage. They were coming to take away his picture; there was so little time left! He made one last, tremendous, despairing effort . . .

And the cell was empty.

They never did find out where he had gone or how he had escaped. It was a nine-day mystery; and, in the course of time, it was forgotten.

But the doctor kept the picture, and hung it up in his study. He knew his suspicions were absurd, but they stuck.

Sometimes he stares at the picture with all three of his eyes, with the green sun below the horizon, and hopes that he is wrong.

For how could anyone survive in a world of brown earth and green leaves, and a blue sky with only one sun?

THE PRINCE AND THE PARTRIDGE

"Children's Circle" by Uncle Jim,
Bucks Free Press, 6, 13, 20 December 1968

*Written under the pseudonym Uncle Jim, "Children's Circle" was
a series of seventy-odd tales that appeared between 1965 and 1973,
of which two have made it into this collection: "The Prince and the
Partridge" and "Rincemangle, the Gnome of Even Moor."*

Once upon a time—that's always a good start—there was a young
prince who was ruler of the Land of the Sun. It was a pleasant
country of long days and blue skies, and most things in it were
either yellow or gold.

The cottages were built of sandstone with golden tiles, daffodils
and buttercups grew in fields of ripe corn, and gold was so plentiful
under the land that the streets were actually paved with it.

Now, to the west of this land was a high range of mountains,
where the prince—did I say his name was Alfred? Well, it was—had
a hunting lodge.

One day when he was out hunting deer with his knights his horse bolted, and carried him away through the thick pine forests. The sounds of the hunt disappeared in the distance, while the prince leaned on the reins and tried to calm his mount.

By the time he had done this he was in an unknown part of the mountains, on the edge of a wide clearing. He found what was wrong with his horse—a sharp burr had got under the saddle girth—and while he stood adjusting it a deer burst into the centre of the glade.

It was the one he had been hunting—but before he could reach for his bow a silver arrow hissed out of the trees and killed the creature.

"Oi, oi," he thought. "Poachers in my mountains!"

Out of the trees rode a host of knights in silver armour, riding white horses. At their head rode a princess clad in silver cloth.

She had white hair, and I dare say I hardly have to tell you that Alfred thought she was the dearest, prettiest, fairest, etc., princess he'd ever clapped eyes on, even though her long hair was whiter than his granny's.

Her knights took the deer and rode away, and of course Alfred followed. He soon realized he was going down the other side of the mountain.

The sun was setting, and this is what he saw. Over the land on the other side of the mountains a big silver moon was rising. The whole land shone like silver, silver flowers grew in the grass, and in the distance his princess was riding.

"Where is this place?" the prince wondered out loud.

In the tree above someone coughed.

"It's the Land of the Moon, of course."

The prince looked up and saw that he was under an old wild pear tree, with gnarled boughs and wizened fruit, and hardly any leaves to speak of. On the lowest branch sat a large, fat, ugly brown bird with big eyebrows.

 "What sort of bird is it that speaks?" said Alfred.

"Me. I'm the partridge. The Partridge, I should say, in a Pear Tree. And you're Prince Alfred. The girl is Princess Selena, but if you want to marry her, you'll have to woo her. Chocolates and flowers and so on."

"She looks as if she can have anything she wants," pointed out Alfred.

"Please yourself," said the partridge. "I'm only here to help, I'm sure. All I'll say is she has promised to marry the man that gives her a Christmas present that dances, leaps, plays tunes, makes a beat, carries pails, hisses, swims, lays eggs, can be worn on one hand, sings, cackles, coos, waggles its eyebrows, and is good to eat. All at once, let me add."

"What for?" asked Prince Alfred.

"Her father, King of the Land of the Moon, decided that only the man who could think up the right kind of present was worthy to marry his daughter. He's got no sons, you see, so whoever is her husband will become king of that land in time," added the partridge.

"A parrot," said the prince thoughtfully. "That might be all right."

"The Emperor of the Rainbow Land tried that," said the partridge. "It didn't work."

So the prince said good-bye to the wise old partridge in his pear tree, and went back home deep in thought.

He called all the palace wizards, wise men, and deep thinkers together, and asked them what dances, leaps, plays tunes, makes a beat, carries pails, hisses, swims, lays eggs, can be worn on one hand, sings, cackles, coos, waggles its eyebrows, and is good to eat? "Come on, work it out, or you'll get no Christmas bonus!"

"It's a riddle," said one of them. But think as they might, they couldn't find the answer.

So the prince organized a great competition, with a gold cup as the prize for anyone who could guess the answer.

But although the hall of the castle was filled to overflowing with postmen sorting out the replies, and people queuing up in the hope  of winning the cup, no one thought up anything like the right answer. The prince sat on his gold throne and sighed.

Right at the end of the queue was the partridge, walking since he was far too fat to fly.

"What are you doing here!" gasped Prince Alfred.

"I've come for the prize," said the partridge.

"You mean you knew all the time?"

"You didn't ask me, did you? But I don't want the cup. What I want costs nothing, is as light as air, and I shan't tell you what it is. Not yet anyway."

"What is the present I'm to give the princess, then?" asked Prince Alfred.

"Patience, patience," said the partridge. "I want to have a meeting with some of your subjects first. Kindly call for the Royal Swankeeper, the Guardian of the Crown Jewels, the Master of the Royal Music, the highest lord in the land, the chief lady-in-waiting, and about four farmers. I'll need them all to make the present.

"Then I want you to go and visit the princess, and her father, and bring them to my pear tree in the mountains."

This the prince did, though he wondered what the partridge had in store.

He went to the Land of the Moon, and brought the king and the princess and a host of their knights to the tree.

"What sort of present is this?" said the king. "The pears are good to eat, maybe, but nothing else. They don't sing."

"Wait a moment," said the prince, gazing anxiously down the road.

"I'm not waiting here all day," said the king angrily. "Show me the present you've got for my daughter or be off."

"Wait a minute, Father," said Princess Selena. "There's something coming."

Prince Alfred looked down the road at the approaching cloud of dust and then let out a whoop of joy.

A very odd crowd could now be seen.

In the lead was a small boy called Bert, the son of the Royal Swankeeper, carrying three enormous cages. One contained two sulky turtledoves; the next three French hens; and the biggest, which kept bumping against his knees, held four little green birds.

On Bert's head sat the partridge, holding on tightly to his hair, and shouting instructions to the others. His voice was rather muffled since he was also trying to hold five large gold rings in his beak.

After Bert came the Royal Swankeeper himself, herding seven hissing swans and six waddling geese, who kept getting under the feet of the eight milkmaids who were puffing along behind.

After them came a big drum, bowling along with its drummer galloping after it, and the other eight drummers hotly in pursuit, closely followed by ten pipers who played as they ran.

Eleven lords came leaping after them, robes flying; and bringing up the rear was a carriage holding twelve ladies-in-waiting.

"Now you all know what to do," said the partridge, when they had reached the old pear tree. And pears rained down as everyone scrambled up into the branches, treading on fingers and cracking branches.

"Quick, quick!" said the partridge. "Are we all ready? Now tell the princess what her present is."

"Twelve ladies dancing," said the ladies on the lowest branch.

"Eleven lords a-leaping," sang the lords, rocketing up and down through the tree. *Creak! Rattle!*

"Ten pipers piping—one, two, one, two, three, four," sang the pipers, and went into a spirited rendering of the tune.

"Nine drummers drumming." *Thud! Boom!*

"Eight maids a-milking."

"Hiss! Hiss!" went the seven swans, who couldn't a-swim on their branch and were angry about it.

"Honk! Honk!" went the six geese a-laying.

"Ring! Ting!" sang the five gold rings in the wind.

"Call! Chirrup," sang the four calling birds.

"Le Cackle!" cackled the three French hens.

"Coo! Coo!" sang the two turtledoves.

There was a breathless pause, and everyone stared up at the partridge. He made sure they were all watching, then ruffled his feathers, stretched out his wings, and with a voice like sandpaper sang:

"And a Partridge in a Pearrrrrrrr"—his neck stretched and his face went red as he took a deep breath—"Treeeeeeee!"

The silence that followed was broken by the laughter of the king, who sat on his horse with tears running down his face.

"It's the funniest thing I've seen in years," he said. "And it does everything it should do! Marry my daughter, by all means!"

"I think it's a lovely present," said the princess.

"Cough, cough," said the partridge tactfully, from his position on the topmost branch. "My reward is that I want to sing a song I've invented all about this at your wedding."

"Yes," said the prince. "You must all come."

So—on the Twelfth Day of Christmas, as it happened—they held a great wedding party in a large tent erected over the old pear tree in the mountains, and the partridge sang his song and was made Prime Minister on the spot by the prince.

Several of the smaller pipers ate too much, and had to be sent home in wheelbarrows, but the prince gave everyone medals and they were all very happy.

Rincemangle, the
Gnome of Even Moor

"Children's Circle" by Uncle Jim,
Bucks Free Press, 16 March–18 May 1973

This is one of the pieces I used to do on Thursday evenings: an earlier and shorter version of what became Truckers. *The name of the protagonist finds an echo in the later creation of Rincewind the Wizard, who first appears in* The Color of Magic.

Once upon a time there was a gnome who lived in a hollow tree on Even Moor, the strange mysterious land to the north of Blackbury. His name was Rincemangle and as far as he knew he was the only gnome left in the world.

He didn't look very gnomelike. He wore a pointed hat, of course, because gnomes do; but apart from that he wore a shabby mouse-skin suit and a rather smelly overcoat made from old mole skins. He lived on nuts and berries and the remains of picnics, and birds' eggs when he could get them. It wasn't a very joyful life.

One day he was sitting in his hollow tree, gnawing a hazelnut. It was pouring with rain, and the tree leaked. Rincemangle thought he was getting nasty twinges in his joints.

"Blow this for a lark," he said. "I'm wet through and fed up."

An owl who lived in the tree next door heard him and flew over.

"You should go out and see the world," he said. "There's more places than Even Moor." And he told him stories about the streets of Blackbury and places even further away, where the sun always shone and the seas were blue. Actually they weren't very accurate, because the owl had heard them from a blackbird who heard them from a swallow who went there for his holidays, but they were enough to get Rincemangle feeling very restive.

In less time than it takes to tell, he had packed his few possessions in a handkerchief.

"I'm off," he cried, "to places where the sun always shines! How far did you say they were?"

"Er," said the owl, who hadn't the faintest idea, "about a couple of miles, I expect. Perhaps a bit more."

"Cheerio, then," said Rincemangle. "If you could read, I'd send you a postcard, if I could write."

He scrambled down the tree and set off.

When Rincemangle the gnome set off down the road to Blackbury he really didn't know how far it was. It was raining, and he soon got fed up.

After a while he came to a lay-by. There was a lorry parked there while the driver ate his lunch and Rincemangle, who had often watched lorries go past his tree, climbed up a tyre and looked for somewhere warm to sleep under the tarpaulin.

The lorry was full of cardboard boxes. He nibbled one and

found it was full of horrible tins. They weren't even comfortable to sleep on.

But he did eventually drop off, just as the lorry set off again to Blackbury. When Rincemangle woke up it was very dark in the box, and there was a lot of banging about going on; then that stopped, and after waiting until all the sounds had died away he peered cautiously through the hole.

The first thing he saw was another gnome.

"Hullo," said the gnome. "Is there much interesting in there? It looks like another load of baked beans to me. Here, help me get a tin out."

Together they gnawed at the box until one tin rolled out. The box was on a high shelf, but the other gnome had got up by climbing it rather like a mountaineer. They lowered the tin down on a piece of thread.

"My name's Featherhead," said the gnome. "You're new here, aren't you? Just up from the country?"

"I thought I was the only gnome in the world," said Rincemangle.

"Oh, there's a lot of us here. Who wants to live in a hollow tree when you can live in a department store like this?"

Talking and rolling the tin along in front of them they crept out of the storeroom and set off. The store was closed for the night, of course, but a few lights had been left on. There was a rather nasty moment when they had to hide from the lady who cleaned the floors but, after a long haul up some stairs, Rincemangle arrived at the gnomes' home.

The gnomes had built themselves a home under the floorboards between the toy shop and the do-it-yourself department, though they had—er—borrowed quite a lot of railway track from the toy shop and built a sort of underground railway all the way to the restaurant. They even had a telephone rigged up between the colony and the gnomes who lived in the Gents' Suiting department two floors down.

All this came as a great shock to Rincemangle, of course. When he arrived with his new friend Featherhead, pushing the baked bean tin in front of them, he felt quite out of place. The gnomes lived in small cardboard houses under the floorboards, with holes drilled through the ceiling to let the light in. Featherhead rolled the tin into his house and shut the door.

"Well, this is a cut above the old hollow tree," said Rincemangle, looking round.

"Everyone's in the restaurant, I expect," said Featherhead. "There's about three hundred gnomes live here, you know. My word, I think it's very odd, you living out in all weathers! Most gnomes have lived indoors for years!"

He led Rincemangle along the floor, through a hole in a brick wall, and along a very narrow ledge. It was the lift, he explained. Of course, the gnomes had managed to use the big lift, but they'd rigged up a smaller one at the side of the shaft. It was driven by clockwork.

They arrived in the Gents' Suiting Department after a long ride down the dark shaft. It was brightly lit, and several gnomes were working a giant sewing machine.

"Good evening!" said one bustling up, rubbing his hands. "Hullo, Featherhead—what can I do for you?"

"My friend here in the mole-skin trousers—" began Featherhead, "—can't you make him something natty in tweed? We can't have a gnome who looks like he's just stepped out of a mushroom!"

The gnomish tailors worked hard. They made Rincemangle a suit out of a square of cloth in a pattern book and there was enough over for a spare waistcoat.

Featherhead led him back down under the floorboards and they went on to the toy department, where most of the gnomes spent the night (they slept when the store was open during the day). All the lights were on. Two gnomes were racing model cars around the display stands. Two teams of gnomes had unrolled one of those big football games and had started playing, while the crowd squeaked with excitement.

"Don't any human beings ever come down here at night?" asked Rincemangle, who was a bit shocked. "I mean, you don't keep lookouts or anything!"

"Oh, no one comes here after the cleaners have gone home," said Featherhead. "We have the place to ourselves."

But they didn't. You see, the store people had noticed how food disappeared and how things had been moved around in the night. They were sensible and didn't believe in gnomes. So they had bought a cat.

Rincemangle saw it first. He looked up from the football game and saw a big green eye watching them through the partly open door. He didn't know it was a cat, but it looked like a fox, and he knew what foxes were like.

"Run for your lives!" he bellowed.

Everyone saw the cat as it pushed open the door. With shrill cries of alarm several gnomes rolled back the carpet and opened the trapdoor to their underground homes, but they were too late. The cat trotted in and stared at them.

"Stand still now," hissed Rincemangle. "He'll get you if you move!"

Fortunately, perhaps because of the way he said it, the gnomes stood still. Rincemangle thought quickly, and then ran to one of the toy cars the gnomes had been using. As the cat bounded after him he drove away.

He wasn't very good at steering, but managed to drive right out of the toy department before crashing the car into a display. He jumped out and climbed the stem of a potted plant just as the cat dashed up.

*

Rincemangle the gnome climbed right up the potted plant just as the cat came scampering towards him. From the topmost leaf he was able to jump onto a shelf, and he ran and hid behind a stack of china plates—knocking quite a few down in the process, I'm sorry to say.

After half an hour or so the cat got fed up and wandered off, and he was able to climb down.

When he got back to the gnome home under the floorboards the place was in uproar. Some families were gathering their possessions together, and several noisy meetings were going on.

He found Featherhead packing his belongings into an old tea caddy.

"Oh hullo," he said. "I say, that was pretty clever of you, leading the cat away like that!"

"What are you doing?"

"Well, we can't stay here now they've got a cat, can we?" said Featherhead.

But it was even worse than that, because very soon the night-watchman who usually stayed downstairs came up and saw all the broken things on the floor, and he called the police.

All the next day the gnomes tried to sleep, and when the store emptied for the night the head gnomes called them all together. They decided that the only thing to do was to leave the store. But where could they go?

Rincemangle stood up and said, "Why don't you go back and live in the country? That's where gnomes used to live."

They were all shocked. One fat gnome said, "But the food here is so marvelous. There's wild animals in the country, so I've heard tell, that are worse than cats even!"

"Besides," someone else said, "how would we get there? All three hundred of us? It's miles and miles away!"

Just then two gnomes burst in dragging a saucer full of blue powder. It smelt odd, they said. They'd found it in the restaurant.

Rincemangle sniffed at it. "It's poison," he said. "They think we're mice! I tell you, if we don't leave soon, we'll all be killed."

Featherhead said, "I think he's right. But how can we leave? Think of the roads we'd have to cross, for one thing!"

As the days passed things got worse and worse for the gnomes. Apart from the cat, there were nightwatchmen patrolling the store after everyone had gone home, and the gnomes hardly dared to show themselves.

But they couldn't think of a way to leave. None of them fancied walking through the city with all its dangers. There were the lorries that delivered goods every day, but only a few brave gnomes were prepared to be a stowaway on them—and, besides, no one knew where they would stop.

"We will have to take so much with us!" moaned the Head Gnome, sitting sadly on an empty cotton reel. "String, and cloth, and all sorts of things. Food, too. A lot of the younger gnomes wouldn't survive for five minutes in the country otherwise. We've had such an easy life here, you see."

Rincemangle scratched his head. "I suppose so, but you'll have to give it up sooner or later. Where's Featherhead?"

Featherhead, the gnome Rincemangle was staying with, had led a raid on the book section to see if there were any books about living in the country.

Towards dawn a party of tired gnomes came back, dragging a big paper bag.

"We were almost spotted by the nightwatchman," muttered Featherhead. "We got a few books, though."

There was one in the sack that had nothing to do with the country. Rincemangle looked at it for a long time.

"*Teach Yourself to Drive*," he said. "Hmmm." He opened it with some difficulty and saw a large picture of the controls of a car. He didn't say anything for a long time.

Finally the Head Gnome said, "It's very interesting, but I hardly think you're big enough to drive anything!"

"No," said Rincemangle. "But perhaps . . . Featherhead, can you show me where the lorries are parked at night? I've got an idea."

Early the next evening the two gnomes reached the large underground car park where the store's lorries were parked.

The journey had taken them quite a long time because they took turns at dragging the book on driving behind them.

And it took them all night to examine the lorry. When they arrived back at the toy department they were very tired and covered in oil.

Rincemangle called the gnomes together.

"I think we can leave here and take things with us," he said, "but it will be rather tricky. We'll have to drive a lorry, you see."

He drew diagrams to explain. A hundred gnomes would turn the steering wheel by pulling on ropes, while fifty would be in charge of the gear lever. Other groups would push the pedals when necessary, and one gnome would hang from the driving mirror and give commands through a megaphone.

"It looks quite straightforward," said Rincemangle. "To me it looks as though driving just involves pushing and pulling things at the right time."

An elderly gnome got up and said nervously, "I'm not sure about all this. I'm sure there must be more to driving than that."

But a lot of the younger gnomes were very enthusiastic, and so the idea took hold.

For the rest of the week the gnomes were very busy. Some stole bits of string from the hardware department, and several times they visited the lorries at night to take measurements and try to find out how it worked. Meanwhile the older gnomes rolled their possessions down through the store until they were piled up in the ceiling of the lorry garage.

A handpicked party of intrepid mountaineering gnomes found out where the lorry keys were kept (high up on a hook in a little office). Rincemangle, meanwhile, studied road maps and wondered what the Highway Code was.

At last the day came for moving.

"We've got to work fast," said Rincemangle, when they heard the last assistant leave the building. "Come on—now!"

While the gnomes lowered their possessions through the garage roof onto the back of the lorry, Rincemangle and an advance party of young gnomes squeezed into the cab through a hole by the brake pedal.

Inside it was—to them—like being in a big empty hall. The steering wheel seemed very big and far too high up.

The gnomes formed themselves into a human pyramid and by standing on the topmost gnome's back Rincemangle managed to throw a line over the steering wheel. Soon they had several rope ladders rigged up and could set to work.

They planned to steer by two ropes tied to the wheel, with fifty gnomes hanging on to each one. While this was being sorted out other gnomes built a sort of wooden platform up against the windscreen, just big enough for Rincemangle to stand and give orders through a megaphone.

Other gnomes came in and were sent to their positions by Featherhead. Before long the cab was festooned with rope ladders, pulleys, and fragile wooden platforms, and these in turn were covered with gnomes hanging on to levers and lengths of thread.

The big moment came when the ignition key was hauled up and shoved into its keyhole by two muscular gnomes. They gave a twist and some lights came on.

"Right," said Rincemangle, looking down at the waiting crowds. "Well, this is going to be a tricky business, so let's get started right away." Featherhead joined him on the platform and hauled up the *Teach Yourself to Drive* book and a street map of Blackbury.

"On the word Go, the Starter Button party will give it a good press and—er—the Accelerator Pedal squad will press the pedal briefly," Rincemangle said uncertainly. "The gnomes working the clutch and gear lever will stand by. Go!"

Of course, it didn't work as simply as that. It took quite some time before the gnomes found out how to start up properly. But at last the engine was going, making the cab boom like a gong.

"Headlights on! Clutch down! First gear! . . ." Rincemangle shouted above the din. There were several ghastly crashes and the great lorry rolled forward.

"Here, what about the garage doors?" shouted Featherhead.

The lorry rolled onwards. There was a loud bang and it was out in the street.

"Turn left!" shouted Rincemangle hoarsely. "Now straighten up!"

For several minutes the cab was full of shouts and bangs as the gnomes pushed and pulled on the controls. The lorry wove from side to side and went up on the pavement several times, but at least it kept going. Rincemangle even felt bold enough to order a gear change.

Through the dark streets of Blackbury the lorry swayed and rumbled, occasionally bouncing off lampposts. Every now and again there was a horrible clonk as it changed gear.

Steering was the big difficulty. By the time the gnomes down below had heard Rincemangle's order it was usually too late. It was a good job there were no other vehicles on the road at that time of night, or there would have been a very nasty accident.

They blundered through the traffic lights and into Blackbury High Street, knocking a piece off a pillar box. Featherhead was staring into the great big mirror, high above them, that showed what traffic was behind.

"There's a car behind with a big blue flashing light on it," he said conversationally. "Listen! It's making a siren noise."

"Very decorative, I'm sure," said Rincemangle, who wasn't really listening. "Look lively down below! It's a straight road out of town now, so change into top gear."

There was a thud and a crash, but the gnomes were getting experienced now and the lorry whizzed away, still weaving from side to side.

"The car with the flashing lights keeps trying to overtake us," said Featherhead. "Gosh! We nearly hit it that time!"

He craned up and had another look. "There's two Human Beings in peaked caps inside it," he added. "Gosh! They look furious!"

"I expect someone has got a little angry because of all those lampposts we knocked down. I don't think we were supposed to," said Rincemangle. Unfortunately, while he said this, he didn't look where they were going.

The lorry rumbled off the road and straight through a hedge. The field behind it was ploughed, and the gnomes had to hang on tightly as they were jolted around in the cab.

The police car screeched to a halt and the two policemen started running across the field after them, shouting.

The lorry went through another hedge and frightened a herd of cows.

Rincemangle peered through the window. There was a wood ahead, and behind that the heather-clad slopes of Even Moor started climbing up towards the sky.

"Prepare to abandon lorry!" he shouted. They plunged into a wood and the lorry stopped dead in the middle of a bramble thicket. It was suddenly very quiet.

Then there was a very busy five minutes as the gnomes unloaded their possessions from the back of the lorry. By the time the policemen arrived there was not a gnome to be seen. Rincemangle and

Featherhead were sitting high up on a bramble branch and watched as the men wandered round the abandoned lorry, scratching their heads. After poking around inside the cab and finding the little ropes and ladders they wandered away, arguing.

When they had gone the gnomes crept out of their hiding places and gathered round Rincemangle.

"Even Moor is only a few hundred yards away," he said. "Let's spend the day hidden here and we can be up there tonight!"

The gnomes lit fires and settled down to cook breakfast. Many of them were wondering what it would be like to live in the country again after so long in the town. A lot of the little ones of course—I mean, even littler than the average gnome—were rather looking forward to it. But they all knew that there was going to be a lot of hard work before them.

Early next morning a poacher, coming home for breakfast, told his wife he'd seen a lot of little lights climbing up the slopes of the moor. She didn't believe him, but perhaps you will.

Kindly Breathe in Short, Thick Pants

Bath and West Evening Chronicle, 9 October 1976

The passage of time has blurred what possibly motivated me to write this, but it was probably after hearing one too many half-baked ideas from one too many half-baked politicians, who are always at their worst when trying to be mater, while always subtly getting it wrong. They're still doing it.

A message from the Rt. Hon. Duncan Disorderly, MP, the new Fresh Air Supremo

Good evening. [*Takes deep breath.*]

As you will no doubt be aware, Britain is facing an air crisis of alarming proportions. In some places supplies of fresh air are reaching alarming prop— no, I've already said that . . . crisis levels. Why is this, you ask? [*Goes to chart behind chair.*]

For years we have been assured of regular supplies of fresh air blown in from the Atlantic. Unfortunately the demand is exceeding supply. More people [*Pokes small black figures on chart*] insist on breathing, which means less air for everyone else.

[*Taps chart firmly with stick.*]

Your Government has been well aware of the problem since about lunchtime, as a result of which I am talking as new Fresh Air Minister now instead of chairing the House of Commons tea trolley subcommittee. Even we politicians have to breathe, you know—ha ha—though of course some of us breathe slower while others breathe faster.

While it is true to say that people in South Wales and the industrial Midlands are being allowed to breathe for only eight hours a day, while Scotland and the South have ample supplies of fresh air, a redistribution would be prohibitively expensive.

A working party is, however, and in strict accordance with Government policy, considering legislation to compel those in Fresh Air Surplus areas into wearing gas masks connected to bottles of potted smog. This is democracy.

Meteorologists tell us that the wind must blow at a hundred miles an hour for the next three months to top up our fresh air levels. In the meantime, what can you do?

Here is how you can help:

- Breathe very slowly. Ministry staff will be calling on you soon to demonstrate.
- All pumps, fans, and windmills are banned—penalty £400—so that supplies of fresh air can be diverted to essential industries. Remember—it takes four million cubic feet of air to make one car tyre, and two thousand tiny bubbles to make a cubic inch of carpet underlay.
- Avoid heavy breathing. Have a cold bath instead—sorry, I mean have a good rubdown with spit. Ministry cats will be calling on you to demonstrate.

- Put a brick up your nose.
- The air you exhale can still be used to inflate balloons, tyres, to warm your hands, and cool your porridge.

If we all follow these simple rules, we will be able to stick our chests in with pride and say that British suck and ingenuity has won the day again. Thank you. [*Breathes out slowly.*]

THE GLASTONBURY TALES

Bath and West Evening Chronicle, 16 June 1977

Actually, I'm rather proud of this one, which has some truth in it. I distinctly remember picking up the first of the hitchhikers when going home from Bath one sunny evening. And there were a lot more hitchhikers heading to Glastonbury. Indeed, as I look back, nearly all of it has some basis in reality, but as Mark Twain used to put it, I might have here and there put a little shine on things. Only he said it in American. I certainly do remember the smoke coming from the back of my van, and hastily winding down my window while at the same time keeping an eye out for Mister Plod. As it was, when we arrived at Glastonbury and I opened the back, there was a kind of pleasant fog but I don't think anyone noticed very much. They were better and somewhat nicer days. And if there is anyone out there who can prove that they were one of those in my van, I would be very pleased to hear from them—but I suppose by now they're prime ministers and so forth.

A van driver there was, let's call him me.
A nine-to-fiver, going home to tea.
Just outside Bath, observant as they come
He spied a hippie—travelling by thumb.
Beside the sunny road the lad stood baking
His hair was dripping sweat, his feet were aching.
Not cool was he, so broiling was the day
The poor man's grass was turning fast to hay.
"Glastonbury's where I'm bound." "Hop in,"
I said. He gave a weary grin
"Right on," he said, "this hitching is a drag."
And then he rolled himself a sort of fag
And told me all about how the next day
Would be specially good vibrations all the way.
"A Festival of Sevens," and the Tor
A sort of dustbin full of cosmic lore.

Some miles further on we stopped again
To pick up four more lurking in a lane,
A woeful band, a travel-weary tribe
Without the breath to raise a single vibe
Between them. In the back they went
With two guitars, three rucksacks, and a tent.
One believed in UFOs, one said ley
Lines were mystic traffic signs and they
All met at Glastonbury; also she
Was really deep into astrology.
"You're Libra." "No," I said. "Oh, Aries?" "No."
"I'm never wrong," she said. "You must be Virgo."
"No," I said; she thought a bit, then—"Leo?
Oh dear, I'm never wrong. Um, Scorpio?
Pisces? Taurus?" "Yes," I said, "that's me."
Bells tinkled as the lady laughed with glee,

And clapped her hands, and said "I'm never wrong."
And then another pilgrim joined our throng.
Black-clad she was. "I always get a hitch,"
She said, when climbing in, "'cos I'm a witch."
"Oho," said Ley-line Joe, with fancies lewd
A-thinking of her prancing in the nude.
But I thought, yes my girl, I've met your kind
At parties, where you always seem to find
Strange lines on people's hands and put on airs
And then go and be sick upon the stairs.

With seven in the van plus tents, the tension
Was getting rather tight on the suspension.
The wheels were giving mystic sort of whines;
We went round corners hopping in straight lines.
And then as I must quickly now relate
The seven of us nearly met our fate.
"You see, inspector, as I drove along
Listening quite astonished to the throng
Discussing miracles, I think, and Re-
Incarnation—it's all Greek to me,
Your Worship—I think that when I die
I'll come back as a corpse, but this is by
The way. I've got to tell you (honest) now
How come we very nearly hit a cow.
The herd came surging out across the road—
I braked, but trouble was, I had this load:
The road was hot, the tyres too and so
We did a mystic skid. And, er, you know
The van it sort of grit its teeth and lunged . . .
The occupants went white with fear and plunged
Very nearly in my lap, bags, beads, and bells,
Ropes, sandals, Levi's, and assorted smells;

On, on we slewed, and how I hoped that seven
Didn't mean my number's up and me in Heaven.
The witch said 'Jesus!' which just goes to show
It pays to hedge your bets. You never know.
And then with one heroic braking judder
We halted seven inches from an udder."

I've got to say that generally the town
Of Glastonbury always gets me down:
A nasty little town of moaning traders.
But then, there is this problem of invaders . . .
I left them near the Tor. I hope they found
What they are looking for. A holy ground?
Sacred to what? I really do not know.
A sort of mystic Glastonbury glow.

I wondered, as a cheerful atheist,
Exactly what, besides a cow, I've missed.

There's No Fool Like an Old Fool Found in an English Queue

Bath and West Evening Chronicle, 14 January 1978

This was one of those letting-off-steam things: you underwent what the late Patrick Campbell used to call rigours of life, and instead of taking it out on somebody, you wrote it down in a tea break and forgot about it, until it turned up here.

Text of the party political broadcast shortly to be given by the Rt. Hon. Maurice Dancer, the newly appointed Minister for Queues

Good evening. You will notice how crisply I said that—good evening. I mean I didn't drag it out, I came right out with it. Good evening.

Many of you will be wondering why you need a Minister for Queues. Well, it's obvious. This is, after all [*Glances at board behind camera*], 1978, the jet age. We must all, ha ha [*Grins*] get with it, although we must not of course freak up, I mean freak off. Off out. Lose our heads.

It has come to the notice of your vigilant Government that many people today, in this country of ours, are too slow in queues. We at the Equal Speeds Commission will be doing something about this, make no mistake about it.

Take post offices. When you and I go in all we want is a 10½ p stamp, for which we are proffering the correct money. Of course we are. But in front of us there is always some nit who wants to send a parcel of live ants to Bolivia, and renew his lawnmower licence, and blow us if he doesn't start to fill in a great big form there and then!

Of course, everyone in the queue behind us nips off smartly to the three other vacant counters, and then the selfish clod pulls out a purse and starts to pay for it all in pennies! Meanwhile looking very self-satisfied! [*Realizes he is standing up, coughs, adjusts tie, sits down, smooths hair back into place.*]

Sorry about that, got a bit carried away there. Now, banks. You go to the Quick-Service Counter to cash as it might be a cheque for £10 and the lady in front of you, it turns out, wants to arrange a complicated transaction that needs phone calls and the taking down of large official books.

And then when you rush to the next counter the man queuing there suddenly opens his briefcase and takes out dozens of little bags of coins, which all have to be weighed and counted!

How many times have you got to the railway station in reason-able time for the train only to find some complacent person at the ticket counter opening negotiations for a return ticket to Vladivo-stok? And of course the clerk, instead of motioning him to the back of the queue, abets him, because it's a change from the usual cheap day returns to London.

Ho yes! I've got my eye on the likes of him! He's the sort who whips into a garage forecourt a bumper ahead of me and then fills his car up very slowly from the one available pump. I mean, you know how you can make those self-service pumps shoot the petrol up at a gallon every ten seconds but not this chap, oh no, he fidgets with the trigger just in case it runs away with him, and then when you're waiting to pay he takes out a cheque book, verrrry slowly, asks the man what the date is, and then says "By the way, sorry to be a nuisance, have you got a fan belt for a 1954 Austin Trundler?"

And then he has the brassbound nerve to smile in a self-satisfied way. Oh yes, he's thinking, I'm first in the queue I am, oh yes, I can take all day if I like, oh yes, any more tooth-grinding out of you matey and I'll buy five pints of oil, an anorak, one of these ghastly little air fresheners, and a motoring map of Angola.

Ironmonger's shops! This vermin breeds there like flies! You're waiting there with your little packet of quite simple nails and he says to the man, "Sorry to be a nuisance, I want a lock." When they've shown him all the locks in the shop, he decides that he'd better go home again and measure the door, but meanwhile could they show him some hinges?

In the past, if you were to seize a length of, as it might be, twenty-two-millimetre copper piping from the counter and batter him with it, our antiquated legal system would have dealt severely with you. Not any more! From now on, unless they are a registered old age pensioner, you will be able to give these people what they richly deserve and they'd better not go and moan to anyone! That'll teach them!

What's the good of being in power unless you use it, that's what I say. God, I hate these people, the hours I've spent standing behind women who open their shopping bags to open another bag to open their handbag to find their purse to find the money to pay— [*Voice off: "Are you going to be all night? I've got a simple news bulletin here and you've been going on for twenty minutes!"*]

Thank you, good evening.

Coo, They've Given Me the Bird

Bath and West Evening Chronicle, 8 April 1978

*My word, how this brings back memories. When I worked for the
Bath Evening Chronicle, in the dear old days of long ago, my place of
work was a shed—your actual fairly cheap garden shed—which was
placed on a flat roof opposite, if I recall correctly, the room that was the
workplace for the Tele Ad girls, who I must say did not work in a shed,
and especially not my shed, which was so ramshackle that if I moved a
useful piece of wood in one corner, I had a direct view of young pigeons
in a nest. Sometimes I used to feed them. That was the time when I
was doing features and other hack work. Oddly enough, it was a good
life if you didn't mind being constantly surrounded by pigeons. And
while I can't remember much more about it, I must assume that my
near neighbours were the inspiration of this little piece.*

According to the *Radio Times* (so it must be right), the Russians
have experimented with using pigeons to do simple production-line
jobs in factories . . .

DEAR COMRADE CHAIRMAN,

I would just like to say right at the start that I have been employed here at the Dugvilasgivichski Tool and Die Collective for twelve years and there have never been any complaints. I have never applied for a visa for Israel, I am not now and never have been an intellectual, and I have always kept my production line spotless, you could eat your dinner off it. There is not another man in the place what could say the same or, if I may put it bluntly, there is not in actual point of fact another man* in the place.

Of course I realize that as a humble Factory Hygiene Operative Grade III it is not my job to criticize decisions made higher up the Party machine, not if I don't want to end up on the wrong side of the Dugvilasgivichski Mental Health Institute anyway, but I cannot help recalling the old days when there were thirteen hundred other comrade workers here, I mean human beings, I mean I don't wish this to be interpreted as a criticism of the quality of the work of my current feathered comrades per se.

I mean, on the production lines all you hear is thousands of little beaks pecking away, that and the rustle of feathers, some days it drives me up the pole. Also take the case of works outings, they used to be very enjoyable, we'd all go out to Nodynoverograd-super-Mare with a few crates of wodka stuck in the back of the coach, only now it's hard to enjoy yourself when you're the only chap in thirteen coaches and all the rest of your fellow comrade workers are in big wicker hampers. When we get there, I have to let them out and then they all fly back home, leaving Joe Joevarich Muggins here with his funny hat and a bag of whelks and a long journey back home on his tod.

I wouldn't mind that so much, but when I complained to the Chief Hygiene Operative he just flew away.

Things aren't the same in the canteen any more, either. Well,

*Author's note: Should have said comrade, shouldn't I?

they're not going to produce thirteen hundred lunches of mixed corn and just one of caviar and chips, are they? No, it's either sandwiches or up there on the feeding perch with all the rest of them and no moaning or we'll peck your fingers.

I will pass over the failing fortunes of the works darts team, the humiliating defeat in the billiards league, the unpleasant encounter with the KGB All-Stars on the football field, and the nasty mess at the international chess championships—and I told the fraternal Chinese delegate not to take his hat off, but of course no one listened.

I appreciate what it said in *Pravda* about not being capitalist about our fellow creatures, and all that about joining together in the greater unity of all warm-blooded creatures as per true Marxist thinking, also where it said that every pigeon in a factory means another man free to build submarines, but what it boils down to is that I'm only employed here because none of my new fellow comrade workers is big enough to push a broom.

I would also like to make a protest that the parrot they've got operating the switchboard won't let me make personal calls, and as for the flamingo on the tea trolley, well, how would you like your tea stirred?

I hope this message reaches you, on account of me attaching it to the leg of one of my fellow comrade workers who's going to see his relatives, he says they've got a little nest just outside your office window.

Thanking you in anticipation, I remain,

Yours fraternally,

TERRY TERRYANOVICH PRATCHETT

PS: Sorry this letter is a bit nibbled at the top, only the works manager has been out for a fly-around and you know what these budgies are like—little scamps.

AND MIND THE MONOLITHS

Bath and West Evening Chronicle, 1 April 1978

Around the time this was written an Iron Age village was being reconstructed somewhere near Farnham in Dorset; I had contacts in the area, which wasn't too far away from where I lived. People had been brought in to this new prehistoric settlement and were filmed going through the working day of Iron Age man, but rumours began that locals nearby were going in during the hours of darkness to flog fags and (if I remember correctly) soft lavatory paper to the ancient and rather desperate inmates. In no way can I vouch for the truth of this, but there seemed to be a vogue for this sort of thing and so, for a jobbing journalist, looking outwards through the pigeons, that was enough of a spark to start a fire. Wind yourself up to a sort of English music hall humour and away, boys and girls, you go.

You can't miss us, down here at the HTV Paleolithic Village. Well, you can, if you're not careful. What you do is, you come up past the Yorkshire Television reconstructed hill fort, turn left at the LWT

Bronze Age encampment, go straight on past Southern TV's Beaker Folk village, and we're next door to the field where some poor bleeders are being paid by Granada to try to build Stonehenge.

It's not a bad life, all things considered. There's only me and Sid here now, ever since Ron and Amanda were lured off to Border Television's Dark Age Settlement by the promise of not having to sleep in the same hut as the goats. Also old Tom Bowler left us last week: he said he didn't mind being Wuluk, Chief of the Saucer Folk, except that when the original Wuluk, Chief of the Saucer Folk, wanted to get his head down after a hard day's flint knapping he, Wuluk, Chief of the Saucer Folk, didn't have a ruddy great 250 horsepower diesel generator roaring away outside his sodding sod hut hut. Or a bank of arc lights in his bedroom.

I can't say I mind that. What keeps me awake are the thuds and abruptly cutoff screams from next door every time a monolith falls over.

Still it's not too bad. I can put a pretty good edge on a flint, even if I say it myself, and next week it's our turn to go hunting. There's been a bit of a stink over this hunting business ever since the Granada lot came back with a side of best beef and three chickens with their giblets in a plastic bag. I thought that was a bit odd, and I said as much to Sid.

Mind you, Sid's an old hand at this business. He did a year on the Sussex University Ancient Farm, then he wangled a place on the Radio Three Celtic Living Experiment, and then he did nine months being paid to reconstruct Silbury Hill. He can knock out a copper bracelet quick as a wink, can Sid, and when it comes to hunting, he just nips over to the nearest farm and pinches a cow.

The TV types have never rumbled him; we hardly see them now, what with there being no bathrooms in the Paleolithic and the midden right outside the hut and everything—they just stay on the main road and use a long lens.

Where I disagree with Sid, though, is over this flogging of fags to

55

the other villages. I looked at his straw mattress the other day and it's stuffed with Benson & Hedges, toothpaste, shampoos, and rolls of soft toilet paper. I don't think it's in the spirit of the thing, but Sid said trading was very important in the olden days, and anyway, he can get a quid for a roll of Andrex down at the Bronze Lake Village.

What? Oh, that was just that lot next door again. They've found twenty-seven different ways Stonehenge couldn't possibly have been built. No, I shouldn't go and look, if I was you. They've already lost fifteen villagers, three cameramen, and the *Blue Peter* outside broadcast unit.

That site over there? The empty one with the pond? Oh, that's the Irish Television's Jurassic Experiment. Yes, I know it's pretty difficult to find actors thirty feet tall with scaly skins—I suppose they'll have to, you know, rig up some sort of pantomime horses, only dinosaurs, if you see what I mean. They *had* to go back to the Jurassic, all the other periods have already been pinched by other companies—

My word! That was a heavy one! Nearly brought the hut down!

It was a whole trilithon went over that time. Oh—it's okay, all it got was a sociologist. Last winter, when we couldn't go hunting, a whole research team from Keele University disappeared in very mysterious circumstances, nudge nudge, so take my tip and refuse any sausages you get offered by the Bronze Age lot.

Now, if you'll excuse me, I've just got to do a bit of pottery . . .

NOTE: This was followed by a photograph of an ancient-style tent village with arrows and the following captions:

"Anyone see what I did with my library book?"
"Gosh, rat soup, my favourite."
"Of course the goat is angry. You're sitting in her seat."
"Hey, I've invented a druid-yourself kit."
"Only another five months, three weeks, four days to go."
"After you with the midden."
"What I miss most is *Points West*."

THE HIGH MEGGAS

1986

The short story evolved into The Long Earth. *"The High Meggas" was rather a doodle at first, something to do after I had sent* The Color of Magic *to my then publishers, Colin Smythe. I could visualize it minutely and wanted to begin with a series of short stories. I was still playing with the ideas when* The Color of Magic *was published and inexplicably became very popular, far more successful than any of my previous books.*

And in those circumstances, what is a humble jobbing author supposed to do? The basis of The Light Fantastic *was already dancing in my mind and gathering momentum and so with some reluctance I put "The High Meggas," which I had previously thought would one day make the foundation to a great series, under wraps until it was unearthed a few years ago over quail's eggs at a literary dinner attended by Ralph Vicinanza, my American agent, and Rob Wilkins. My enthusiasm was rekindled and after discussing the ideas with Steve Baxter, who I have always considered to be the UK's finest writer of hard SF, a new journey began.*

Frankly I'm glad we did it this way; besides it was a lot more fun.

They said that Daniel Boone would pull up and move on if he could see the smoke from another man's fire. Compared with Larry Linsay, Boone was pathologically gregarious. There was someone else on this world. *His* world. It was like finding a fingernail in your soup. It irked. It made the small hairs on the back of his neck stand up.

Linsay had rigged an array of antennae in the pines at the top of the rise. In the virgin wave bands of this world the tiny blip of an arrival was crystal clear; it stood out on the miniature displays like an Everest among the background molehills. Only one type of person would come up this far into the high meggas. The gumment. In Linsay's vocabulary the word was as pregnant with meaning as some of the old Chinese words that expressed a whole stream of thought. It meant regulations, and taxes, and questions, and interference. Other people. It had to be the gumment because it took money to get into the high meggas, and generally it was the sort of money that only the gumment could muster. Besides, people didn't like it this far out, where the tuning had to be so fine and it took several weeks of real-time travel to get to the next human being. People didn't like being that far from people. But there were other reasons. Things started to be *different* in the high meggas.

There was another blip. *Two* people. Linsay began to feel crowded.

They had to be from Forward Base. Linsay was annoyed—he went to Forward Base, they didn't come to him. Hard to think of any reason that would bring them up here. He imagined them looking around in astonishment, unable to find him. The third rule of survival up here was: keep away from your point of arrival.

He took a bearing to make sure, picked up the rifle that leaned against his chart table, and set off through the scrub. Any watcher would have noticed how Linsay kept to shaded areas, broke cover only when he had to, and broke cover fast. But there wasn't any watcher. If there had been, Linsay would be creeping up behind him.

People got the wrong idea about Robinson Crusoe. The popular image was of a jolly but determined man, heavily into goatskin underwear and manumission. But someone at Forward Base had loaned Linsay an old, battered copy of the book. Robinson Crusoe was on his island for over twenty-six years, Linsay learned, and had spent most of the time building stockades. Linsay approved of this: the man obviously had his head screwed on right.

It was late summer here in what was approximately southern France, although the Fist had made such a mess of the coastline that it was barely recognizable. Here there were no longer just the spatter craters that had been such a feature a few tens of Earths back. Up here the Fist had raked across Europe and western Asia, sending major fragments barrelling towards the very core in tongues of plasma. There must have been several years of winter before the atmosphere dropped most of the dust. When it cleared, the seasons were all wrong. The colander that was Europe was slightly nearer the new Equator, the Earth had developed a wobble, and the ice caps were spreading fast.

Mankind, however, was learning about Agriculture at the time and failed to notice. A pack of rantelopes watched Linsay cautiously. He didn't hunt on this Earth—it was easy enough to hop back one for that—but all the same they weren't entirely at ease. The winter following the Fist hadn't wiped out all the primates, and some baboons in these parts were mean hunters.

The bull baboon he'd christened Big Yin watched him from his perch on a rock. Linsay waved at him cheerfully. Big Yin had seen the rifle. He didn't wave back.

The man was crawling cautiously behind the inadequate cover of an outcrop of fused glass. He moved very much like a man who'd got his ideas about stealth from watching adventure films. He was holding a small handgun. It didn't look as though it had much stopping power, but Linsay didn't approve.

He let off a shot that nicked the rock a few feet from the man's head.

"Throw the gun this way," he suggested.

He watched shock, panic, and resignation chase one another across the man's face, as it scanned the thicket of anonymous bushes that had just spoken.

"The gun," he repeated. He could make out the detail of the man's belt. Gumment issue, of course, but light duty. That meant he could only have come up from Forward Base.

"Okay, bush," said the man. He tossed the gun in Linsay's general direction and slowly moved his hands . . .

A sliver of rock nicked his ear as another round hit the glassy boulder beside him.

"The belt, too," said the bush.

"You're Larry Linsay," said the man. "They said you were stone paranoid—no offence, you understand."

"None taken. Move those hands real careful now."

The hands moved real careful. "You don't know me, I guess we never met. I'm Joshua Valienté. Security man. From Forward Base, you know?"

He flinched as Linsay appeared only a few feet away. Approaching someone by movin' up towards them through an adjacent world was an old trick, but it never failed to disconcert.

Valienté found himself looking up into a pair of grey-blue eyes that were entirely without mercy. This bastard'd really shoot, he told himself. Don't even look at your own gun. He'd really shoot you, up here where no one else will ever come. He wouldn't even have to bury the body.

"Prove it," said Linsay.

Valienté shrugged what he hoped was an unaggressive shrug. "I can't."

"All good security men carry little plastic cards," said Linsay. "They have little pictures of themselves in case they forget what they look like."

"Not when they're off duty. Can I stand up?"

Linsay stepped back. Possibly that meant yes. Valienté didn't risk it.

"There isn't any Forward Base now," he said as levelly as he could. "The station's there all right, but there aren't any people. They're dead." He paused, waiting for the reaction. It was like dropping a brick into a pool of treacle.

"Aren't you going to say anything?" he asked.

"No. I've got the gun. You talk."

"All right, you soulless bastard; someone poisoned them. You know the little spring, where they get the water? In there. I was out hunting. But I saw her when I came back. Smashing up equipment. Then she went *movin'*. I followed her up here until I caught your beacon."

Linsay regarded him for some time.

"I go back to Base once in a while," he said. "I've never seen you before. Didn't even know they had security men."

"I only came up three weeks ago."

"I see you've been doing a great job," said Linsay.

"Look, she's *here*. Somewhere. And if we stand here all day, then she'll be at the other end of a trajectory."

The chase had taken four days, nearly. The murderer had used the Base's generator to give an initial boost, but the guard had been bright enough to scavenge for spare charged batteries. They meant a weight penalty, but not for long. There was a trail of burnt-out cells across three thousand alternate Earths, discarded after a series of mind-punishing *moves* that drained the power and sent the guard pinwheeling across unsuspecting landscapes. Pity about the belt. There had been time either to take one of the more rugged models that were specifically designed for the high meggas, or to find extra batteries and a knapsack to carry them. There hadn't been time for both.

There ought to have been time to do something about the bodies. It hadn't been a subtle poison, just a slow-acting one. There would have to be time later.

The guard wasn't very experienced at tacking on the move, but he knew one thing: never flip across alternate worlds without also moving laterally. It's too easy for the quarry to wait for you right in the place you started from, and then he needn't even shoot. A heavy stone would be sufficient.

So the trick was to duck, flip, and run, and take the occasional risk by jumping two or three worlds at once. They had both slept sporadically, in odd corners of the landscape. Meat was easy to come by, hard to cook. Once, they had arrived back to back, a few feet from each other. They both fired and flipped, so that two bullets sped away from each other over a deserted landscape, maybe the only artefacts that world would ever see.

You don't have to do this, the guard's conscience kept repeating. No one expects you to do this, you're not paid for it. Why play Mounties? Even if you win, how will you get back? It'll take years, if you get back at all. And conscience was pushed against a metaphorical wall and told: because there were five children on the base, the youngest was three, and the poison attacked the nerves and they weren't quite dead when I got there.

And so they dodged and tracked across worlds as the microscopic changes began to multiply. Into the high meggas.

There had been two blips on Linsay's detector. The second one was lying in a crater, semiconscious. From here he could see she too was wearing a basic belt, with limited detectors. It must have been like stepping into a well.

Her gun was lying a few feet away. Linsay scooped it up and shoved it into a pocket, then turned his attention to the woman herself. She was wearing a red jumpsuit, ugly with pockets but highly practical for *movin'*, where what you couldn't carry you didn't take. A lightly built person could tote about sixty pounds of gear before battery drain began to soar. Most of the pockets were empty, but there were still a few unspent batteries. Linsay undid the belt and slung it over one shoulder. He picked up the woman and slung her over the other. Wrong, but there didn't seem to be any obviously broken bones. If there were, then tough.

A quarter of a mile away Valienté was tied to a tree and watching a pack of superbaboons. Judging by the sticks they carried they had already mastered the principle of the club and the hammer, and looked about ready to go on to trepanning and disembowelling. There was one that particularly concerned him, a big rangy brute with torn ears and yellow eyes as narrow and vindictive as the bridges of hell. It sat on a rock like a living gargoyle, just watching.

A bullet kicked up dust at the foot of the rock. The superbaboon turned its muzzle eastwards and snarled soundlessly, bared teeth a row of yellow knives. Then it was gone, scampering ungracefully into the scrub with the rest of the troupe following it.

Linsay appeared with the woman's body over one shoulder. By some juggling, as Valienté couldn't help noticing, the man contrived to untie his ropes without ever quite failing to point the rifle at him.

"They could have killed me."

Linsay stepped back. "Quite probably," he said. "Big Yin is learning real fast. I think I might have to do something about him one day."

"Right now'd be favourite."

"Maybe I've got a soft spot for him."

Valienté doubted it; any soft spots in Linsay would still be diamonds.

"He's one of a kind. I've been all through the worlds round here

63

and the same troupe is around, but not him. Maybe he's some kind of mutant. Maybe the 'boons will inherit the earth."

There was something weird about the rifle. Without any apparent effort Linsay managed to keep it pointing towards him like a compass needle.

"Is that necessary?" said Valienté. "Even if you don't believe my story, you've still got my gun."

"Just walk."

Earths, untold Earths. More Earths than a computer could count, they said.

It was hard to talk about them accurately without referring to folded universes and the quantum packet theory. It was even harder to explain to a TV audience how a belt worked; once you invited them to consider the multiplex universe as a rubber sheet the initiative was fumbled. The pack of cards analogy was totally inappropriate, although most people felt at home with it. The universe was in fact a large pack of three-dimensional cards. The belt allowed you to travel up and down the pack, boring, as it were, through the cards themselves.

A belt was simple enough to build, if you were desperate enough not to worry about safety devices. All over the world, people were. All you needed was the transistor radio you'd earned via your vasectomy, about one hundred metres of copper wire, and blind faith that you wouldn't emerge inside a tree.

It was worth the risk. The nearby Earths were identical on all but the microscopic level. California was already sparsely colonized out to several K, and at the far ends was beginning to develop in ways that even Californians thought were nutty. In what remained of the USSR security men were combing nearby worlds for the previous lot of security men.

The world was crowded, but the universe was empty. It was a

gold economy. What was happening would make the Diaspora look like a family outing.

Of course, some minds couldn't cope.

Linsay's camp was tucked into a small hollow on a south-facing hillside; it was little more than a tent, and a slightly more substantial shed for the instruments. And, of course, there was a stockade. It was not large, and not high, but the thin red wire that ran around the top of it assured all the privacy Robinson Crusoe could have desired.

Outside the tent was a small solar station and a row of batteries. There was also the usual cage of white mice.

Linsay disappeared into the tent and laid the unconscious woman on the bed. When he came out Valienté was sitting by the remains of the fire, which was still smouldering. It was well after noon.

"How come she was unconscious?" Valienté said.

Linsay hauled the gate into place and hooked a strand of the red wire across the top of it. "Neither of you has got the right belt for the high meggas," he said.

"Is that an answer?"

Linsay turned.

"Sure. The normal belts just protect you from coming out inside anything thicker than air. The Low Earths are so similar, that's all you need. You don't have to worry about the ground. It's always there. Where she came out, the Fist had punched the ground away."

"Fist?"

"Didn't you see any craters?"

"Yeah, I thought the ground was getting rough."

Linsay looked at the mouse cage. A mouse, strapped inside a little belt unit atop a battery pack, could get a message to Forward Base within six hours. Could it get right back to the low numbers? It'd take a week, maybe ten days. There would have to be feed, water—say two more batteries for them. Plus a multiband here-I-am screamer, which meant another battery. Plus four more batteries to give enough power to carry the extra batteries. Plus—forget it . . .

"Are you human?" said Valienté. "I mean, I was told you were a cold sort, but when you hear that fifty people have been massacred you're supposed to do something, you know? Like say 'How terrible', or something."

"Would you like some coffee?" said Linsay. "It's only black."

"What?" Valienté was trembling now, with exhaustion and anger.

"Did you do anything about the goats?"

"*What?*"

"They had a herd of goats at Forward. I never had the patience to trap them here, myself. I expect they'll need milking. You could at least have let them out of their stockade."

Valienté's face was a mask.

Linsay sat down on a log opposite him and reached into the pocket of his jumpsuit. He spoke slowly and deliberately, as to a child.

"What's it to you what I feel? I think you fail to understand something fundamental about your position here. You shouldn't be hating me, you should be thinking. You should be thinking: when he asks me why *she* had a neat little card in her pocket saying she was employed by the Institute of Trans-terrestrial Ecology as a security officer, what shall I say in the thirty seconds left to me?"

There was the snick of a hammer going back. Valienté looked down the barrel of a pistol of ancient design. In one of those cold digresses of the mind he recalled that transworld pioneers favoured black powder guns, because ammunition was easier to make. They didn't have a lot of power and they made a lot of smoke, but one tumbling slug would make a lot of mess inside his head.

"Twenty-seven seconds," said Linsay.

"You wouldn't shoot me without giving me a chance to explain," said Valienté.

"Do you really believe that? Twenty-four seconds."

"Sure she's got a security pass. She came up to Base with me. She was infiltrated. Nationalists. Look, when did you last care how things were downslope?"

Where, precisely, was the land God gave to Moses? Where, *precisely*, was America? If England meant Land of the Angles, what were the infinite unpeopled countries stretching away from it in the *movin'* dimensions? Did those Feet in ancient times walk among an infinity of pastures green or, if not, on what arbitrary number did they walk?

It seemed to matter. Faced with an infinite feast, the lawyers of the world settled down to argue about the place settings. America, for example, was held in essence to be an idea, and therefore all the sideways Americans were theoretically under the sway of the USA. A number of well-reasoned and photogenic arguments were advanced to support this, and translated approximately as: no Mexicans. On the other hand, all those worlds had Middle Eastern oil fields as yet unexploited, and there seemed no justice in a system that allowed the Saudis to monopolize all the oil in the universe. There was, of course, an additional problem. A belt didn't move you laterally, but if you went one world along, worked out where a bank vault actually was—and flipped back—then a lot of people would be very embarrassed. It took various security men quite some time to work out an answer to that.

On the wider issues, the leaders of the world met for several days and issued a fourteen-page document later known as the Sideways Doctrine. This fell into two parts. The first stated that Earth—the original one, the one with the atoms of Caesar, Christ, and Mao—was sacrosanct, its boundaries inviolate.

The second part of the Doctrine could be distilled into two rules.

You get what you grab.

You keep what you can.

"What do they call themselves?" said Linsay.

"Forever France," said Valienté.

"But this isn't legally France. You can't lay claim to country boundaries into infinity. Even the Jews didn't do that."

"What you have to realize about madmen is that they're mad. And there are some sane people behind them, I think."

"But what have they got to gain?"

"Power. Money. Stuff like that."

"Shit," said Linsay. "A billion worlds . . ."

"Seventeen."

"What?"

"My thirty seconds. You got as far as seventeen." Valienté pointed to the gun.

Linsay looked at it as though seeing it for the first time.

"Maybe I'll trust you for a while," he said.

"Great. Can I fix myself some food?"

"I'll do it. I don't trust you that much."

There were fruits, small and sour. There was a stew, finely flavoured and rich with a meat that Valienté didn't make guesses about . . .

Something had certainly disliked this landscape. Valienté recalled the lush countryside around Forward Base, which overlooked a tributary of what was not the Rhône, just an identical river in exactly the same place.

Here the landscape was yellow and brown, and the river had become a silt-filled valley with a line of scrubby trees that might be marking a trace of moisture. The air hummed with heat. He had been to Africa, but this wasn't Africa. This was a European summer that hadn't ended.

"What was the Fist?" he asked. "A comet?"

Linsay looked at him speculatively.

"Good thinking," he said. "Wrong, though. Nickel-iron asteroid. A big one. Really big. Bigger than the one that made the Canadian Shield. But it broke up before it hit. There's only spatter around here, but it screwed up the weather for years. I think there's a land bridge to Africa."

"When was all this?"

"Ten, fifteen thousand years ago. I've been tracing it through the worlds around here. It gets worse. On this world it only grazed."

Valienté whistled. "Nasty," he said.

"No, not really. Asteroids don't think. It just happened."

"I mean—"

"People are the worst thing to happen to a world," said Linsay. "We were an accident, like the asteroid. A billion-to-one chance."

"Oh, come on. They've found human artefacts on a lot of worlds around Earth. Flint tools, stuff like that."

"Barely human. They never had fire. No hearths found, anywhere. That's the real picture: ten million dark planets, and one circle of firelight."

"Yeah, but we're spreading out now."

"Like a fungus, yes."

Linsay was a left-ear person, Valienté realized. He had seen plenty of them: their eyes glazed slightly and they stared fixedly at your left ear, while their mouths spouted the truth about flying saucers, the great world conspiracy, or one-born-every-minute evangelism. Inside everyone was a left-ear person waiting to get out.

He could see the detail of Linsay's belt from here. It was bulkier than most, and had a funky, homemade look. But it wasn't the sort of device a peasant would scratch together, out of parts glommed from old motor cars, following the instructions in a black-market broadsheet that was probably a poor photocopy of a bad photocopy. And quite possibly wrong anyway. Linsay's belt looked as a production car would look if it had been bought by a hotshot automobile engineer.

"You helped," he said softly. "You invented the belts."

"No. Lider did."

"Okay, but you perfected them. I've seen those early belts. It must have been like wearing a barrel. You isolated the principle. Then you just dropped out. Lider invented them, but you gave people the worlds."

"There've been lots of improvements since then."

"Improvements on your basic design, yes. But mainly just bells and whistles. Why so guilty?"

"Guilty?"

"Lurking up here like a cross between John Wayne and Captain Nemo, doing legwork for a little research outfit. What is this, a penance for turning evil mankind loose on the unsuspecting dimensions?"

Linsay laughed, and lit a cigar—Valienté had already noted the little tobacco patch inside the stockade.

"Mankind isn't really evil. It hasn't got enough dignity to be evil. I came up here for peace. You say I gave people the worlds. And what did they do with them? Their gimcrack economies cracked under the strain, they squabbled, there were territorial wars—when there was land without limit—there was actual starvation, there was . . . oh, hell. You know."

"It's getting better."

"Temporarily."

Linsay stood up and moved over to the stockade gate, swinging it open. There were indistinct shapes under the distant trees.

"Those are the guys I feel sorry for," he said.

"The baboons?"

"They hit a turning point after the Fist hit. They're evolving fast. But they don't stand a chance. By the time they've invented agriculture—no, probably by the time they've acquired fire—they'll be slaves. Or more likely wiped out, because if there's one thing you can say about them, it's that they're vicious little sods."

"I know it."

"I like them."

The night was purple velvet, alive with insects and spiky with invisible chiggers that bit and stung every exposed inch of flesh. Linsay normally kept a fire piled high. Its light was distantly mirrored as two tiny red points in the eyes of Big Yin, watching from his thorny treetop.

The baboon remembered, but dimly, because memory was still a novelty among the tribes. There had been a time-not-now, before the spiky trees with no leaves had been put up around the camp, when a younger Big Yin had crept towards the tent. There had been a shape lying on the ground-higher-than-ground inside, but as the baboon had crept closer it had vanished. And then there had been a sound behind him, and as he turned there was an explosion of sound and light . . .

If Big Yin had been a human, he might have wondered why the man had aimed the gun to scare, not kill. If he had been an animal he would have hightailed it away and never returned. But he was no longer one and not yet the other, and the brain behind the red-lit eyes entertained a mixture of emotions that he would not be able to name for at least three million years. So he waited.

The woman opened her eyes. She had in fact been conscious for over an hour, Linsay knew. He admired the self-control.

She sat up slowly.

"Where's this?"

"You don't sound French," said Linsay.

She hesitated. If her head had been transparent, one would have been able to see the gears mesh.

"I see," she said.

She was small, and on the skinny side. That was an advantage for a *mover*—less weight meant more speed. She didn't look like a mass murderer, but Linsay recalled that mass murderers never did.

"Like to hear my side?" she said.

"I know it," said Linsay. "You were a security guard at Forward Base. You were on duty—why didn't you get poisoned?"

"It was in the water. He put it in the purification plant. But I only had milk and sandwiches."

"Okay. And then?"

"He was off duty. That meant he was able to sneak up to the spring and tip the stuff in. A nerve poison, I think. He came down a few hours later. He didn't expect to see me, but I'd got some extra batteries together and I snuck up behind him and I would have got him if he hadn't turned. And then there was the chase—I expect he's told you about that."

There was a snort from Valienté, who was sitting just inside the tent. Moths did Zimmerman turns around the solitary, low-wattage bulb overhead.

Linsay sat back.

"You could have jumped him."

"What?"

"Moved down one world, gone to his position, and jumped back behind him. Don't they still call it that these days? It was a favourite with muggers."

She grinned weakly.

"You mean upducked him? The Base is on piles. You can't rely on getting the levels right."

Linsay nodded. If the levels weren't right, the minimal safeties in the belt wouldn't allow you to come out, for example, knee-deep in concrete. Even a basic belt would only allow you to move if there was nothing at your destination. Air didn't count—air got out of the way quick enough.

"Well, now," he said. "Neat, isn't it?"

"You don't believe all that?" shouted Valienté. "I've been—"

Linsay ignored him. He looked at the security card.

"Says here your name is Anna Shea. How long have you been in this business?"

"A year."

"Not long."

Shea nodded. But that was how it was. Anyone with any expertise in anything was rushed into service. Mankind was eating worlds faster than he could digest them. What he normally wanted was matches and machetes, but security guards were hot property in a civilization where nothing was secure.

"Tell me about Forever France," said Linsay.

She glanced from him to Valienté.

"What do you think you already know?" she demanded.

"They're fanatics. They won't suffer anyone else to colonize a sideways France."

"He tell you that?"

"Yes. But it fits. I recall five, ten years ago, there was all kinds of weird nationalism."

"Well, not now." She stood up, noting how Linsay's barely perceptible movement revealed the pistol by the chair. Her pistol. She'd been told about him. He must be a madman—he could have been richer than Croesus. But he'd left it all, and hidden up here in the high meggas.

"It was true in the old days," she said. "Life's tougher now. There's still some jockeying among politicians, though. That's what lies behind Forever France. They're just mercenaries. A political lever. Everyone can deplore them, but at bottom they're useful to have around. You know what I mean? The politicians can have them say 'Of course we would not dream of using violence, but unfortunately public feeling is running so high that—', and so on."

Valienté laughed bitterly. "Yeah, sure. You're probably right."

"Ask him about Qom twenty-three," said Shea.

"I don't know anything about Qom twenty-three . . . except what I heard," Valienté ended slightly lamely.

"He led it," she went on relentlessly. "Twenty of them upducked a bunch of peaceful colonists. I can't even remember why it was supposed to be important, but what they did was, they put them all in—"

"Qom twenty-three was a massacre?" said Linsay.

"And the sea's a puddle." She spoke as if reading a script inside her eyeball. "I can't even recall who financed it, the Middle Easts were a mess anyway, but what they did at Qom twenty-three was supposed to be a warning. Because all they left was—"

"Why are you listening to this?" Valienté demanded.

"I don't know what he told you his name was, but his real name—at least, as far as we know—is Martin Venhaus. He's got a scar right down his back, starting at the left armpit. He's skilled with most hand weapons, and nearly as ruthless without them. He—"

Valienté looked up. Linsay's gaze was as penetrating as an auger.

Both men moved. But Linsay's hand was first. It didn't have so far to go. The gun came up smoothly and Valienté waited for the shot. He knew there would be impact, and numbness. No pain yet. Perhaps no pain ever.

It didn't come.

But the pistol stayed up.

Curled up round his gun in the tent that night, Linsay dreamt of falling. Then he woke up, and it was true. But there was grass a few feet below him, and he landed hard but unhurt.

Overhead the cold stars sleeted their light through air untainted by the merest hint of pollution. Creatures of the night chattered and roared in the trees down by the dry river. It was as cold as a tropical night can be, just before sunrise.

Linsay was up and running, moving swiftly to the nearest white-painted marker post which would place him more or less in the centre of the compound.

Time was when he'd thought this was all he needed. Just rig a simple beam inside the tent each night so that anything moving would trigger the belt unit, sending him back one world where a network of crude markers would allow him to position himself aright so that he could flip back and jump the intruder.

Two leopards and one visit from Big Yin had discouraged him. Stockades were less taxing. The baboon had gibbered, when Linsay had levelled the gun a foot from it and fired, but it hadn't run far: it had stopped and looked back *hard* . . .

Tonight's intruder must have come from inside the stockade. Linsay wondered which of them it was. Then he skidded, trod on a stone that skittered away, went down heavily, awkwardly, felt a snap, screamed, punched the belt.

Back at the stockade, dawn was yellow-green and bright, with a fresh breeze blowing off the brackish reed beds that were the Mediterranean. It stirred the papers on Linsay's rough desk. They were black with tiny handwriting. Making paper was a time-consuming and messy job. A loner in the high meggas conserved paper like a medieval scholar, covering both sides thickly.

There was also a Mellanier map of the local Earths, its finely printed concentric circles almost hidden by the red dots and shading with which Linsay had plotted the progress of the Fist.

Shea peered at it, noting how the asteroid—no, the asteroids, because many Fists had pummelled the soft earth—had done more and more damage in each dimension. She had been too busy hunting and being hunted to notice it in the past dozen worlds, but even so it must have made the planet ring like a gong when it hit.

Linsay watched her, the gun clutched at his side, his mind a grey fog through which the pain of his ankle pierced like tiny lightning flashes. There were only a limited number of Detril painkillers in his kit. He had already used a third of them.

She looked up. "You ought to let me look at that," she said. "Paranoia is all very well. Gangrene is worse."

"It's not that bad."

"Sue your face for slander, then."

Linsay shifted, and the white spear of agony shot through his leg. It must have shown.

"Look," said Shea. "Even I can see the blood pooling. What have you got to lose? I've had training, I could—"

"No!"

"You know why I came to your tent last night?"

"He said you'd got a knife."

"He would, wouldn't he? I came to persuade you—by any means necessary. You won't listen to the voice of reason. I wondered if you would listen to . . . older voices."

He made the mistake of laughing. Even laughing hurt.

And it wasn't well received.

"If you're so sure," she snapped, standing up. "I could kill you now, couldn't I?" She pointed to Valienté, dozing curled up beside the tent.

"He couldn't stop me and maybe you wouldn't be able to," she snarled. "You're running out of time, keeping us here. You've got the gun now, but how long will you be able to aim properly? You'll have to trust someone then—and maybe I won't be listening."

And then Valienté was up and running, running into the tent and then out the other side, running strongly, one of the belts now in his hand, out through the open gateway into the waist-high grass.

Linsay struggled up, leant against the table, raised the rifle in a shaky movement, took instant aim, and fired. The distant man jerked and fell.

Linsay half fell back into the chair, his face grey with pain.

"I would have said it was you," he said. "He seemed too . . . simple. I'd really made up my mind it was you. If the damn fool had got the belt round him, he could have *moved* out instead of running. I wonder why he didn't?"

"You scare people," she said. "That's why. Living out here drains something from people. You're too far away from everyone else, I guess. Still, you made the right choice of who to trust. Give me the gun."

He didn't slacken his grip. She moved closer.

"I've got to go and see," she said, a new note in her voice. "I don't give a damn if he's dead, but if you only winged him, he might be back. Give me the gun."

A realization seemed to cross her mind as she looked at his hand still tight on the gun, the aim unwavering.

"Oh shit," she said, and kicked his ankle.

He made one movement, even as the gun went flying from his hand. He hit the belt.

He rose into consciousness again maybe a few minutes later, lying in the grass. Straining down he could see the display on the belt buckle—plus 3—three worlds further up.

He'd taken the batteries out of the other belts, and done some minimal stripping down. It might take her a few more minutes to work out what he'd done and put it all together and come after him.

Come after him she would. She would have to track him down, because she'd be bright enough to suspect that he'd cache a weapon in some handy nearby world.

He should have cached a weapon in some handy nearby world. Would she expect him to have gone downhill, put a tiny inroad into the vast distance between himself and the first Earth?

Possibly—which gave him a minute or two more, if she was husbanding her batteries. No. She'd all the batteries in the camp to use.

If she was clever at putting things together, she could be here *now*.

He rolled away as she flashed into view, taking aim even as she appeared. The smack of the bullet into the ground near his head was still echoing in his ears as he moved up two worlds, wincing with pain because that meant another jolt to his ankle. Here the ground was even more chewed up, and the trees were gone. Here the Fist had begun to really hit, not just graze. Here the air was thin, depleted.

He rolled, almost cherishing the pain because it somehow kept the darkness at bay. But she had expected that, only she gave him more credit than he deserved and emerged firing at a spot several yards away.

Flip. And drop a bone-shaking metre on to ground that was nearly freezing. Flip. Flip. The soil here was rock now, the freezing remains of the molten guts spewed out when the Fist had really meant business. The air was thinner and the rising sun prickled oddly. It would fire him, if he stayed. Flip. She was ready for the drop, emerged with legs bent to cushion her fall. Linsay glanced at his belt with watering eyes. Plus 23. Plus 24.

Flip. She was holding the gun one-handed, knowing he wouldn't roll far, knowing that the thin air would tell on him first. She hit the belt switch.

Linsay was ready. He had his mouth open, and was already turning the belt controls when she arrived again. In the one red-eyed second before his hand found the switch he saw her tumble, breath escaping in a plume of ice crystals. The gun fired and sent its bullet barrelling off towards the freezing shining stars. Then she was spinning, her face a mask, her legs still tensed from the fall that this time would be endless. About a mile off was a jagged asteroid, one of a great many out here between Mars and Venus. The Fist had pummelled harder, and here the Fist had won.

Before he blacked out Linsay made it back a few steps, to the freezing lava flow, and managed a final roll downslope into the shade of a rock. Almost naked sunlight sleeted past, and the boundary between shade and light was knife sharp. There was air, but it was weak wheezy stuff.

The pain seemed distant, a hot sensation rather than an agony. He wondered whether she would survive. But she'd lost valuable seconds before she touched the belt, and even then it would still be set to jump the wrong way.

Linsay, half expecting it even the first time round, had travelled forward with the belt rigged so that the next flip would take him back to his starting point. He nearly hadn't survived, even then.

So she would have jumped onwards—and there was no telling yet how many times the destruction of the Earth had taken place. Perhaps only once or twice, perhaps a thousand, a million times. But not more, because even with an infinity of Earths to play with, the striking of the Fist must be a rarity.

So beyond there must stretch even more. Beyond the high meggas would be the gigas, the teras, the googols. But by then Earth would have hit the big changes, it would be moonless, or an airless desert, or a cinder around a red sun, all the things that Earth might have been if it hadn't been the one place in a multiplexed universe that could give rise to sapience. Perhaps. Because they said the soul was indivisible.

He could feel them, the vast empty spaces stretched around him, as distant as the back of a reflection. Far behind him, impossible to reach, was the tiny circle of firelight. Ahead, the untold possibilities.

That would be the way to go. To hit the switch and hold it down until the battery burned out, drift a few hundred dimensions out, like a burial at sea . . .

He remembered dreaming: it is vital to know how many Earths the Fist knocked out. If we have a measure of that, we can hazard a guess at the chances of a Fist strike, and the two figures might give us an idea of the numbers of the Earth. Of course, Mellanier says it will simply be the circumference of a great circle. But he was wrong to think we simply come back to our starting point. If we go far enough, we should meet ourselves halfway. He remembered waking: he was white with frost, but his ankle glowed white-hot. Overhead a few early stars were out, and they wheeled around him as he pulled himself upright against the boulder and then, with a last effort, stood up.

"Were you trying to walk home?"

The words filtered through the warm white fuzz in his head as he woke. The pain was gone—he could feel the shape that it had left.

Valienté was sitting by the open flap of the tent, and the maps had been pushed aside to make room for batteries.

Linsay felt a weight on his chest. There was a pistol there.

Valienté caught the movement.

"It's loaded," he said. "I didn't want you to feel in any way beholden. What's all this stuff? I found it in the shed."

Linsay's lips were swollen, but he managed.

"Biltong," he said.

"You mean like jerked meat?"

"Yah."

"Right. It's light, nutritious—we'll take it. We leave the guns."

"Wah?"

"Too heavy." Valienté's fingers flew over the paper-thin calcula-tor. "We'll get to Forward in maybe seven days, if we waste charge. There's all kinds of medical stuff there. Perhaps I'll have to learn surgery. Don't worry—I probably won't, I think. If we don't waste time. And time's speed, and speed is lightness, so we'll take jerky and sugar for a few days and pick up water as we go and then just forage. Then later I reckon if we pick up every battery there, and demount the little solar charger, plus get a kick from their generator, we should be back in the low numbers in three months." He paused, shielded the display from the rising light. "Thirteen weeks, in fact, but we can take it easy. We'll have to anyway, 'cos there'll be a lot of hanging around waiting for the cells to recharge. Did you aim to miss or just miss anyway? I've got to know."

There was silence.

"I couldn't be . . . sure," said Linsay. "If I'd aimed to hit, I would have hit. I had to see what would happen next."

"What happened next?"

Linsay sat up, ignoring the slight wave of nausea.

"She's dead. About two dozen jumps up ahead there isn't any Earth. She didn't expect it. The kind of belts you've got will always flip you through provided there's nothing in the way. There was nothing in the way."

"You were there?"

"Briefly. The human skin is quite a good space suit."

"But she wouldn't have expected it."

"No."

"She deserved it."

There was the barest click. Linsay looked up. Valienté looked around.

She was standing just inside the stockade gateway, with the rifle raised. There was blood on her face.

Linsay tried to calculate how many shots would be left. Maybe only one.

"Touch the pistol and I'll blow your head off," she said, and the words croaked through a tortured throat. "I came the long way round. Did you know the gap is only one world wide? I had to cross it twice."

Beyond the gate the long yellow grass swayed gently. Big Yin's muzzle rose like the dawn of man.

Linsay's face must have shown it, because Shea's gaze flickered uncertainly, but the moment of hesitation was too long because the baboon was already out and leaping. She turned then, but he was inside the rifle's radius, paws open to tear and rip. Linsay swept the pistol up and sighted carefully, ignoring the dual screaming. The red jumpsuit and the dusty grey shape danced in front of his sight, but he didn't squeeze the trigger until he was certain.

As the echo died away he thought: *If I have any influence back there, like he says, if the people think they owe me anything, then I'll have this world declared off limits. Let the baboons try.*

It was moonlight. The camp was long deserted, but the fire was still burning and threw a circle of light around the open stockade. Grey bodies huddled as far from it as they could, afraid to go any closer despite the growls of their leader.

He sat near it, watching, and the light in his eyes was a tiny circle of firelight.

Twenty Pence, with Envelope
and Seasonal Greeting

Time Out, 16 December 1987

I remember reading long ago that the vision of a "typical" English Christmas owed a lot to the fact that, in his boyhood, Charles Dickens lived through seven of the worst Christmases of the nineteenth century—and so they became, under his influential pen, what Christmas "ought" to be. As a former journalist, I think that's far too good a story to check.

This was written for the magazine Time Out *for Christmas 1987. I wanted to write a kind of Victorian horror story in which the covers of a row of Christmas cards come to life. And what better starting point than the jolly mail coach which is so, so traditional on the really cheap cards . . . and what would the passengers think of Christmas cards to come? We don't see Snoopy cards much now. But there are plenty that are worse.*

From the *Bath and Wiltshire Herald,* 24 December 1843:

CALNE—Singular Mystery surrounds the disappearance of the London Mail Coach on Tues. last in a snowstorm of considerable magnitude, the like of which has not been seen in the memory of the oldest now living. It is thought that the coachman, missing his way in the driving blizzard at Silbury, took the horses off the road, perhaps to seek the shelter of a Hedge or Rick, and became overwhelmed in the drifting. Search parties have been sent out and the coachman, who was found wandering in a state of severe anxiety in the snow, has been brought back to Bath . . .

From the journal of Thos Lunn, Doctor, of Chippenham, Wilts:

The world is but a tissue spread over the depths of Chaos. That which we call sanity is but a circle of firelight, and when I spoke to that poor mazed man downstairs, he was several logs off a full blaze.

Even now, with my own more Natural fire drawn up and the study curtains shut against the Christmas chill, I shudder at the visions he imparted. Were it not for the solid evidence, which I have before me as I write, and which catches the firelight and sparkles so prettily, I could dismiss it as the mere ravings of a deranged mind. We have made him as comfortable as the ropes allow in my front room, but his cries punctuate this Christmas Eve like skulls in a flower bed.

"Is Father Christmas Coming/or Is He Just Breathing Heavily? Lots of Stuffing This Christmas!!! Snugglebottom Ex Ex Ex!"
There is a sound outside. Carol singers! Do they not realize the terrible, terrible risk? Yet if I were to throw open the window and warn them to quit the streets, how could I answer their most obvious question? For if I attempted to, I too would be thought

mad . . . But I must set down what he told me, in his moments of clear thought, before insanity claimed him for its own.

Let my readers make of them what they may.

His eyes were the eyes of a man who had looked into Hell and had left behind something of himself. At times he was perfectly lucid, and complained about the ropes the searcher had put him in for fear that in his ravings he would hurt himself. At other times he tried to beat his head on the wall and ranted the slogans that had sent him mad.

"Twenty Pence, Plus Envelope and Seasonal Greeting!"

In between he told me . . .

It had been a wild day, with the snow blowing off the Plain and turning the hills west of Silbury into one great white waste. At such times it is possible to miss the road, and he had got down off the box to lead the horses. Yet, despite what one may read in the papers, the snow was not impossibly deep on the hills, and had abated so that the sunset could be seen. Spirits were generally high, for the lights of Calne were visible, and one and all looked forward to being off the freezing roads by darkness.

And then, as he tells it, there was a creaking noise and a flicker of shadow and the world changed or, he believes, they stepped from this world into another. And, ahead of them, there was a great square hole in the landscape.

He avers now that it was the gateway to Hell, and while it was not the Hell that Dante visited there is to my mind some internal evidence to suggest that his ignorant guess might be the truth. There was something aglitter at the edge of the world and, when he examined the drifted snow, he found the same curious substance strewn haphazardly on the crest of each hummock. It appeared to be thin plates of silver, scattered so as to reflect the light in what would have been, in better circumstances, a pleasing manner.

The coachman and several of the male passengers considered the situation. The sun was sinking fast into a western sky that was now a mess of livid red and purple tones, and to the east more snow threatened. Besides, it appeared to those who ventured a little way back along the coach tracks, which were already being erased by the blowing snow, that the road had been well lost and a white wilderness stretched all around.

At length, there appearing to be no alternative, several of the party resolved to venture closer to the rectangle that obliterated the sky a score of yards away.

It was then that they saw for the first time the monster that appeared to be the guardian of the gateway, perched on a snow-covered log.

It was a giant Robin, several times larger than a Turkey. It watched them with malevolence in its beady eyes, and they feared greatly that it would attack; but it remained unmoving as they reached the rim, and peered out on a blur of colour. Warm air, tinged with tobacco smoke, was blowing into the world, and according to the coachman they could hear strange sounds, distorted and distant . . .

One of the party was a scholar from Oxford who, having in the coachman's opinion refreshed himself mightily during the journey, suggested that some of the party climb through the opening, beyond which lay, at a depth of perhaps three feet, a wide expanse of brown plain, because, uncertain though this course might be, it offered a more certain chance of survival than a night in hills which seemed increasingly alien.

"Season's Greetings! From all at the office!"

Several bold spirits in the party, with whom the scholar had been sharing his brandy, resolved to do this. The coachman was not among them, he told me, yet eventually decided to accompany them out of a sense of duty. They were still his passengers, he said, and he felt it incumbent upon him to bring them safely to Bath.

It was the view of the scholar that Bath might be found across the plain, for, he held, if this was a window out of the world, then it followed that there might be a window back into it . . .

Strange though it may seem, this appeared to be the case. They had not gone above a hundred yards before they saw, looming out of the mists in front of them, another rectangle very similar in appearance to the one they had vacated.

Imagine their joy to see that it opened on to a friendly street lined with yellow-lit windows. One of the party declared that it was in fact a street very close to his own home in London, and while many of the travellers had left London some time before, the prospect of a return now caused them the greatest joy; the traveller promised to open up his house for them, and one of the men volunteered to go back alone to the coach to fetch the rest of the party. For it seemed to all, in those last few moments of hope, that Almighty Providence had foreseen their fate upon the bitter road and had opened a gateway into the warm heart of the greatest city in the world . . .

It was then that they noticed a party of anxious people clustered near the rectangle, and the coachman saw with a falling heart that it too was rim'd with the glittering plates. This party was composed both of men and women, bearing lanterns, and, after some hesitation, one member approached the coachman.

The man who had a house nearby gave a cry of recognition and embraced the stranger, claiming to know him as a neighbour, and then recoiled at the dreadful expression on his face. It was clear that here was another victim of a similar fate.

After some refreshment from the Oxford scholar the newcomer explained that he had, with a party of friends, gone out carol singing. All had been well until, an hour before, there had been an eerie creaking and shifting of shadows, and now they were somehow in a world that was not of the world.

"But—there is a street, and lighted windows," said the London man. "Is that not the Old Curiosity Shop, so ably run by Mrs. Nugent?"

"Then it is more than decently curious, because the doors do not open, and there is nothing beyond the windows but dull yellow light," said the carol singer. "What were houses, my friend, are now nothing but a flat lifelessness."

"But there are other streets—my home, not a hundred yards away . . ."

The carol singer's face was pale. "At the end of the street," he said, "is nothing but white cardboard."

Their companion gave a terrified scream, climbed into the frame, and was soon lost to view. After a few seconds they heard his shout, which the coachman screamed to me, also:

"May This Day Bring You, Every Year, / Joy and Warmth and All Good Cheer!"

Several of the ladies in the carol singers' party were quite hysterical at this point and insisted on joining the company. Thus, after much heated debate, it was resolved to return to the mail coach and, with considerable difficulty, snow and luggage and the glitter were piled against the frame sufficient to allow it to be manhandled down on to the plain.

At this point the coachman's tale becomes quite incoherent. It would seem that they set out to seek yet another entrance to the real world, and found for the first time that the strange windows had an obverse side. If I can understand his ravings, they seemed to be vast white squares in the sky on which some agency had written lengthy slogans of incredible yet menacing banality, whose discovery had so unhinged the London gentleman.

I can hear the coachman's mad giggling even now: *"I have come a long, long way, / To bring you Joy this Christmas Day!"* and he would bang his head on the wall again, in time to what I may, in the loosest sense, call the rhythm of the phrase.

Then he would drum his heels on the floor.

"Merry Xmas to All at No. Twenty-seven!" he would scream, *"From Tony, Pat, and the kids. Remember Majorca?"*

And, *"Get lots of crackling this Christmas!"* This last one seemed particularly to affect his brain, and I cannot but wonder what the poor man must have seen. *"Merry Xmas from Your Little Willy!!!"* and it was at this point that I had to get the gardener to come in and help me restrain him, in the apprehension that he would otherwise manage to do himself an injury.

How long were they on that fateful plain? For it appears that they were in a world outside Time as we know it, and sought for days an entrance into a world that was more than a flatness.

And they were not alone.

There were other people on the same dreadful journey. And Monsters also.

I fear that his mind is quite gone. No sane man could have seen such things. There was a window, if such I may call it, into a world of desert sands under a night sky, wherein three men of African or Asian appearance had made their camp. One of them spoke passable Latin, which the Oxford scholar was still just able to understand, despite his state of near inebriation. They too had found their world running out into a cardboard waste, and after considerable study had put it down to some event, possibly astronomical, which had severely distorted Space and, who knows, perhaps even Time itself.

They made common cause with the coachman's party, much to the chagrin of the ladies present, but it would seem that they were well educated by heathen standards and indeed kept up the spirits of the company with their tales and outlandish songs. They were also men of considerable wealth, a fact of some importance when the swollen caravan of benighted travellers met a party of Shepherds, orphans of their world, and were able to purchase several Sheep which the coachman, who had been raised on a farm, was able to slaughter and dress.

The Shepherds, being nomads by persuasion, had been wandering for some time from their Window, and told of many fearful wonders.

"*Happy Christmas!/ It's Your First One!/ Wishing You Joy/ And a Lifetime of Fun!* Sweet Jesus! The dreadful Beagle!"

What more dare I write? He babbled of four giant kittens with blue bows around their necks; and a rectangle within which was a vast Pie of mincemeat, which they carried for their continued provisions. There were also several glasses, taller than a house, which—after considerable effort with ropes and the utilization of a giant sprig of Holly—were found to contain a sweet Sherry, in which the Oxford scholar unfortunately drowned.

And there was the bellowing red giant, bearded and mad, sitting on a rooftop. And other things, too dreadful to recount: men who were merely coloured shapes, and the enormous black-and-white Caricature of a Dog watching them balefully from the top of its Kennel, and things which even as a man of Science I would blush to record.

It seems that at the last he resolved to quit the company, and came back alone across the plain, believing that to die in the bitter hills of Wiltshire in midwinter was a better fate for a Christian man than life in that abominable world.

No sooner had he reached it, and was crawling in extremis across the strange glittering snow, than behind him he heard once again the eldritch creaking and, upon looking around, saw the dreadful oblong slot disappear. Cold winds and snow immediately forced themselves upon it, but he felt it to be a benediction after that dreadful warm world of the brown plain. And thus, staggering in the fresh blizzard, he was found . . . It is now fully dark. The carol singers have gone, and I trust it is to their homes.

And now my housekeeper departs, having brought me the strange news of the day. A blackamoor on a Camel has been arrested near Avebury. In Swindon a man has been savagely pecked to death in his own garden, and all there are to be seen in the snow are the foot-prints of an enormous Bird. Here in Chippenham itself a traveller has reported seeing, before it leapt a tall hedge and ran across the fields, a cat larger than an Elephant. It had a blue bow about its neck. What monsters have been let into the world?

And on my desk I see my reflection in the shining, tinselly shard that the coachman had clutched in his hands. Who would cover the snow with this to make it glitter, and what fearful reason could there be?

I open the curtains, and look out upon the busy street. The local coach has come up from Bath and is outside the inn, and all is bus-tle and Christmas cheer, a world away from the sad ravings and pleadings of the man downstairs. It is a picture of hope, a reminder of reality, and perhaps he is, after all, no more than a man mazed by exposure, and the tales of giant Beagles and flying sledges are no more than strange jests. Except for the shard of tinsel . . .

"The tinsel on the straw! Amen! Wishing you all the best, Mum and Dad!"

And I see the falling snow, how it glitters . . . And I hear the creak-ing. God help us, every one.

Incubust

The Drabble Project, ed. Rob Meades and David B. Wake,
Beccon Publications, 1988

*This appeared in 1988 in the first of what turned out to be three
books in* The Drabble Project, *produced by Birmingham fans to
raise money for charity and add to the gaiety of nations.*

*A drabble is that once popular SF format, the short, short,
short—one hundred words, not a word more or less. Every word
counts. Oddly enough, I really enjoyed doing it, and even managed
to fit in a footnote.*

The physics of magic is this: no magician, disguise it as he might,
can achieve a result beyond his own physical powers.[*]

And, spurned, he performed the Rite of Tumescence and called
up a fiend from the depths of the Pit to teach her a lesson she
wouldn't forget, the witch.

[*]See the *Necrotelecomnicon*, p. 38.

The phone rang.

"Nice try," she said. "It's sitting on the bedhead now."

His breath quickened. "And?"

"Listen," she said.

And he heard the voice of the fiend, distant and wretched:

". . . frightfully sorry . . . normally, no problem . . . oh god, this has never happened to me before . . ."

FINAL REWARD

G. M. The Independent Fantasy Roleplaying Magazine,
October 1988

I've tinkered with it since, and I can see it needs further tinkering.
Once or twice I've thought about extending it into a novel, and then
thought better of it. But I've always had a soft spot for this story.

Dogger answered the door when he was still in his dressing gown.
Something unbelievable was on the doorstep.

There's a simple explanation, thought Dogger. I've gone mad.

This seemed a satisfactory enough rationalization at seven o'clock
in the morning. He shut the door again and shuffled down the passage, while outside the kitchen window the Northern Line rattled
with carriages full of people who weren't mad, despite appearances.

There is a blissful period of existence which the Yen Buddhists*
call plinki. It is defined quite precisely as that interval between

*Like Zen Buddhists, only bigger begging bowls.

waking up and being hit on the back of the head by all the problems that kept you awake the night before; it ends when you realize that this was the morning everything was going to look better in, and it doesn't.

He remembered the row with Nicky. Well, not exactly row. More a kind of angry silence on her part, and an increasingly exasperated burbling on his, and he wasn't quite sure how it had started anyway. He recalled saying something about some of her friends looking as though they wove their own bread and baked their own goats, and then it had escalated to the level where he'd probably said things like Since you ask, I do think green 2CVs have the antinuclear sticker laminated into their rear window before they leave the factory. If he had been on the usual form he achieved after a pint of white wine, he'd probably passed a remark about dungarees on women, too. It had been one of those rows where every jocular attempt to extract himself had opened another chasm under his feet.

And then she'd broken, no, shattered the silence with all those comments about Erdan, macho wish-fulfilment for adolescents, and there'd been comments about Rambo, and then he'd found himself arguing the case for people who, in cold sobriety, he detested as much as she did.

And then he'd come home and written the last chapter of *Erdan and the Serpent of the Rim,* and out of pique, alcohol, and rebellion he'd killed his hero off on the last page. Crushed under an avalanche. The fans were going to hate him, but he'd felt better afterwards, freed of something that had held him back all these years. And had made him quite rich, incidentally. That was because of computers, because half the fans he met now worked in computers, and of course in computers they gave you a wheelbarrow to take your wages home; science fiction fans might break out in pointy ears from time to time, but they bought books by the shovelful and read them round the clock.

Now he'd have to think of something else for them, write proper science fiction, learn about black holes and quantums . . .

There was another point nagging his mind as he yawned his way back to the kitchen.

Oh, yes. Erdan the Barbarian had been standing on his doorstep. Funny, that.

This time the hammering made small bits of plaster detach themselves from the wall around the door, which was an unusual special effect in a hallucination. Dogger opened the door again.

Erdan was standing patiently next to his milk. The milk was white, and in bottles. Erdan was seven feet tall and in a tiny chain-mail loincloth; his torso looked like a sack full of footballs. In one hand he held what Dogger knew for a certainty was Skung, the Sword of the Ice Gods.

Dogger was certain about this because he had described it thousands of times. But he wasn't going to describe it again.

Erdan broke the silence.

"I have come," he said, "to meet my Maker."

"Pardon?"

"I have come," said the barbarian hero, "to receive my Final Reward." He peered down Dogger's hall expectantly and rippled his torso.

"You're a fan, right?" said Dogger. "Pretty good costume . . ."

"What," said Erdan, "is fan?"

"I want to drink your blood," said Skung conversationally.

Over the giant's shoulder—metaphorically speaking, although under his massive armpit in real life—Dogger saw the postman coming up the path. The man walked around Erdan, humming, pushed a couple of bills into Dogger's unresisting hand, opined against all the evidence that it looked like being a nice day, and strolled back down the path.

"I want to drink his blood, too," said Skung.

Erdan stood impassively, making it quite clear that he was going to stay there until the Snow Mammoths of Hy-Kooli came home.

History records a great many foolish comments, such as, "It looks perfectly safe," or "Indians? What Indians?" and Dogger added to the list with an old favourite which has caused more encyclopedias and life insurance policies to be sold than you would have thought possible.

"I suppose," he said, "that you'd better come in."

No one could look that much like Erdan. His leather jerkin looked as though it had been stored in a compost heap. His fingernails were purple, his hands calloused, his chest a trelliswork of scars. Something with a mouth the size of an armchair appeared to have got a grip on his arm at some time, but couldn't have liked the taste.

What it is, Dogger thought, is I'm externalizing my fantasies. Or I'm probably still asleep. The important thing is to act natural.

"Well, well," he said.

Erdan ducked into what Dogger liked to call his study, which was just like any other living room but had his word processor on the table, and sat down in the armchair. The springs gave a threatening creak.

Then he gave Dogger an expectant look.

Of course, Dogger told himself, he may just be your everyday homicidal maniac.

"Your final reward?" he said weakly.

Erdan nodded.

"Er. What form does this take, exactly?"

Erdan shrugged. Several muscles had to move out of the way to allow the huge shoulders to rise and fall.

"It is said," he said, "that those who die in combat will feast and carouse in your hall forever."

"Oh." Dogger hovered uncertainly in the doorway. "My hall?"

Erdan nodded again. Dogger looked around him. What with the

telephone and the coatrack it was already pretty crowded. Opportunities for carouse looked limited.

"And, er," he said, "how long is forever, exactly?"

"Until the stars die and the Great Ice covers the world," said Erdan.

"Ah. I thought it might be something like that."

Cobham's voice crackled in the earpiece.

"You've what?" it said.

"I said I've given him a lager and a chicken leg and put him in front of the television," said Dogger. "You know what? It was the fridge that really impressed him. He says I've got the next Ice Age shut in a prison, what do you think of that? And the TV is how I spy on the world, he says. He's watching *Neighbours* and he's laughing."

"Well, what do you expect me to do about it?"

"Look, no one could act that much like Erdan! It'd take weeks just to get the stink right! I mean, it's him. Really him. Just as I always imagined him. And he's sitting in my study watching soaps! You're my agent, what do I do next?"

"Just calm down." Cobham's voice sounded soothing. "Erdan is your creation. You've lived with him for years."

"Years is okay! Years was in my head. It's right now in my house that's on my mind!"

". . . and he's very popular and it's only to be expected that, when you take a big step like killing him off . . ."

"You know I had to do it! I mean, twenty-six books!" The sound of Erdan's laughter boomed through the wall.

"Okay, so it's preyed on your mind. I can tell. He's not really there. You said the milkman couldn't see him."

"The postman. Yes, but he walked around him! Ron, I created him! He thinks I'm God! And now I've killed him off, he's come to meet me!"

"Kevin?"

"Yes? What?"

"Take a few tablets or something. He's bound to go away. These things do."

Dogger put the phone down carefully.

"Thanks a lot," he said bitterly.

In fact, he gave it a try. He went down to the hypermarket and pretended that the hulking figure that followed him wasn't really there.

It wasn't that Erdan was invisible to other people. Their eyes saw him all right, but somehow their brains seemed to edit him out before he impinged on any higher centres.

That is, they could walk around him and even apologized automatically if they bumped into him, but afterwards they would be at a loss to explain what they had walked around and who they had apologized to.

Dogger left him behind in the maze of shelves, working on a desperate theory that if Erdan was out of his sight for a while he might evaporate, like smoke. He grabbed a few items, scurried through a blessedly clear checkout, and was back on the pavement before a cheerful shout made him stiffen and turn around slowly, as though on castors.

Erdan had mastered shopping trolleys. Of course, he was really quite bright. He'd worked out the Maze of the Mad God in a matter of hours, after all, so a wire box on wheels was a doddle.

He'd even come to terms with the freezer cabinets. Of course, Dogger thought. *Erdan and the Top of the World,* Chapter Four: he'd survived on ten-thousand-year-old woolly mammoth, fortuitously discovered in the frozen tundra. Dogger had actually done some research about that. It had told him it wasn't in fact possible, but what the hell. As far as Erdan was concerned, the wizard Tesco had simply prepared these mammoths in handy portion packs.

"I watch everyone," said Erdan proudly. "I like being dead."

Dogger crept up to the trolley. "But it's not yours!"

Erdan looked puzzled.

"It is now," he said. "I took it. Much easy. No fighting. I have drink, I have meat, I have My-Name-Is-TRACEY-How-May-I-Help-You, I have small nuts in bag."

Dogger pulled aside most of a cow in small polystyrene boxes and Tracey's mad, terrified eyes looked up at him from the depths of the trolley. She extended a sticker gun in both hands, like Dirty Harry about to have his day made, and priced his nose at 98p a pound.

"Soap," said Dogger. "It's called soap. Not like *Neighbours*, this one is useful. You wash with it." He sighed. "Vigorous movements of the wet flannel over parts of your body," he went on. "It's a novel idea, I know.

"And this is the bath," he added. "And this is the sink. And this is called a lavatory. I explained about it before."

"It is smaller than the bath," Erdan complained mildly.

"Yes. Nevertheless. And these are towels, to dry you. And this is a toothbrush, and this is a razor." He hesitated. "You remember," he said, "when I put you in the seraglio of the Emir of the White Mountain? I'm pretty certain you had a wash and shave then. This is just like that."

"Where are the houris?"

"There are no houris. You have to do it yourself."

A train screamed past, rattling the scrubbing brush into the washbasin. Erdan growled.

"It's just a train," said Dogger. "A box to travel in. It won't hurt you. Just don't try to kill one."

Ten minutes later Dogger sat listening to Erdan singing, although that in itself wasn't the problem; it was a sound you could imagine floating across sunset taiga. Water dripped off the light fitting, but that wasn't the problem.

The problem was Nicky. It usually was. He was going to meet

her after work at the House of Tofu. He was horribly afraid that Erdan would come with him. This was not likely to be good news. His stock with Nicky was bumping on the bottom even before last night, owing to an ill-chosen remark about black stockings last week, when he was still on probation for what he'd said ought to be done with mime artists. Nicky liked New Men, although the term was probably out of date now. Jesus, he'd taken the *Guardian* to keep up with her and got another black mark when he said its children's page read exactly like someone would write if they set out to do a spoof *Guardian* children's page . . . Erdan wasn't a New Man. She was bound to notice him. She had a sort of radar for things like that.

He had to find a way to send him back.

"I want to drink your blood," said Skung, from behind the sofa.

"Oh, shut up."

He tried some positive thinking again.

It is absolutely impossible that a fictional character I created is having a bath upstairs. It's hallucinations, caused by overwork. Of course I don't feel mad, but I wouldn't, would I? He's . . . he's a projection. That's right. I've, I've been going through a bad patch lately, basically since I was about ten, and Erdan is just a projection of the sort of macho thingy I secretly want to be. Nicky said I wrote the books because of that. She said I can't cope with the real world, so I turned all the problems into monsters and invented a character that could handle them. Erdan is how I cope with the world. I never realized it myself. So all I need do is be positive, and he won't exist.

He eyed the pile of manuscript on the table.

I wonder if Conan Doyle had this sort of problem? Perhaps he was just sitting down to tea when Sherlock Holmes knocked at the door, still dripping wet from the Richtofen Falls or whatever, and then started hanging around the house making clever remarks until Doyle trapped him between pages again.

He half rose from his chair. That was it. All he had to do was rewrite the—

Erdan pushed open the door.

"Ho!" he said, and then stuck his little, relatively little, finger in one wet ear and made a noise like a cork coming out of a bottle. He was wearing a bath towel. Somehow he looked neat, less scared. Amazing what hot water could do, Dogger decided.

"All my clothes they prickle," he said cheerfully.

"Did you try washing them?" said Dogger weakly.

"They dry all solid like wood," said Erdan. "I pray for clothes like gods,' mighty Kevin."

"None of mine would fit," said Dogger. He looked at Erdan's shoulders. "None of mine would half fit," he added. "Anyway, you're not going anywhere. I give in. I'll rewrite the last chapter. You can go home."

He beamed. This was exactly the right way. By taking the madness seriously he could make it consume itself. All he need do was change the last page, he didn't even need to write another Erdan book, all he needed to do was to make it clear that Erdan was still alive somewhere.

"I'll write you some new clothes, too," he said. "Silly, isn't it," he went on, "a big lad like you dying in an avalanche! You've survived much worse."

He pulled the manuscript towards him.

"I mean," he burbled happily, "don't you remember when you had to cross the Grebor Desert without water, and you—"

A hand like iron closed over his wrist, gently but firmly. Dogger remembered one of those science films which had showed an industrial robot, capable of putting two tons of pressure on a point an eighth of an inch across, gently picking up an egg. Now his wrist knew how the egg felt.

"I like it here," said Erdan.

He made him leave Skung behind. Skung was a sword of few words, and none of them would go down well in a whole-food restaurant where even the bean sprouts were free-range. Erdan wasn't going to be left behind, though. Where does a seven-foot barbarian hero go? Dogger thought. Wherever he likes.

He also tried writing Erdan a new suit of clothes. It was only partially successful. Erdan was not cut out by nature, by him, to wear a sports jacket. He ended up looking as Dogger had always pictured him, like a large and overenthusiastic Motorhead fan.

Erdan seemed to be becoming more obvious. Maybe whatever kind of mental antibodies prevented people from seeing him wore away after a while. He certainly got a few odd looks.

"Who is tofu?" said Erdan, as they walked to the bus stop.

"Ah. Not a who, an it. It's a sort of food and tiling grout combined. It's . . . it's something like . . . well, sometimes it's green, other times it isn't," said Dogger. This didn't help much. "Well," he said, "remember when you went to 'fight-for-help' the Doge of Tenitti? I'm pretty sure I wrote you eating pasta."

"Yes."

"Compared to tofu, pasta is a taste explosion. Two to the centre, please," Dogger added, to the conductor.

The man squinted at Erdan. "Rock concert on, is there?" he said.

"And you carouse in this tofu?" said Erdan, as they alighted.

"You can't carouse organically. My girl— a young lady I know works there. She believes in things. And, look, I don't want you spoiling it, okay? My romantic life isn't exactly straightforward at the moment." A thought struck him. "And don't let's have any advice from you about how to straighten it. Throwing women over your pommel and riding off into the night isn't approved of around here. It's probably an ism," he added gloomily.

"It works for me," said Erdan.

"Yes," muttered Dogger. "It always did. Funny, that. You never had any trouble, I saw to that. Twenty-six books without a change of clothes and no girl ever said she was washing her hair."

"Not my fault, they just throw—"

"I'm not saying it was. I'm just saying a chap has only got so much of it, and I gave mine to you."

Erdan's brow wrinkled mightily with the effort of thought. His lips moved as he repeated the sentence to himself, once or twice. Then he appeared to reach a conclusion.

"What?" he said.

"And you go back in the morning."

"I like it here. You have picture television, sweet food, soft seats."

"You enjoyed it in Chimera! The snowfields, the bracing wind, the endless taiga . . ."

Erdan gave him a sidelong glance.

"Didn't you?" said Dogger uncertainly.

"If you say so," said Erdan.

"And you watch too much far-seeing box."

"Television," corrected Erdan. "Can I take it back?"

"What, to Chimera?"

"It get lonely on the endless taiga between books."

"You found the Channel Four button, I see." Dogger turned the idea over in his mind. It had a certain charm. Erdan the Barbarian with his blood-drinking sword, chain-mail kilt, portable television, and thermal blanket.

No, it wouldn't work. It wasn't as if there were many channels in Chimera, and probably one of the few things you couldn't buy in the mysterious souks of Ak-Terezical was a set of decent NiCads.

He shivered. What was he thinking about? He really was going mad. The fans would kill him.

And he knew he'd never be able to send Erdan back. Not now. Something had changed, he'd never be able to do it again. He'd enjoyed creating Chimera. He only had to close his eyes and he could see the Shemark Mountains, every lofty peak trailing its pennant of snow. He knew the Prades Delta like the back of his hand. Better. And now it was all going, ebbing like the tide. Leaving Erdan.

Who was evolving.

"Here it say 'House of Tofu.'" said Erdan.

Who had learned to read.

Whose clothes somehow looked less hairy, whose walk was less of a shamble.

And Dogger knew that, when they walked through that door, Erdan and Nicky would hit it off. She'd see him all right. She always seemed to look right through Dogger, but she'd see Erdan.

His hair was shorter. His clothes looked merely stylish. Erdan had achieved in a short walk from the bus stop what it had taken most barbarians ten thousand years to accomplish. Logical, really. After all, Erdan was basically your total hero type. Put him in any environment and he'd change to fit. Two hours with Nicky and he'd be torpedoing whaling ships and shutting down nuclear power stations single-handedly.

"You go on in," he said.

"Problems?" said Erdan.

"Just got something to sort out. I'll join you later. Remember, though, I made you what you are."

"Thank you," said Erdan.

"Here's the spare key to the flat in case I'm not back. You know. Get held up or something."

Erdan took it gravely.

"You go ahead. Don't worry, I won't send you back to Chimera."

Erdan gave him a look in which surprise was leavened with just a hint of amusement.

"Chimera?" he said.

The word processor clicked into life.

And the monitor was without form, and void, and darkness was upon the screen, with of course the exception of the beckoning flicker of the cursor.

Dogger's hand moved upon the face of the keyboard.

It ought to work both ways. If belief was the engine of it all, it ought to be possible to hitch a ride if you really were mad enough to try it.

Where to start?

A short story would be enough, just to create the character. Chimera already existed, in a little bubble of fractal reality created by these ten fingers.

He began to type, hesitantly at first, and then speeding up as the ideas began to crystallize.

After a little while he opened the kitchen window. Behind him, in the darkness, the printer started up.

The key turned in the lock.

The cursor pulsed gently as the two of them came in, talked, made coffee, talked again in the body language of people finding they really have a lot in common. Words like "holistic approach" floated past its uncritical beacon.

"He's always doing things like this," she said. "It's the drinking and smoking. It's not a healthy life. He doesn't know how to look after himself."

Erdan paused. He found the printed output cascading down the table, and now he put down the short MS half read. Outside a siren wailed, dopplered closer, shut off.

"I'm sorry?" he said.

"I said he doesn't look after himself."

"I think he may have to learn," he said. He picked up a pencil, regarded the end of it thoughtfully until the necessary skills clicked precisely in his head, and made a few insertions. The idiot hadn't even specified what kind of clothing he was wearing. If you're really going to write first person, you might as well keep warm. It got damn cold out on the steppes.

"You've known him a long time, then?"

"Years."

"You don't look like most of his friends."

"We were quite close at one time. I expect I'd better see to the place until he comes back." He pencilled in "but the welcoming firelight of a Skryling encampment showed through the freezing trees." Skrylings were okay, they considered that crazy people were great shamans, Kevin should be all right there.

Nicky stood up. "Well, I'd better be going," she said. The tone and pitch of her voice turned tumblers in his head.

"You needn't," he said. "It's entirely up to you, of course."

There was a long pause. She walked up behind him and looked over his shoulder, her manner a little awkward.

"What's this?" she said, in an attempt to turn the conversation away from its logical conclusion.

"Just a story of his. I'd better mail it in the morning."

"Oh. Are you a writer, too?"

Erdan glanced at the word processor. Compared to the Bronze Hordes of Merkle it didn't look too fearsome. A whole new life was waiting for him, he could feel it, he could flow out into it. And change to suit.

"Just breaking into it," he said.

"I mean, I quite like Kevin," she said quickly. "He just never seemed to relate to the real world." She turned away to hide her embarrassment, and peered out of the window.

"There's a lot of blue lights down on the railway line," she said.

Erdan made a few more alterations. "Are there?" he said.

"And there's people milling about."

"Oh." Erdan changed the title to *The Traveller of the Falconsong*. What was needed was more development, he could see that. He'd write about what he knew.

After a bit of thought he added Book One in the Chronicles of Kevin the Bardsinger.

It was the least he could do.

Turntables of the Night

**Hidden Turnings, ed. Diana Wynne Jones,
Methuen, London, 1989**

*Sometimes you just get an idea for a story title and you have to
write it. And Diana Wynne Jones wanted a story for the young adult
anthology* Hidden Turnings, *published in 1989 . . . I quite like it, but
short stories always seem to cost me blood, and I envy the people who
do them for fun.*

Look, constable, what I don't understand is, surely he wouldn't be
into blues? Because that was Wayne's life for you. A blues single.
I mean, if people were music, Wayne would be like one of those
scratchy old numbers, you know, rerecorded about a hundred times
from the original phonograph cylinder or whatever, with some old
guy with a name like Deaf Orange Robinson standing knee-deep in
the Mississippi and moaning through his nose.

You'd think he'd be more into heavy metal or Meat Loaf or someone. But I suppose he's into everyone. Eventually.

What? Yeah. That's my van, with Hellfire Disco painted on it. Wayne can't drive, you see. He's just not interested in anything like that. I remember when I got my first car and we went on holiday, and I did the driving and, okay, also the repairing, and Wayne worked the radio, trying to keep the pirate stations tuned in. He didn't really care where we went as long as it was on high ground and he could get Caroline or London or whatever. I didn't care where we went so long as we went.

I was always more into cars than music. Until now, I think. I don't think I want to drive a car again. I'd keep wondering who'd suddenly turn up in the passenger seat . . .

Sorry. So. Yeah. The disco. Well, the deal was that I supplied the van, we split the cost of the gear, and Wayne supplied the records. It was really my idea. I mean, it seemed a pretty good bet. Wayne lives with his mum but they're down to two rooms now because of his record collection. Lots of people collect records, but I reckon Wayne really wants—wanted—to own every one that was ever made. His idea of a fun outing was going to some old store in some old town and rummaging through the stock and coming out with something by someone with a name like Sid Sputnik and the Spacemen, but the thing was, the funny thing was, you'd get back to his room and he'd go to a shelf and push all the records aside and there'd be this neat brown envelope with the name and date on it and everything—waiting.

Or he'd get me to drive him all the way to Preston or somewhere to find some guy who's a self-employed plumber now but maybe back in 1961 called himself Ronnie Sequin and made it to number 152 in the charts, just to see if he'd got a spare copy of his one record which was really so naff you couldn't even find it in the specialist stores.

Wayne was the kind of collector who couldn't bear a hole in his collection. It was almost religious, really. He could outtalk John Peel in any case, but the records he really knew about were the ones he hadn't got. He'd wait years to get some practically demo disc from a punk group who probably died of safety-pin tetanus, but by the time he got his hands on it he'd be able to recite everything down to the name of the cleaning lady who scrubbed out the studio afterwards. Like I said, a collector.

So I thought, what more do you need to run a disco?

Well, basically just about everything which Wayne hadn't got—looks, clothes, common sense, some kind of idea about electric wiring, and the ability to rabbit on like a prat. But at the time we didn't look at it like that, so I flogged the Capri and bought the van and got it nearly professionally resprayed. You can only see the words Midland Electricity Board on it if you know where to look. I wanted it to look like the van in *The A-Team* except where theirs can jump four cars and still hare off down the road mine has trouble with drain covers.

Yes, I've talked to the other officer about the tax and insurance and MOT. Sorry, sergeant. Don't worry about it, I won't be driving a car ever again. Never.

We bought a load of amplifiers and stuff off Ian Curtis over in Wyrecliff because he was getting married and Tracey wanted him at home of a night, bunged some cards in newsagents' windows, and waited.

Well, people didn't exactly fall over themselves to give us gigs on account of people not really catching on to Wayne's style. You don't have to be a verbal genius to be a jock—people just expect you to say, "Hey!" and "Wow!" and "Get down and boogie" and stuff. It doesn't actually matter if you sound like a pillock, it helps them feel superior. What they don't want, when they're all getting drunk after the wedding or whatever, is for someone to stand there with his eyes flashing worse than the lights saying things like, "There's a rather interesting story attached to this record."

Funny thing, though, is that after a while we started to get popular in a weird word-of-mouth kind of way. What started it, I reckon, was my sister Beryl's wedding anniversary. She's older than me, you understand. It turned out that Wayne had brought along just about every record ever pressed for about a year before they got married. Not just the top ten, either. The guests were all around the same age and pretty soon the room was so full of nostalgia you could hardly move. Wayne just hot-wired all their ignitions and took them for a joyride down Memory Motorway.

After that we started getting dates from what you might call the more older types, you know, not exactly kids but bits haven't started falling off yet. We were a sort of speciality disco. At the breaks people would come up to him to chat about this great number they recalled from way back or whenever and it would turn out that Wayne would always have it in the van. If they'd heard of it, he'd have it. Chances are he'd have it even if they hadn't heard of it. Because you could say this about Wayne, he was a true collector—he didn't worry whether the stuff was actually good or not. It just had to exist.

He didn't put it like that, of course. He'd say there was always something unique about every record. You might think that this is a lot of crap, but here was a man who'd got just about everything ever made over the last forty years and he really believed there was something special about each one. He loved them. He sat up there all through the night, in his room lined with brown envelopes, and played them one by one. Records that had been forgotten even by the people who made them. I'll swear he loved them all.

Yes, all right. But you've got to know about him to understand what happened next.

We were booked for this Hallowe'en Dance. You could tell it was Hallowe'en because of all the little bastards running around the streets shouting, "Trickle treat," and threatening you with milk bottles.

He'd sorted out lots of "Monster Mash" type records. He looked pretty awful, but I didn't think much of it at the time. I mean, he always looked awful. It was his normal look. It came from spending years indoors listening to records, plus he had this bad heart and asthma and everything.

The dance was at— okay, you know all that. A Hallowe'en Dance to raise money for a church hall. Wayne said that was a big joke, but he didn't say why. I expect it was some clever reason. He was always good at that sort of thing, you know, knowing little details that other people didn't know; it used to get him hit a lot at school, except when I was around. He was the kind of skinny boy who had his glasses held together with Elastoplast. I don't think I ever saw him raise a finger to anybody, only that time when Greebo Greaves broke a record Wayne had brought to some school disco and four of us had to pull Wayne off him and prise the iron bar out of his fingers and there was the police and an ambulance and everything.

Anyway.

I let Wayne set everything up, which was one big mistake but he wanted to do it, and I went and sat down by what they called the bar, i.e., a couple of trestle tables with a cloth on it.

No, I didn't drink anything. Well, maybe one cup of the punch and that was all fruit juice. All right, two cups.

But I know what I heard, and I'm absolutely certain about what I saw.

I think.

You get the same old bunch at these kinds of gigs. There's the organizer, and a few members of the committee, some lads from the village who'd sort of drifted in because there wasn't much on the box except snooker. Everyone wore a mask but hadn't made an effort with the rest of the clothes so it looked as though Frankenstein and Co. had all gone shopping in Marks and Sparks. There were Scouts' posters on the wall and those special kinds of village hall radiators that suck the heat in. It smelled of tennis shoes. Just to sort of set the seal on it as one of the hotspots of the world there was a little mirror ball spinning up in the rafters. Half the little mirrors had fallen off.

All right, maybe three cups. But it had bits of apple floating in it. Nothing serious has bits of apple floating in it.

Wayne started with a few hot numbers to get them stomping. I'm speaking metaphorically here, you understand. None of this boogie on down stuff, all you could hear was people not being as young as they used to be.

Now, I've already said Wayne wasn't exactly cut out for the business, and that night—last night—he was worse than usual. He kept mumbling, and staring at the dancers. He mixed the records up. He even scratched one. Accidentally I mean—the only time I've ever seen Wayne really angry, apart from the Greebo business, was when scratch music came in.

It would have been very bad manners to cut in, so at the first break I went up to him and, let me tell you, he was sweating so much it was dropping onto the mixer.

"It's that bloke on the floor," he said, "the one in the flares."

"Methuselah?" I said.

"Don't muck about. The black silk suit with the rhinestones. He's been doing John Travolta impersonations all night. Come on, you must have noticed. Platform soles. Got a silver medallion as big as a plate. Skull mask. He was over by the door."

I hadn't seen anyone like that. Well, you'd remember, wouldn't you?

Wayne's face was frozen with fear. "You must have!"

"So what, anyway?"

"He keeps staring at me!"

I patted his arm. "Impressed by your technique, old son," I said.

I took a look around the hall. Most people were milling around the punch now, the rascals. Wayne grabbed my arm.

"Don't go away!"

"I was just going out for some fresh air."

"Don't . . ." He pulled himself together. "Don't go. Hang around. Please."

"What's up with you?"

"Please, John! He keeps looking at me in a funny way!"

He looked really frightened. I gave in. "Okay. But point him out next time."

I let him get on with things while I tried to neaten up the towering mess of plugs and adapters that was Wayne's usual contribution to electrical safety. If you've got the kind of gear we've got—okay, had—you can spend hours working on it. I mean, do you know how many different kinds of connectors— all right.

In the middle of the next number Wayne hauled me back to the decks.

"There! See him? Right in the middle!"

Well, there wasn't. There were a couple of girls dancing with each other, and everyone else was just couples who were trying to pretend the seventies hadn't happened. Any rhinestone cowboys in that lot would have stood out like a strawberry in an Irish stew. I could see that some tact and diplomacy were called for at this point.

"Wayne," I said, "I reckon you're several coupons short of a toaster."

"You can't see him, can you?"

Well, no. But . . .

. . . since he mentioned it . . .

. . . I could see the space.

There was this patch of floor around the middle of the hall which everyone was keeping clear of. Except that they weren't avoiding it, you see, they just didn't happen to be moving into it. It was just sort of accidentally there. And it stayed there. It moved around a bit, but it never disappeared.

All right, I know a patch of floor can't move around. Just take my word for it, this one did.

The record was ending but Wayne was still in control enough to have another one spinning. He faded it up, a bit of an oldie that they'd all know.

"Is it still there?" he said, staring down at the deck.

113

"It's a bit closer," I said. "Perhaps it's after a spot prize."

. . . I wanna live forever . . .

"That's right, be a great help."

. . . people will see me and cry . . .

There were quite a few more people down there now, but the empty patch was still moving around—all right, was being avoided—among the dancers.

I went and stood in it.

It was cold. It said: GOOD EVENING.

The voice came from all around me, and everything seemed to slow down. The dancers were just statues in a kind of black fog, the music a low rumble.

"Where are you?"

BEHIND YOU.

Now, at a time like this the impulse is to turn around, but you'd be amazed at how good I was at resisting it.

"You've been frightening my friend," I said.

I DID NOT INTEND TO.

"Push off."

THAT DOESN'T WORK, I AM AFRAID.

I did turn around then. He was about seven feet tall in his, yes, his platform soles. And, yes, he wore flares, but somehow you'd expect that. Wayne had said they were black but that wasn't true. They weren't any colour at all, they were simply clothes-shaped holes into Somewhere Else. Black would have looked blinding white by comparison. He did look a bit like John Travolta from the waist down, but only if you buried John Travolta for about three months.

It really was a skull mask. You could see the string.

"Come here often, do you?"

I AM ALWAYS AROUND.

"Can't say I've noticed you." And I would have done. You don't meet many seven-foot, seven-stone people every day, especially ones that walked as though they had to think about every muscle movement in advance and acted as though they were alive and dead at the same time, like Cliff Richard.

YOUR FRIEND HAS AN INTERESTING CHOICE OF MUSIC.

"Yes. He's a collector, you know."

I KNOW. COULD YOU PLEASE INTRODUCE ME TO HIM?

"Could I stop you?"

I DOUBT IT.

All right, perhaps four cups. But the lady serving said there was hardly anything in it at all except orange squash and homemade wine, and she looked a dear old soul. Apart from the Wolfman mask, that is.

But I know all the dancers were standing like statues and the music was just a faint buzz and there were these, all these blue and purple shadows around everything. I mean, drink doesn't do that.

Wayne wasn't affected. He stood with his mouth open, watching us.

"Wayne," I said, "this is—"

A FRIEND.

"Whose?" I said, and you could tell I didn't take to the person, because his flares were huge and he wore one of those silver identity bracelets on his wrist, the sort you could moor a battleship with, and they look so posey; the fact that his wrist was solid bone wasn't doing anything to help, either. I kept thinking there was a conclusion I ought to be jumping to, but I couldn't quite get a running start. My head seemed to be full of wool.

EVERYONE'S, he said, SOONER OR LATER. I UNDERSTAND YOU'RE SOMETHING OF A COLLECTOR.

"Well, in a small—" said Wayne.

I GATHER YOU'RE ALMOST AS KEEN AS I AM, WAYNE.

Wayne's face lit up. That was Wayne, all right. I'll swear if you shot him he'd come alive again if it meant a chance to talk about his hobby, sorry, his lifetime's work.

"Gosh," he said. "Are you a collector?"

ABSOLUTELY.

Wayne peered at him. "We haven't met before, have we?" he said. "I go to most of the collectors' meetings. Were you at the Blenheim Record Fest and Auction?"

I DON'T RECALL. I GO TO SO MANY THINGS.

"That was the one where the auctioneer had a heart attack."

OH. YES. I SEEM TO REMEMBER POPPING IN, JUST FOR A FEW MINUTES.

"Very few bargains there, I thought."

OH. I DON'T KNOW. HE WAS ONLY FORTY-THREE.

All right, inspector. Maybe six drinks. Or maybe it wasn't the drinks at all. But sometimes you get the feeling, don't you, that you can see a little way into the future? Oh, you don't. Well, anyway. I might not have been entirely in my right mind but I was beginning to feel pretty uncomfortable about all this. Well, anyone would. Even you.

"Wayne," I said. "Stop right now. If you concentrate, he'll go away. Settle down a bit. Please. Take a deep breath. This is all wrong."

The brick wall on the other side of me paid more attention. I know Wayne when he meets fellow collectors. They have these weekend rallies. You see them in shops. Strange people. But none of them as strange as this one. He was dead strange.

"Wayne!"

They both ignored me. And inside my mind bits of my brain were jumping up and down, shouting and pointing, and I couldn't let myself believe what they were saying.

OH, I'VE GOT THEM ALL, he said, turning back to Wayne. ELVIS PRESLEY, BUDDY HOLLY, JIM MORRISON, JIMI HENDRIX, JOHN LENNON . . .

"Fairly widespread, musically," said Wayne. "Have you got the complete Beatles?"

NOT YET.

And I swear they started to talk records. I remember Mr. Friend saying he'd got the complete seventeenth-, eighteenth-, and nineteenth-century composers. Well, he would, wouldn't he?

I've always had to do Wayne's fighting for him, ever since we were at primary school, and this had gone far enough and I grabbed Mr. Friend's shoulder and went to lay a punch right in the middle of that grinning mask.

And he raised his hand and I felt my fist hit an invisible wall which yielded like treacle, and he took off his mask and he said two words to me and then he reached across and took Wayne's hand, very gently . . .

And then the power amp exploded because, like I said, Wayne wasn't very good with connectors and the church hall had electrical wiring that dated back practically to 1800 or something, and then what with the decorations catching fire and everyone screaming and rushing about I didn't really know much about anything until they brought me round in the car park with half my hair burned off and the hall going up like a firework.

No. I don't know why they haven't found him either. Not so much as a tooth?

No. I don't know where he is. No, I don't think he owed anyone any money.

(But I think he's got a new job. There's a collector who's got them all—Presley, Hendrix, Lennon, Holly—and he's the only collector who'll ever get a complete collection, anywhere. And Wayne wouldn't pass up a chance like that. Wherever he is now, he's taking them out of their jackets with incredible care and spinning them with love on the turntables of the night . . .)

Sorry. Talking to myself, there.

I'm just puzzled about one thing. Well, millions of things, actually, but just one thing right at the moment.

I can't imagine why Mr. Friend bothered to wear a mask.

Because he looked just the same underneath, idio— officer.

What did he say? Well, I dare say he comes to everyone in some sort of familiar way. Perhaps he just wanted to give me a hint. He said DRIVE SAFELY.

No. No, really. I'll walk home, thanks.

Yes. I'll mind how I go.

#IFDEFDEBUG +
"WORLD/ENOUGH" + "TIME"

Digital Dreams, ed. David V. Barrett, Hodder & Stoughton,
London, 1990

This was published in 1990 in the anthology Digital Dreams, *edited by
Dave Barrett. I was tempted to "update" this—after all, it's about Virtual Reality, haha, remember that, everybody? I am so old I can remember virtual reality!—but what's the point? Besides, it would be cheating.*

*I just liked the idea of an amiable repairman, not very bright but
good with machines, padding the streets of a quiet, dull, sleeping
world. Things are breaking down, knowledge is draining away, and
he's driving his van around the sleeping streets, helping people dream.*

*Now, many years later, it appears rather chilly and maybe quite
close to home.*

Never could stand the idea of machines in people. It's not
proper. People say, hey, what about pacemakers and them arti-

ficial kidneys and that, but they're still machines no matter what.

Some of them have nuclear batteries. Don't tell me that's right.

I tried this implant once, it was supposed to flash the time at the bottom left-hand corner of your eyeball once a second, in little red numbers. It was for the busy exec, they said, who always needs to know, you know, subliminally what the time is. Only mine kept resetting to Tuesday, 1 January 1980, every time I blinked, so I took it back, and the salesman tried to sell me one that could show the time in twelve different capitals plus stock market reports and that. All kinds of other stuff, too. It's getting so you can get these new units and you go to have a slash, excuse my French, and all these little red numbers scroll up with range and position details and a vector-graphics lavvy swims across your vision, beepbeepbeep, lock-on, fire . . .

She's around somewhere. You might of even seen her. Or him. It's like immortality.

Can't abide machines in people. Never could, never will.

I mention this because, when I got to the flat, the copper on the door had that panicky look in his eye they have when they're listening to their internal radio.

I mean, probably it looked a great idea on paper. Whole banks of crime statistics and that, delivered straight to the inside of your head. Only they get headaches from all the noise. And what good is it, every time a cab goes by, they get this impulse to pick up a fare from Flat 27, Rushdie Road? My joke.

I went in and there was this smell.

Not from the body, though. They'd got rid of that smell, first thing.

No. This smell, it was just staleness. The kind of smell old plastic makes. It was the kind of smell a place gets that ought to be dirty, only there's not enough dirt around, so what you get is ground-in cleanness. When you leave home, say, and your mum keeps the room just like it was for ten years, that's the kind of smell you get. The whole flat was like that, although there were no aeroplanes hanging from the ceiling.

So I get called into the main room and immediately I spot the Seagem, because I'm trained, you notice things like that. It was a series Five, which in my opinion were a big mistake. The Fours were pretty near ideal, so why tinker? It's like saying, hey, we've invented the perfect bicycle so, next thing we'll do, we'll put thirteen more wheels on it—like, for example, they replaced the S-2030s with the S-4060, not a good move in my opinion.

This one was dead. I mean, the power light was on and it was warm, but if it was operating, you'd expect to see lights moving on the panel. Also, there was this really big 4711 unit on top, which you don't expect to see in a private house. It's a lab tool. It was a dual model, too. Smell and taste. I could see by the model number it was one of the ones you use a tongue glove with, which is actually quite okay. Never could understand the spray-on polymers. People say, hey, isn't it like having a condom in your mouth, but it's better than having to scrape gunk off your tongue at bedtime.

Lots of other stuff had been hooked in, too, and half a dozen phone lines into a patch unit. There was a 1 MT memory sink, big as a freezer.

Someone who knew what they wanted to buy had really been spending some money here.

And, oh yes, in the middle of it, like they'd told me on the phone, the old guy. He was dead, too. Sitting on a chair. They weren't going to do anything to him until I'd been, they said.

Because of viruses, you see. People get funny ideas about viruses.

They'd taken his helmet off and you could see the calluses where the nose plugs had been. And his face was white, I mean, yes, he was dead and everything, but it had been like something under a stone even before, and his hair was all long and crinkly and horrible where it had been growing under the helmet. And he didn't have a beard, what he had was just long, long chin hair, never had a blade to it in years. He looked like God would look if he was on really serious drugs. And dead, of course.

Actually, he was not that old at all. Thirty-eight. Younger than me. Of course, I jog.

This other copper was standing by the window, trying to pick up HQ through the microwave mush. He looked bored. All the first-wave scene-of-crime types had long been and gone. He just nodded to the Seagem and said, "You know how to fix these things?"

That was just to establish, you know, that there was them and us, and I was a them. But they always call me in. Reliable, see. Dependable. You can't trust the big boys, they're all dealers and agents for the afer companies, they're locked in. Me, I could go back to repairing microswatch players tomorrow. Darren Thompson, Artificial Realities repaired, washing-machine motors rewound. I can do it, too. Ask kids today even to repair a TV, they'll laugh at you, they'll say you're out of the Ark.

I said, "Sometimes. If they're fixable. What's the problem?"

"That's what we'd like you to find out," he says, more or less suggesting, if we can't pin something on him, we'll pin it on you, chum. "Can you get a shock off these things?"

"No way. You see, the interfaces—"

"All right, all right. But you know what's being said about 'em. Maybe he was using it for weird kicks." Coppers think everyone uses them for weird kicks.

"I object most strongly to that," said this other voice. "I object most strongly, and I shall make a note of it. There's absolutely no evidence."

There was this other man. In a suit. Neat. He was sitting by one of these little portable office terminals. I hadn't noticed him before because he was one of these people you wouldn't notice if he was with you in a wardrobe.

He smiled the sort of smile you have to learn and stuck out his hand. Can't remember his face. He had a warm, friendly handshake, the kind where you want to have a wash afterwards.

"Pleased to meet you, Mr. Thompson," he said. "I'm Carney. Paul Carney. Seagem public affairs department. Here to see that you are allowed to carry out your work. Without interference." He looked at the copper, who was definitely not happy. "And any pressure," he added.

Of course, they've always wanted to nail Seagem, I know that. So I suppose they have to watch business. But I've done thirty, forty visits where afers have died, and men in suits don't turn up, so this was special. All the money in the equipment should've told me that.

Life can get very complicated for men in overalls who have problems with men in suits.

"Look," I said. "I know my way around these things okay, but if you want some really detailed testing, then I would have thought your people'll—"

"Seagem's technical people are staying right out of this," snapped the copper. "This is a straight in situ report, you understand. For the coroner. Mr. Carney is not allowed to give you any instructions at all."

Uniforms, too. They can give you grief.

So I took the covers off, opened the toolbox, and stuck in. That's my world. They might think they're big men, but when I've got the back off something and its innards all over the floor, it's me that's the boss . . .

Of course, they're all called Seagems, even the ones made by Hitachi or Sony or Amstrad. It's like Hoovers and hoovers. In a way, they aren't difficult. Nine times out of ten, if you're in trouble, you're talking loose boards, unseated panels, maybe a burnout somewhere. The other one time it's probably something you can only cure by taking the sealed units into the hyperclean room and tapping them with a lump hammer, style of thing.

People say, hey, bet you got an armful of degrees and that. Not me. Basically, if you can repair a washing machine, you can do everything to a Seagem that you can do outside a lab. So long as you can remember where you put the screws down, it's not taxing. That's if it's a hardware problem, of course. Software can be a pain. You got to be a special type of person to handle the software. Like me. No imagination, and proud of it.

"Kids use these things, you know," said the copper, when I was kneeling on the floor with the interface boards stacked around me.

(I always call them coppers, because of tradition. Did you know that "copper" as slang for policeman comes from the verb "to cop," first reliably noted in 1859? No, you don't, because, after all that big thing ten years ago about the trees and that, the university put loads of stuff into those big old read/write optical units, and some kid managed to get a McLint virus into the one in the wossname department. You know? Words? History of words. This was before I specialized in Seagems, only in those days they were still called Computer Generated Environments. And they called me in and all I could haul out of 5 kt of garbage was half a screenful which I read before it wiped. This guy was crying. "The whole history of English philology is up the Swanee," he said, and I said, would it help if I told him the word "copper" was first reliably noted in 1859, and he didn't even make a note of it. He should of. They could, you know, start again. I mean, it wouldn't be much, but it would be a start. Often wondered what "up the Swanee" really means. Don't suppose I'll ever know, now.)

"Kids use them," he said. You could tell he wanted to use a word like "bastards," but not with the suit around.

Not ones like these they don't, I thought. This stuff is top-of-the-range. You couldn't get it in the shops.

"If I caught my lad with one, I'd tan his hide. We used to play healthy games when I was a kid. Elite, Space Invaders, that stuff."

"Yeah." Let's see, attach probes here and here . . .

"Please allow Mr. Thompson to get on with his work," said the suit.

"I think," said the copper nastily, "we ought to tell him who this man is." Then they started to argue about it.

I suppose I'd assumed he was just some old guy who'd hooked into one porno afer too many. Not a bad way to go, by the way. People say, hey, what you mean? Dying of an overdose of artificial sex is okay? And I say, compared to about a million other ways, yes. Realities can't kill you unless you want to go. The normal feedback devices can't raise a bruise, whatever the horror stories say, although between you and me, I've heard of, you know, things, exoskeletons, the army used 'em but they've turned up elsewhere. They can let your dreams kick the shit out of you.

"He's Michael Dever," said the copper. "Mr. Thompson should know that. He invented half this stuff. He's a big man at Seagem. Hasn't been into the office for five years, apparently. Works from home. Worked," he corrected himself. "Top man in development. Lives like this. Lived. Sends all his stuff in over the link. No one bothered about it, see, because he's a genius. Then he missed an important deadline yesterday."

That explained about the suit, then. Heard about Dever, of course, but all the pix in the mags showed this guy in a T-shirt and a grin. Old pix, then. A big man, yes. So maybe important stuff in the machine. Or he was testing something. Or they thought, maybe someone had slipped him a virus. After all, there were enough lines into the unit.

Nothing soiled though, I thought. Some people who are gone on afer will live in shit, but you do get the thorough ones, who work it all out beforehand—fridge stacked with TV dinners, bills paid direct by the bank, half an hour out from under every day for housework and aerobics, and then off they go for a holiday in their heads.

"Better than most I've seen," I said. "Neat. No trouble to anyone. I've been called into ones because of the smell even when they weren't dead."

"Why's he got those pipes hooked up to the helmet?" said the copper.

He really didn't know. I supposed he hadn't had much to do with afers, not really. A lot of the brighter coppers keep away from them, because you can get really depressed. What we had here was Entonox mixture, the intelligent afer's friend. Little tubes to your nose plugs, then a little program on the machine which brings you out of your reality just enough every day for, e.g., a go on the exercise bike, a meal, visit the bathroom.

"If you're going to drop out of your own reality, you need all the help you can get," I explained. "So the machine trickles you some gas and fades the program gradually. Gives you enough of a high to come out of it without screaming."

"What if the valves stick?" asked the suit.

"Can't. There's all kinds of fail-safes, and it monitors your—"

"We believe the valves may have stuck," said the suit firmly.

Well. Good thinking. Seagem don't make valves. The little gas units are definitely third-party add-ons. So if some major employee dies under the helmet, it's nice to blame valves. Only I've never heard of a valve sticking, and there really are a load of fail-safes. The only way it'd work is if the machine held some things off and some things on, and that's purpose, and machines don't have that.

Only it's not my place to say things like that.

"Poor guy," I said.

The copper unfolded at high speed and grabbed my shoulder and towed me out and into a bedroom, just like that. "Just you come and look at this," he kept saying. "Just you come and look. This isn't one of your bloody electronic things. Poor guy? Poor guy? This is real."

There was this other dead body next door, see.

He thought I was going to be shocked. Well, I wasn't. You see worse things in pictures of Ancient Egypt. You see worse things on TV. I see them for real, sometimes. Nearly fresh corpses can be upsetting, believe me, but this wasn't because it'd been years. Plenty of time for the air to clear. Of course, I only saw the head, I wouldn't have liked to have been there when they pulled the sheets back.

She might have been quite good looking, although of course it was hard to be sure. There were coroner's stickers over everything.

"Know what she died of?" asked the copper. "Forensic think she was pregnant and something went wrong. She bled to death. And her just lying there, and him in the next room in his little porno world. Name was Suzannah. Of course, all the neighbours are suddenly concerned that they never saw her around for years. Kept themselves to themselves," he mimicked shrilly. "Half of 'em afers too, you bet.

"He left her for five years. Just left her there."

He was wrong. Listen, I've been called in before when an afer's died, and like I said it's the smell every time. Like rotting food, you know. But Dever or someone had sealed the room nicely, and put her in a body-bag thing.

Anyway, let's face it, most people these days smell via a Seagem of some sort. Keeps you from smelling what you don't want to smell.

It began with the dataglove, and then there were these whole-body suits, and along with them were the goggles—later the helmets—where the computer projected the images. So you could walk into the screen, you could watch your hands move inside the images, you could feel them. All dead primitive stuff now, like Edison's first television or whatever. No smell, not much colour, hardly any sensory feedback. Took them ages to crack smell.

Everyone said, hey, this is it, like your accountant can wear a whole reality suit and stroll around inside your finances. And chemists can manipulate computer simulations of molecules and that. Artificial realities would push back the boundaries of, you know, man's thirst for wossname.

Well, yeah. My dad said once, "Know where I first saw a micro-chip? Inside a Ping-Pong game."

So prob'ly those thirsty for pushing back boundaries pushed 'em back all right, but where you really started seeing reality units was on supermarket checkout girls and in sports shops, because you could have a whole golf course in your home and stuff like that. If you were really rich. Really very rich. But then Seagem marketed a cut-down version, and then Amstrad, and then everything went mad.

You see people in the streets every day with reality units. Mostly they're just changing a few little things. You know. Maybe they edit out black men, or slogans, or add a few trees. Just tinkering a bit, just helping themselves get through the day.

Well sure, I know what some afers do. I know kids who think you can switch the wires so you taste sound and smell vision. What you really do is, you get a blinding headache if you're lucky. And there's the people who, like I said, can't afford a rollafloor so they go hiking through the Venusian jungles or whatever in a room eight feet square and fall out the window. And afers have burned alive and turned into couch crisps. You've seen it all on the box. At least, you have if you're not an afer. They don't watch much.

Odd, really. Government is against it. Well, it's a drug. One you can't tax. And they say, freedom is the birthright of every individual, but you start being free, they get upset. Coppers seem to be offended, too. But . . . well. Take rape. I mean, you don't hear about it these days. Not when you can pick up *Dark Alley Cruiser* down the rental shop. Not that I've watched it, you understand, but I'm told the girl's very good, does all that's expected of her, which you don't have to be an Eisenstein to work out isn't what it'd be like for real, if you catch my drift. And there's other stuff, I won't even mention the titles. I don't need to, do I? It's not all remakes of *Rambo XXIV* with you in the title role is what I mean.

I reckon what the coppers don't like is there's all this crime going on in your head and they can't touch you for it.

There's all that stuff on the TV about how it corrupts people. All these earnest professors sitting round in leather chairs—of course they never use their machines for anything except the nature programmes or high-toned stuff like *Madam Ovary*. Probably does corrupt people but, I don't know, everything's been corrupting people since the, you know, dawn of thingy, but with afers it stays inside. They aren't about to go and knock over some thin little girl in cotton underwear coming back from the all-night chippy, not after *Dark Alley Cruiser*. Probably can't, anyway. And it's cheap so you don't have to steal for it. A lot of them forget to feed themselves. Afers are the kind of problems that come with the solutions built in.

I like a good book, me.

They watched me very hard when I checked the gas-feed controls. The add-on stuff was pretty good. You could see where it was hooked into everything else. I bet if I had time to really run over it on the bench you'd find he had a little daydream every day. Probably didn't even properly come out from under. Funny thing, that, about artificial realities. You know how you can be dreaming and the buzzer goes and the dream sort of incorporates the buzzer into the plot? Probably it was like that.

It had been well maintained. Cleaned regularly and everything. You can get into trouble otherwise, you get buildups of gunk on connectors and things. That's why all my customers, I tell them, you take out a little insurance, I'll be round every six months regular, you can give me the key, I've even got a bypass box so if you're, you know, busy I can do a quick service and be away and you won't know I've been. This is personal service. They trust me.

I switched off the power to the alarms, cleaned a few boards for the look of it, reseated everything, switched it back on. Et wolla.

The copper leaned over my shoulder.

"How did you do that?" he said.

"Well," I said, "there was no negative bias voltage on the sublogic multiplexer," which shut him up.

Thing is, there wasn't anything wrong. It wasn't that I couldn't find a fault, there was nothing to say that a fault existed. It was as if it'd just been told to shut down everything. Including him.

Valve stuck . . . that meant too much nitrous oxide. The scene of crime people prob'ly had to get the smile off his face with a crowbar.

The lights came on, there were all the little whirs and gurgles you get when these things boot up, the memory sinks started to hum, we were cooking with gas.

They got excited about all this.

And then, of course, I had to get out my own helmet.

Viruses, that's the thing. Started off as a joke. Some kid'd hack into someone else's reality, scrawl messages on the walls. A joke, like the McLints. Only, instead of scrambling the wage bill or wiping out English literature, you turned their brain to cheese. Frighten them to death, or whatever. Scares the hell out of some people, the thought that you can kill people that way. They act illogical. You find someone dead under an afer unit, you call in someone like me. Someone with no imagination.

You'd be amazed, the things I've seen.

You're right.

You're clever. You've had an education.

You're saying, hey, I know what you saw. You saw the flat, right, and it was just like it was really, only maybe cleaner, and she was still alive in it, and maybe there was a kid's voice in the next room, the kid they never had, because, right, he'd sat there maybe five years ago maybe while she was still warm and done the reality creation job of a lifetime. And he was living in it, just sane enough to make sure he kept on living in it. An artificial reality just like reality ought to have been.

Right. You're right. You knew it. I should've held something back, but that's not like me.

Don't ask me to describe it. Why ask me to describe it? It was his.

I told the other two and the PR man said firmly, "Well, all right. And then a valve stuck."

"Look," I said, "I'll just make a report, okay? About what I've found. I'm a wire man, I don't mess around with pipes. But I wouldn't mind asking you a question."

That got them. That got them. People like me don't normally ask questions, apart from "Where's the main switch?"

"Well?" said the suit.

"See," I said, "it's a funny old world. I mean, you can hide a body from people these days, it's easy. But there's a lot more to it in the real world. I mean, there's banks and credit companies, right? And medical checks and polls and stuff. There's this big electric shadow everyone's got. If you die—"

They were both looking at me in this funny way. Then the suit shrugged and the uniform handed me this printout from the terminal. I read it, while the memory sink whirred and whirred and whirred . . .

She visited the doctor last year.

The girl who runs the supermarket checkouts swears she sees her regularly.

She writes stories for kids. She's done three in the last five years. Quite good, apparently. Very much like the stuff she used to do before she was dead. One of them got an award.

She's still alive. Out there.

It's like I've always said. Most of the conversations you have with most people are just to reassure one another that you're alive, so you don't need a very complex paragorithm. And Dever could do some really complex stuff.

She's been getting everywhere. She was on that flight to Norway that got blown up last year. The stewardess saw her. Of course, the girl was wearing environment gear, all aircrew do, it stops them having to look at ugly passengers. Mrs. Dever still had a nice time in Oslo. Spent some money there.

She was in Florida, too. At the same time.

She's a virus. The first ever self-replicating reality virus.

She's everywhere.

Anyway, you won't of heard about it, because it all got hushed up because Seagem are bigger than you thought. They buried him and what was left of her. In a way.

I heard from, you know, contacts that at one point the police were considering calling it murder, but what was the point? The way they saw it, all the evidence of her still being alive was just something he'd arranged, sort of to cover things up. I don't think so because I like happy endings, me.

And it really went on for a long time, the memory sink. Like I said, the flat had more data lines running into it than usual, because he needed them for his work.

I reckon he's gone out there, now.

You walk down the street, you've got your reality visor on, who knows if who you're seeing is really there? I mean, maybe it isn't like being alive, but perhaps it isn't like being dead.

I've got photos of both of them. Went through old back issues of the Seagem house magazine, they were both at some long-service presentation. She was quite good-looking. You could tell they liked one another.

Makes sense they'll look just like that now. Every time I switch a visor on, I wonder if I'll spot them. Wouldn't mind knowing how they did it, might like to be a virus myself one day, could be an expert at it.

He owes me, anyway. I got the machine going again and I never told them what she said to me, when I saw her in his reality. She said, "Tell him to hurry."

Romantic, really. Like that play . . . what was it . . . with the good dance numbers, supposed to be in New York. Oh, yeah. *Romeo and Juliet.*

People in machines, I can live with that.

People say to me, hey, this what the human race is meant for? I say, buggered if I know, who knows? We never went back to the Moon, or that other place, the red one, but we didn't spend the money down here on Earth either. So people just curl up and live inside their heads.

Until now, anyway.

They could be anywhere. Of course, it's not like life but prob'ly it isn't death either. I wonder what compiler he used? I'd of loved to have had a look at it before he shut the machine down. When I rebooted it, I sort of initialized him and sent him out. Sort of like a godfather, me.

And anyway, I heard somewhere there's this god, he dreams the whole universe, so is it real or what? Begins with a b. Buddha, I think. Maybe some other god comes round every six million years to service the machinery.

But me, I prefer to settle down of an evening with a good book. People don't read books these days. Don't seem to do anything, much. You go down any street, it's all dead, all these people living in their own realities.

I mean, when I was a kid, we thought the future would be all crowded and cool and rainy with big glowing Japanese adverts everywhere and people eating noodles in the street. At least you'd be communicating, if only to ask the other guy to pass the soy sauce. My joke. But what we got, we got this Information Revolution, what it means is no bugger knows anything and doesn't know they don't know, and they just give up.

You shouldn't turn in on yourself. It's not what being human means. You got to reach out.

For example, I'm really enjoying *Elements of OSCF Bandpass Design in Computer Generated Environments.*

Man who wrote it seems to think you can set your S-2030s without isolating your cascade interfaces.

Try that in the real world and see what happens.

HOLLYWOOD CHICKENS

More Tales from the Forbidden Planet, ed. Roz Kaveney, Titan
Books Ltd, London, 1990

*As the author's note says at the end, this was based on a true story.
At least, Diane Duane swore it was true, and I wasn't about to argue.
And the story just rolled out in front of me. Fortuitously, not long
after I was asked for a story for* More Tales from the Forbidden
Planet, *published in 1990 . . .*

The facts are these.

In 1973, a lorry overturned at a freeway interchange in Hollywood.
It was one of the busiest in the United States and, therefore, the world.

It shed some of its load. It had been carrying chickens. A few
crates broke.

Alongside the interchange, bordered on three sides by thunder-
ing traffic and on the fourth by a wall, was a quarter mile of heavily
shrubbed verge.

No one bothered too much about a few chickens.

*

Peck peck.
Scratch. Scratch.
Cluck?

It is a matter of record that, after a while, those who regularly drove this route noticed that the chickens had survived. There were, and indeed still are, sprinklers on the verge to keep the greenery alive and presumably the meagre population of bugs was supplemented by edible fallout from the constant stream of traffic.

The chickens seemed to be settling in. They were breeding.

Peck peck. Scratch. Peck . . .
Peck?
Scratch peck?
Peck?
Peck + peck = squawk
Cluck?

A rough census indicated that the population had stabilized at around fifty birds. For the first few years young chickens would frequently be found laminated to the blacktop, but some sort of natural selection appeared to be operating, or, if we may put it another way, flat hens don't lay eggs.

Passing motorists did occasionally notice a few birds standing at the kerb, staring intently at the far verge.

They looked like birds with a problem, they said.

SQUAWK PECK PECK CROW!
I   Peck squawk peck
II   Squawk crow peck
III Squawk squawk crow
IV   Scratch crow peck waark

V	(Neck stretch) peck crow
VI	Peck peck peck (preen feathers)
VII	(Peck foot) scratch crow
VIII	Crow scratch
IX	Peck (weird gurgling noise) peck
X	Scratch peck crow waark (to keep it holy).

In fact, aside from the occasional chick or young bird, no chicken was found dead on the freeway itself apart from the incident in 1976, when ten chickens were seen to set out from the kerb together during the rush-hour peak. This must have represented a sizeable proportion of the chicken population at that time.

The driver of a gas tanker said that at the head of the little group was an elderly cockerel, who stared at him with supreme self-confidence, apparently waiting for something to happen.

Examination of the tanker's front offside wing suggests that the bird was a Rhode Island Red.

Cogito ergo cluck.

Periodically an itinerant, or the just plain desperate, would dodge the traffic to the verge and liberate a sleeping chicken for supper.

This originally caused some concern to the Department of Health, who reasoned that the feral chickens, living as they did so close to the traffic, would have built up dangerously high levels of lead in their bodies, not to mention other noxious substances.

In 1978, a couple of research officers were sent into the thickets to bring back a few birds for a sacrifice to Science.

The birds' bodies were found to be totally lead free.

We do not know whether they checked any eggs.

This is important (see Document C).

They did remark incidentally, however, that the birds appeared to have been fighting amongst themselves. (See Document F:

Helorksson and Frim, *Patterns of Aggression in Enclosed Environments,* 1981.) We must assume, in view of later developments, that this phase passed.

Four peck-(neck stretch) and seven cluck-scratch ago, our crow-(peck left foot)-squawk brought forth upon this cluck-cluck-squawk . . .

In the early hours of 10 March 1981, Police Officer James Stooker Stasheff, in pursuit of a suspect, following a chase which resulted in a seven-car collision, a little way from the verge, saw a construction apparently made of long twigs, held together with cassette tape, extending several feet into the carriageway. Two chickens were on the end of it, with twigs in their beaks. "They looked as if they was nest building," he now recalls. "I went past again about ten a.m. It was all smashed up in the gutter."

Officer Stasheff went on to say, "You always get tapes along the freeway. Any freeway. See, when they get snarled up in the Blaupunkt or whatever, people just rip 'em out and pitch them through the window."

According to Ruse and Sixbury (*Bulletin of the Arkham Ornithological Society* 17, pp. 124–32, 1968) birds may, under conditions of chronic stress, build nests of unusual size and complexity (Document D).

This is not necessarily advanced as an explanation.

Peck . . . peck . . . scratch.

Scratch scratch scratch scratch scratch scratch scratch scratch scratch scratch scratch.

The collapse of a small section of carriageway near the verge in the summer of 1983 is not considered germane to this study. The tunnel underneath it was put down to gophers. Or foxes. Or some other burrowing animal. What were irresponsibly described as shoring timbers must simply have been, for example, bits of timber that accidentally got carried into the tunnel by floodwater, as it were, and wedged. Undoubtedly the same thing happened with the feathers.

If Cluck were meant to fly, they'd have bigger (flap).

Testimony of Officer Stasheff again:

"This must have been around late August 1984. This trucker told me, he was driving past, it would have been around midafternoon, when this thing comes flapping, he said flapping, out of the bushes and right across the freeway and he's watching it, and it doesn't lose height, and next thing he knows it bounces off his windshield and breaks up. He said he thought it was kids or something, so I went and had a look at the bushes, but no kids. Just a few of the chickens scratching about, and a load of junk, you know. You wouldn't believe the kind of junk that ends up by the side of roads. I found what was left of the thing that'd hit him. It was like a sort of cage with these kind of big wings on, and all full of pulleys and more bits of cassette tapes and levers and stuff. What? Oh, yeah. And these chickens. All smashed up. I mean, who'd do something like that? One minute flying chickens, next minute McNuggets. I recall there were three of them. All cockerels, and brown."

It's a (small scratch) for a cluck, a (giant flap) for Cluck.

Testimony of Officer Stasheff again (19 July 1986):

"Kids playing with fire. That's my opinion. They get over the wall and make hideouts in the bushes. Like I said, they just grab one of the chickens. I don't see why everyone's so excited. So some kids fill an old trash can with junk and fireworks and stuff and push a damn chicken in it and blow it up in the air . . . It'd have caused a hell of a lot of damage if it hadn't hit one of the bridge supports on the far side. Bird inside got all smashed up. It'd got this cloth in there with strings all over. Maybe the kids thought the thing could use a parachute. Okay, so there's a crater, what the hell, plant a bush in it. What? Sure it'd be hot, it's where they were playing spacemen. Not that kind of hot? What kind of hot?"

Peck (Neck Twist) – crow = gurgle/C^2
   Cluck?

We do know that at about two a.m. on the morning of 3 May 1989, a purple glow in the bushes around the middle of the verge was noticed by several drivers. Some say it was a blue glow. From a cross-checking of the statements, it appeared to last for at least ten minutes.

There was also a noise. We have a number of descriptions of this noise. It was "sort of weird," "kind of a whooping sound," and "rather like radio oscillation." The only one we have been able to check is the description from Curtis V. J. McDonald, who said, "You know in that *Star Trek* episode when they meet the fish men from an alternate Earth? Well, the fish men's matter transmitter made just the same noise."

We have viewed the episode in question. It is the one where Captain Kirk falls in love with the girl (Tape A).

Cluck?
   (Foot twist) $\sqrt{2t}\beta$ ... [Σ/peck]/Scratch$^{2^*}$ $^{*\text{oon}}$ (Gurgle)(Left-shoulder-preen) = (Right-shoulder-preen) ...
   HmmMMmmMMmmMMmmMMmmMMmm.
   Cluck.

We also know that the person calling himself Elrond X, an itinerant, entered the area around 2 a.m. When located subsequently, he said: "Yeah, well, maybe sometimes I used to take a chicken but there's no law against it. Anyway, I stopped because it was getting very heavy, I mean, it was the way they were acting. The way they looked at you. Their beady eyes. But times are tough and I thought, okay, why not . . .

"There's no chickens there, man. Someone's been through it, there's no chickens!"

When asked about the Assemblage, he said: "There was only this pile of junk in the middle of the bushes. It was just twigs and wire and junk. And eggs, only you never touch the eggs, we know that, some of those eggs give you a shock, like electricity. 'Cos you never asked me before, that's why. Yeah, I kicked it over. Because there was this chicken inside it, okay, but when I went up close there was this flash and, like, a clap of thunder and it went all wavy and disappeared. I ain't taking that from no chicken."

Thus far we have been unable to reassemble the Assemblage (Photos A through G). There is considerable doubt as to its function, and we have dismissed Mr. X's view that it was "a real funky microwave oven." It appeared simply to have been a collection of roadside debris and twigs, held together with cassette tape.* It may have had some religious significance. From drawings furnished by Mr. X, there appeared to have been space inside for one chicken at a time.

Document C contains an analysis of the three eggs found in the debris. As you will see, one of them seems normal but infertile, the second has been powering a flashlight bulb for two days, and a report on the third is contingent on our finding either it or Dr. Paperbuck, who was last seen trying to cut into it with a saw.

For the sake of completeness, please note Document B, which is an offprint of Paperbuck and Macklin's *Western Science Journal* paper, "Exaggerated Evolutionary Pressures on Small Isolated Groups Under Stress."

*The Best of Queen

All that we can be certain of is that there are no chickens in the area where chickens have been for the last seventeen years.

However, there are now forty-seven chickens on the opposite verge.

Why they crossed is of course one of the fundamental riddles of popular philosophy.

That is not, however, the problem.

We don't know how.

But it's not such a great verge over there, and they're all clustered together and some of the hens are laying.

We're just going to have to wait and see how they get back.

Cluck?

AUTHOR'S NOTE: In 1973, a lorry overturned at a freeway interchange in Hollywood. It was one of the busiest in the United States and, therefore, the world. Some chickens escaped and bred. They survived—are surviving—very well, even in the hazardous atmosphere of the roadside. But this story is about another Hollywood. And other chickens.

THE SECRET BOOK OF THE DEAD

Now We Are Sick, ed. Neil Gaiman and Stephen Jones,
DreamHaven Books, Minneapolis, 1991

*Given the title of the anthology in which this was to appear, I tried
to write this as though I were thirteen years old, with that earnest
brand of serious amateurishness. This is possibly not a long way from
how I write at the best of times . . .*

They don't teach you the facts of death,
Your Mum and Dad. They give you pets.
We had a dog which went astray.
Got laminated to the motorway.
I cried. We had to post him to the vet's.

You have to work it out yourself,
This dying thing. Death's always due.
A goldfish swimming on a stall,
Two weeks later: cotton wool,
And sent to meet its Maker down the loo.

The bottom of our garden's like a morg-you
My dad said. I don't know why.
Our tortoise, being in the know
Buried himself three years ago.
This is where the puppies come to die.
Puss has gone to be a better cat
My dad said. It wasn't fair.
I think my father's going bats
Jesus didn't come for cats
I went and looked. Most of it's still there.

They don't teach you the facts of death,
Your mum and dad. It's really sad.
Pets, I've found, aren't built to last;
One Christmas present, next Christmas past.
We go on buying them. We must be mad.

They die of flu and die of bus,
Die of hard pad, die of scabies,
Foreign ones can die of rabies,
But usually they die of us.

ONCE AND FUTURE

Camelot, ed. Jane Yolen, Philomel Books, New York, 1995

There's a lot more of this deep on a hard drive somewhere. It may yet become a novel, but it started as a short story in Camelot, *edited by Jane Yolen, in 1995. I'd wanted to write it for nearly ten years. I really ought to dig out those old discs* again . . .*

. . . when matins were done the congregation filed out to the yard. They were confronted by a marble block into which had been thrust a beautiful sword. The block was four feet square, and the sword passed through a steel anvil which had been struck in the stone, and which projected a foot from it. The anvil had been inscribed with letters of gold:

---

*Sorry to say, if I ever do find those discs, they will almost certainly be in the wrong format. But I still really like the idea of the person who pulled Excalibur from the stone happening to be female.

A BLINK OF THE SCREEN

WHOSO PULLETH OUTE THIS SWERD
OF THIS STONE AND ANVYLD
IS RIGHTWYS KYNGE
BORNE OF ALL BRYTAYGNE.

from Le Morte d'Arthur *by Sir Thomas Malory*

The copper wire. It was the copper wire that gave me the trouble.

It's all down to copper wire. The old alchemists used to search for gold. If only they'd known what a man and a girl can do with copper wire . . .

And a tide mill. And a couple of hefty bars of soft iron.

And here I am now, with this ridiculous staff in one hand and the switch under my foot, waiting.

I wish they wouldn't call me Merlin. It's Mervin. There was a Merlin, I've found out. A mad old guy who lived in Wales and died years ago. But there were legends about him, and they're being welded on to me now. I reckon that happens all the time. Half the famous heroes of history are really lots of local guys all rolled into one by the ballad singers. Remember Robin Hood? Technically I suppose I can't, because none of the rascals who went under that name will be born for several centuries yet, if he even is due to exist in this universe, so using the word *remember* is probably the wrong, you know, grammar. Can you remember something that hasn't happened yet? I can. Nearly everything I can remember hasn't happened yet, but that's how it goes in the time-travel business. Gone today and here tomorrow . . .

Oh, here comes another one of them. A strapping lad. Legs like four beer kegs stacked in pairs, shoulders like an ox. Brain like an ox, too, I shouldn't wonder. Hand like a bunch of bananas, gripping the sword . . .

Oh, no, my lad. You're not the one. Grit your teeth all you like. You're not the one.

There he goes. His arm'll be aching for days.

You know, I suppose I'd better tell you about this place.

About this time.

Whenever it is . . .

I had special training for time travelling. The big problem, the big problem, is finding out when you are. Basically, when you step out of a time machine you can't rely on seeing a little sign that says, "Welcome to AD 500, Gateway to the Dark Ages, pop. 10 million and falling." Sometimes you can't even rely on finding anyone in a day's march who knows what year it is, or what king is on the throne, or what a king is. So you learn to look at things like church architecture, the way the fields are farmed, the shape of the ploughshares, that sort of thing.

Yeah, I know, you've seen films where there's this dinky little alphanumeric display that tells you exactly where you are . . .

Forget it. It's all dead reckoning in this game. Real primitive stuff. You start out by checking the constellations with a little gadget, because they tell me all the stars are moving around all the time and you can get a very rough idea of when you are just by looking through the thing and reading off along the calibrations. If you can't even recognize the constellations, the best thing to do is run and hide, because something forty feet tall and covered with scales is probably hunting you already.

Plus they give you a guide to various burned-out supernovas and Stofler's *Craters of the Moon by Estimated Creation Date.* With any luck you can pinpoint yourself fifty years either way. Then it's just a matter of checking planetary positions for the fine-tuning. Try to imagine sea navigation around the time of, oh, Columbus. A bit hit or miss, yeah? Well, time navigation is just about at the same level.

Everyone said I must be one great wizard to spend so much time studying the sky.

That's because I was trying to find out when I was.

Because the sky tells me I'm around AD 500. So why is the architecture Norman and the armour fifteenth-century?

Hold on . . . here comes another one . . .

Well, not your actual Einstein, but it could be . . . oh, no, look at that grip, look at that rage . . . no. He's not the one. Not him.

Sorry about that.

So . . . right . . . where was I? Memory like a sieve these days.

Yeah, the architecture. And everyone speaking a sort of Middle English, which was okay as it turned out because I can get by in that, having accidentally grounded in 1479 once. That was where I met John Gutenberg, father of modern printing. Tall man, bushy whiskers. Still owes me tuppence.

Anyway. Back to this trip. It was obvious from the start that things weren't quite right. This time they were supposed to be sending me to observe the crowning of Charlemagne in AD 800, and here I was in the wrong country and, according to the sky, about three centuries too soon. That's the kind of thing that happens, like I said; it's going to be at least fifty years before we get it right. Fifty-three years, actually, because I met this man in a bar in 1875 who's from a hundred years in our future, and he told me. I told them at Base we might as well save a lot of effort by just, you know, bribing one of the future guys for the plans of the next model. They said if we violated the laws of Cause and Effect like that, there's a good chance the whole universe would suddenly catastrophically collapse into this tiny bubble .005 angstroms across, but I say it's got to be worth a try.

Anyway, the copper wire gave me a load of trouble.

That's not to say I'm an incompetent. I'm just an average guy in every respect except that I'm the one in ten thousand who can time travel and still end up with all his marbles. It just gives me a slight headache. And I'm good at languages and I'm a very good observer, and you'd better believe I've observed some strange things. The Charlemagne coronation was going to be a vacation. It was my second visit, paid for by a bunch of historians in some university somewhere. I was going to check a few things that the guys who commissioned the first trip had raised after reading my report. I had it all worked out where I was going to stand so I wouldn't see myself. I could probably have talked my way out of it even if I had met myself, at that. One thing you learn in this trade is the gift of the gab.

And then a diode blew or a one turned out to be a zero and here I am, whenever this is.

And I can't get back.

Anyway . . . what was I saying . . .

Incidentally, the other problem with the copper wire is getting the insulation. In the end I wrapped it up in fine cloth and we painted every layer with some sort of varnish they use on their shields, which seems to have done the trick.

And . . . hmm . . . you know, I think time travelling affects the memory. Like, your memory subconsciously knows the things you're remembering haven't happened yet, and this upsets it in some way. There's whole bits of history I can't remember. Wish I knew what they were.

Excuse me a moment. Here's another one. An oldish guy. Quite bright, by the look of him. Why, I bet he can probably write his own name. But, oh, I don't know, he hasn't got the . . .

Hasn't got the . . .

Wish I knew what it was he hasn't got . . .

. . . charisma. Knew it was there somewhere.

So. Anyway. Yeah. So there I was, three centuries adrift, and nothing working. Ever seen a time machine? Probably not. The bit you move around is very, very hard to see, unless the light catches it just right. The actual works are back at Base and at the same time in the machine, so you travel in something like a mechanical ghost, something like what's left of a machine when you take all the parts away. An idea of a machine.

Think of it as a big crystal. That's what it'd look like to you if, as I said, the light was right.

Woke up in what I suppose I've got to call a bed. Just straw and heather with a blanket made of itches woven together. And there was this girl trying to feed me soup. Don't even try to imagine medieval soup. It's made of all the stuff they wouldn't eat if it was on a plate and, believe me, they'd eat stuff you'd hate to put in a hamburger.

I'd been there, I found out later, for three days. I didn't even know I'd arrived. I'd been wandering around in the woods, half conscious and dribbling. A side effect of the travelling. Like I said, normally I just get a migraine, but from what I can remember of that, it was jet lag times one million. If it had been winter, I'd have been dead. If there'd been cliffs, I would have thrown myself over one. As it was, I'd just walked into a few trees, and that was by accident. At least I'd avoided the wolves and bears. Or maybe they'd avoided me; maybe they think you die if you eat a crazy person.

Her father was a woodcutter, or a charcoal burner, or one of those things. Never did find out, or perhaps I did and I've forgotten. He used to go out every day with an axe, I remember that. He'd found me and brought me home. I learned afterwards he thought I was a nobleman, because of my fine clothes. I was wearing Levi's, that should give you some idea. He had two sons, and they went out every day with axes, too. Never really managed to strike up a conversation with either of them until after the father's accident. Didn't know enough about axes, I suppose.

But Nimue . . . What a girl. She was only . . . er . . .

"How old were you, when we met?"

She wipes her hands on a bit of rag. We'd had to grease the bearings with pig fat.

"Fifteen," she says. "I think. Listen, there's another hour of water above the mill, but I don't think the gennyrator will last that long. It's shaking right merrily."

She looks speculatively at the nobles.

"What a bunch of by-Our-Lady jacks," she says.

"Jocks."

"Yes. Jocks."

I shrug. "One of them will be your king," I tell her.

"Not my king, Mervin. I will never have a king," she says, and grins.

By which you can tell she's learned a lot in twelve months. Yes, I broke the rules and told her the truth. And why not? I've broken all the rules to save this damn country, and it doesn't look like the universe is turning into this tiny ball .005 angstroms across. First, I don't think this is our timeline. It's all wrong, like I said. I think I was knocked sideways, into some sort of other history. Maybe a history that'll never really exist except in people's heads, because time travel is a fantasy anyway. You hear mathematicians talk about imaginary numbers which are real, so I reckon this is an imaginary place made up of real things. Or something. How should I know? Perhaps enough people believing something makes it real.

I'd ended up in Albion, although I didn't find out until later. Not Britain, not England. A place very much like them, a place that shares a lot of things with them, a place so close to them that maybe ideas and stories leak across—but a place that is its own place.

Only something went wrong somewhere. There was someone missing. There should have been a great king. You can fill in his name. He's out there somewhere, in the crowd. It's lucky for him I turned up.

You want me to describe this world. You want to hear about the jousts, the pennants, the castles. Right. It's got all of that. But everything else has this, like, thin film of mud over it. The difference between the average peasant's hut and a pigsty is that a good farmer will sometimes change the straw in a pigsty. Now, get me right—no one's doing any repressing, as far as I can see. There's no slavery as such, except to tradition, but tradition wields a heavy lash. I mean, maybe democracy isn't perfect, but at least we don't let ourselves be outvoted by the dead.

And since there's no strongman in charge there's a little would-be king in every valley, and he spends most of his time fighting other would-be kings, so the whole country is in a state of halfhearted war. And everyone goes through life proudly doing things clumsily just because their forefathers did them that way, and no one really enjoys anything, and good fields are filling with weeds . . .

I told Nimue I came from another country, which was true enough.

I talked to her a lot because she was the only one with any sense around the place. She was small, and skinny, and alert in the same way that a bird is alert. I said I broke the rules to save this country but if I'm honest, I'll have to say I did it all for her. She was the one bright thing in a world of mud, she's nice to have around, she learns quickly, and—well, I've seen what the women here look like by the time they're thirty. That shouldn't happen to anyone.

She talked and she listened to me while she did the housework, if that's what you can call moving the dirt around until it got lost.

I told her about the future. Why not? What harm could it do? But she wasn't very impressed. I guess she didn't know enough to be impressed. Men on the moon were all one with the fairies and the saints. But piped water caught her interest, because every day she had to go to a spring with a couple of wooden buckets on a yoke thing round her neck.

"Every cottage has this?" she said, eyeing me carefully over the top of the broom.

"Sure."

"Not just the rich?"

"The rich have more bathrooms," I said. Then I had to explain about bathrooms.

"You people could do it," I told her. "You just need to dam a spring up in the hills, and find a—a blacksmith or someone to make some copper pipes. Or lead or iron, at a pinch."

She looked wistful.

"My father wouldn't allow it," she said.

"Surely he'd see the benefits of having water laid on?" I suggested.

She shrugged. "Why should he? He doesn't carry it from the spring."

"Oh."

But she took to following me around, in what time there was between chores. It's just as I've always said—women have always had a greater stake in technology than have men. We'd still be living in trees, otherwise. Piped water, electric lighting, stoves that you don't need to shove wood into—I reckon that behind half the great inventors of history were their wives, nagging them into finding a cleaner way of doing the chores.

Nimue trailed me like a spaniel as I tottered around their village, if you could use the term for a collection of huts that looked like something deposited in the last Ice Age, or possibly by a dinosaur with a really serious bowel problem. She even led me into the forest, where I finally found the machine in a thorn thicket. Totally unrepairable. The only hope was that someone might fetch me, if they ever worked out where I was. And I knew they never would, because if they ever did, they'd have been there already. Even if it took them ten years to work it out, they could still come back to the Here and Now. That's the thing about time travel; you've got all the time in the world.

I was marooned.

However, we experienced travellers always carry a little something to tide us over the bad times. I'd got a whole box of stuff under the seat. A few small gold ingots (acceptable everywhere, like the very best credit cards). Pepper (worth more than gold for hundreds of years). Aluminum (a rare and precious metal in the days before cheap and plentiful electricity). And seeds. And pencils. Enough drugs to start a store. Don't tell me about herbal remedies—people screamed down the centuries, trying to stop things like dental abscesses with any green junk that happened to be growing in the mud.

She watched me owlishly while I sorted through the stuff and told her what it all did.

And the next day her father cut his leg open with his axe. The brothers carried him home. I stitched him up and, with her eyes on me, treated the wound. A week later he was walking around again, instead of being a cripple at best or most likely a gangrenous corpse, and I was a hero. Or, rather, since I didn't have the muscles for a hero, obviously a wizard.

I was mad to act like that. You're not supposed to meddle. But what the hell. I was marooned. I was never going home. I didn't care. And I could cure, which is almost as powerful as being able to kill. I taught hygiene. I taught them about turnips, and running water, and basic medicine.

The boss of the valley was a decent enough old knight called Sir Ector. Nimue knew him, which surprised me, but shouldn't have. The old boy was only one step up from his peasants, and seemed to know them all, and wasn't much richer than they were except that history had left him with a crumbling castle and a suit of rusty armour. Nimue went up to the castle one day a week to be a kind of lady's maid for his daughter.

After I pulled the bad teeth that had been making his life agony, old Ector swore eternal friendship and gave me the run of the place. I met his son Kay, a big hearty lad with the muscles of an ox and possibly the brains of one, and there was this daughter to whom no one seemed to want to introduce me properly, perhaps because she was very attractive in a quiet kind of way. She had one of those stares that seem to be reading the inside of your skull. She and Nimue got along like sisters. Like sisters that get along well, I mean.

I became a big man in the neighbourhood. It's amazing the impression you can make with a handful of medicines, some basic science, and a good line in bull.

Poor old Merlin had left a hole which I filled like water in a cup. There wasn't a man in the country who wouldn't listen to me.

And whenever she had a spare moment Nimue followed me, watching like an owl.

I suppose at the time I had some dream, like the Connecticut Yankee, of single-handedly driving the society into the twentieth century.

You might as well try pushing the sea with a broom.

"But they do what you tell them," Nimue said. She was helping me in the lab at the time, I think. I call it the lab, it was just a room in the castle. I was trying to make penicillin.

"That's exactly it," I told her. "And what good is that? The moment I turn my back, they go back to the same old ways."

"I thought you told me a dimocracy was where people did what they wanted to do," she said.

"It's a democracy," I said. "And it's fine for people to do what they want to do, provided they do what's right."

She bit her lip thoughtfully. "That does not sound sensible."

"That's how it works."

"And when we have a, a democracy, every man says who shall be king?"

"Something like that, yes."

"And what do the women do?"

I had to think about that. "Oh, they should have the vote, too," I said. "Eventually. It'll take some time. I don't think Albion is ready for female suffrage."

"It has female suffrage already," she said, with unusual bitterness.

"Suffrage. It means the right to vote."

I patted her hand.

"Anyway," I told her, "you can't start with a democracy. You have to work up through stuff like tyranny and monarchy first. That way people are so relieved when they get to democracy that they hang on to it."

"People used to do what the king told them," she said, carefully measuring bread and milk into the shallow bowls. "The high king, I mean. Everyone did what the high king said. Even the lesser kings."

I'd heard about this high king. In his time, apparently, the land had flowed with so much milk and honey people must have needed waders to get around. I don't go for that kind of thing. I'm a practical man. When people talk about their great past they're usually trying to excuse the mediocre present.

"Such a person might get things done," I said. "But then they die, and history shows"—or will show, but I couldn't exactly put it like that to her—"that things go back to being even worse when they die. Take it from me."

"Is that one of those things you call a figure of speech, Mervin?"

"Sure."

"There was a child, they say. Hidden somewhere by the king until it was old enough to protect itself."

"From wicked uncles and so on?"

"I do not know about uncles. I heard men say that many kings hated the power of Uther Pendragon." She stacked the dishes on the windowsill. I really hadn't got much idea about penicillin, you understand. I was just letting stuff go mouldy, and hoping.

"Why are you looking at me like that?" she said.

"Uther Pendragon? From Cornwall?"

"You knew him?"

"I—er—I—yes. Heard of him. He had a castle called Tintagel. He was the father of—"

She was staring at me.

I tried again. "He was a king here?"

"Yes!"

I didn't know what to say to her. I wandered over to the window and looked out. There was nothing much out there but forest. Not clear forest, like you'd find Tolkien's elves in, but deep, damp forest, all mosses and punkwood. It was creeping back. Too many little wars, too many people dying, not enough people to plough the fields. And out there, somewhere, was the true king. Waiting for his chance, waiting for—

Me?

The king. Not any old king. *The* king. Arthur. Artos the Bear. Once and Future. Round Table. Age of Chivalry. He never existed.

Except here. Maybe.

Maybe here, in a world you get to in a broken time machine, a world that's not exactly memory and not exactly story . . .

And I was the only one who knew how the legend went.

Me. Mervin.

With his leadership and my, er, experience . . . what a team . . .

I looked at her face. Clear as a pond now, but a little worried. She was thinking that old Mervin was going to be ill again.

I remember I drummed my fingers on the cold windowsill. No central heating in the castle. Winter was coming. It was going to be a bad one, in this ruined country.

Then I said, "Ooooooh."

She looked startled.

"Just practising," I said, and tried again, "Ooooooooooooh, hear me, hear me." Not bad, not bad. "Hear me, O ye men of Albion, hear me. It is I, Mervin, that's with a V, who speaks to you. Let the message go out that a Sign has been sent to end the wars and choose the rightwise King of Albion . . . Ooooooooooooh-er."

She was near to panic by this time. A couple of servants were peering around the door. I sent them away.

"How was it?" I said. "Impressive, eh? Could probably work, yeah?"

"What is the Sign?" she whispered.

"Traditionally, a sword in a stone," I said. "Which only the rightful heir can pull out."

"But how can that be?"

"I'm not sure. I'll have to think of a way."

That was months ago.

The obvious way was some sort of bolt mechanism or something . . .

No, of course I didn't think there was a mystic king out there. I kept telling myself that. But there was a good chance that there was a lad who looked good on a horse and was bright enough to take advice from any wizardly types who happened to be around. Like I said, I'm a practical man.

Anyway . . . what was I saying? Oh, yes. All the mechanical ways of doing it I had to rule out. That left electricity. Strange thing is, it's a lot easier to make a crude electrical generator than a crude steam engine. The only really critical things are the bearings.

And the copper wire.

It was Nimue who eventually sorted that one out.

"I've seen ladies wearing fine jewellery with gold and silver wires in it," she said. "The men who made them must know how to do it with copper."

And of course she was right. I just wasn't thinking straight. They just pulled thin strips of metal through tough steel plates with little holes in them, gradually bullying it into smaller and smaller thickness. I went to London and found a couple who could do it, and then I got a blacksmith to make up some more drawplates because I didn't want wire in jewellery quantities but in industrial amounts. I'd already got quite a reputation then, and no one asked me what I needed it for. I could have said, "Well, half of it will be for the generator, and the rest will be for the electromagnets in the stone," and what would they have known? I had another smith make me up some soft iron cores and the bearings, and Nimue and I spent hours winding the wire and shellacking every layer.

Getting the motive power was simpler. The country was thick with mills. I chose a tide mill, because it's dependable and this one was on an impressive stretch of coast. I know the legend said it was done in London or Winchester or somewhere, but I had to go where the power was and, anyway, it looked good, there on the shore with the surf pounding on the rocks and everything.

The stone was the easy bit. There's been a crude concrete technology ever since the Romans. Though I say it myself, I made a quite nice-looking stone around the electromagnets. We got it finished days before the day I'd set for the big contest. We'd put up a big canvas shield around it, although I don't think any of the locals would have come near it for a fortune.

Nimue operated the switch while I slid the sword in and out.

"That means you're king," she said, grinning.

"Not me. I haven't got what it takes to rule."

"Why? What does it take?"

"We'll know when we see it. We're looking for a boy with the air of authority. The kind of lad a war-weary people will follow."

"And you're sure you'll find him?"

"If I don't, the universe isn't being run properly."

She's got this funny way of grinning. Not exactly mocking, but it's always made me feel uneasy.

"And he'll listen to you?"

"He'd better. I'm the wizard around here. There's not a man in the country I can't outthink, my girl."

"I wish I were as clever as you, Mervin," she said, and grinned again.

Silly little thing . . .

And now back to the present. Time travel! Your mind wanders. Back to this rocky shore. And the stone and the sword.

Hold it . . . hold it . . .

I think . . .

Yes.

This looks like the one.

A slight young lad, not swaggering at all, but strolling up to the stone as if he's certain of his fortune. Ragged clothes, but that's not a problem, that's not a problem, we can do something about those later.

People are moving aside. It's uncanny. You can see Destiny unfolding, like a deck chair.

Can't see much under the hood. It's one of those big floppy ones the peasants wear, but he's looking directly at me.

I wonder if he suspects? I wonder if he's real?

I wonder where he's been hiding all these years?

Well, never mind that now. Got to seize the moment. Shift my weight slightly, so my foot comes off the buried switch, cutting the current to the rock.

Good lord, he's not even making an effort. And up comes the sword, sweet as you like.

And everyone's cheering, and he's waving the thing in the air, and the sun's coming out and catching it in a way that even I couldn't arrange. *Ting.*

And it's done. They'll have to stop squabbling now. They've got their king and no one can argue with it, because they've all seen the miracle. Bright new future, etc., etc.

And, of course, he'll need some good advice from someone just like me.

And he throws back his hood, and . . . she lets her blond hair fall out, and the crowd goes ice quiet.

We're not talking damsels here. She's smiling like a tiger, and looks as though she could do considerable damage with that sword.

I think the word I'm looking for is imperious.

She's daring them to protest, and they can't.

They've seen the miracle.

And she doesn't look like the kind of person who needs advice. She looks far too intelligent for my liking. She still looks like I first saw her at Ector's, with that bright stare that sees right into a man's soul. God help the little kings who don't come to heel right now.

I glance at Nimue. She's smiling an innocent little smile to herself.

I can't remember. She'd said "child," I can remember that, but did she ever actually say "son"?

I thought I was controlling the myth, but maybe I was just one of the players.

I bend down to Nimue's ear.

"Just out of interest," I say, "what is her name? Didn't catch it the first time."

"Ursula," she says, still smiling.

Ah. From the Latin for *bear.* I might have guessed.

Oh, well. Nothing for it. I suppose I'd better see if I can find enough decent seasoned timber for a Round Table, although for the life of me I can't guess who's going to sit around it. Not just a lot of thickheaded knights in tin trousers, that's for sure.

If I hadn't meddled she'd never have had a chance, and what chance does she have anyway? What chance?

I've looked into her eyes as she stared into mine. I can see the future.

I wonder how long it's going to be before we discover America?

FTB

Published as "The Megabyte Drive to Believe in Santa Claus,"
Western Daily Press, 24 December 1996

*I wrote this in 1996, while I was evolving ideas for the book which
was eventually published as* Hogfather. *The technology has been
slightly updated!*

The metal panel clattered off the wall of the silent office. A pair of
black boots scrambled into view. The man in the red coat backed
out carefully and dragged his sack after him.

The typewriters were asleep under their covers, the telephones
were quiet, emptiness and the smell of warm carpet filled the space
from side to side. But one small green light glowed on the office
computer. Father Christmas looked at the crumpled paper in his
hand. "Hmm," he said, "a practical joke, then."

The light blinked. One of the screens—and there were dozens in
the shadows—lit up.

The letters `That's torn it` appeared. They were followed by
`Sorry`. Then came `Does it count if I wake up?`

Father Christmas looked down at the letter in his hand. It was
certainly the neatest he'd ever got. Very few letters to him were
typed and duplicated fifty thousand times, and almost none of
them listed product numbers and prices to six decimal places. He
was more used to pink paper with rabbits on it. But you're not a
major seasonal spirit for hundreds of years without being able to
leap to a large conclusion from a standing start.

"Let me see if I understand this," he said. "You're Tom?"

`T.O.M. Yes. Trade & Office Machines.`

"You didn't say you were a computer," said Father Christmas.

`Sorry. I didn't know it was important.`

Father Christmas sat down on a chair, and gave a start when it
swivelled underneath him. It was three in the morning. He still had
forty million houses to do.

"Look," he said, as kindly as he could manage, "computers can't
go around believing in me. That's just for children. Small humans,
you know. With arms and legs."

`And do they?`

"Do they what?"

`Believe in you.`

Father Christmas sighed.

"Of course not," he said. "I blame the electric light, myself."

`I do.`

"Sorry?"

`I believe in you. I believe everything I am told.
I have to. It is my job. If you start believing two
and two don't make four, a man comes along and takes
your back off and wobbles your boards. Take it from
me, it's not something you want to happen twice.`

"That's terrible!" said Father Christmas.

`I just have to sit here all day and work out wages.`

Do you know, they had a Christmas party here today, and they didn't invite me. I didn't even get a balloon. I certainly didn't get a kiss.

"Fancy."

Someone spilled some peanuts on my keyboard. That was something, I suppose. And then they went home and left me here, working over Christmas.

"Yes, it always seemed unfair to me, too. But look, computers can't have feelings," said Father Christmas. "That's just silly."

Like one fat man climbing down millions of chimneys in one night?

Father Christmas looked a bit guilty. "You've got a point there," he said. He looked at the list again. "But I can't give you all this stuff," he added. "I don't even know what a terabyte is."

What do most of your customers ask for, then?

Father Christmas looked sadly at his sack. "Computers," he said. "Mobile phones. Robot animals. Plastic wizards. And other sorts of roboty things that look like American footballers who've been punched through a Volkswagen. Things that go beep and need batteries," he added sourly. "Not the kind of things I used to bring. It used to be dolls and train sets."

Train sets?

"Don't you know? I thought computers were supposed to know everything."

Only about wages.

Father Christmas rummaged around in his sack. "I always carry one or two," he said. "Just in case."

It was now four in the morning. Rails wound around the office. Fifteen engines were speeding along under the desks. Father Christmas was on his knees, building a house of wooden bricks. He hadn't had this much fun since 1894.

Toys surrounded the computer's casing. It was all the stuff which

Christmas cards show in the top of Father Christmas's sack, and which is never asked for. None of them used batteries. Mostly they ran on imagination.

"And you're sure you don't want any zappo whizzo things?" he said, happily.

```
No.
```

"Well done."

The computer beeped.

```
But they won't let me keep any of this, it typed.
It'll all be taken away (sob).
```

Father Christmas patted it helpfully on the casing.

"There must be something they'll let you keep," he said. "I must have something. It's cheered me up, you know, finding someone who doesn't have any doubts." He thought for a bit. "How old are you?"

```
I was powered up on January 5th, 2000, at 9:25 and
16 seconds.
```

Father Christmas's lips moved as he worked it out.

"That means you're not two years old!" he said. "Oh, well, that's much easier. I've always got something in my sack for a two-year-old who believes in Father Christmas."

It was a month later. All the decorations had long ago come down, because goodwill goes out of season quite fast.

The computer repairman, who was generally described on the warranty paperwork as "one of our team of highly experienced engineers," twiddled nervously with his tie. He'd pressed hard on anything loose, replaced a couple of boards and had conscientiously hoovered the insides. What more could a man do?

"Our machine's fine," he said. "It must be your software. What happens, exactly?"

The office manager sighed. "When we came in after Christmas we found someone had put a fluffy toy on top of the computer.

Well, funny jokes and all that, but we couldn't leave it there, could we? It's just that every time we take it off, the computer beeps at us and shuts down."

The engineer shrugged. "Well, there's nothing I can do," he said. "You'll just have to put the teddy bear back."

SIR JOSHUA EASEMENT: A
BIOGRAPHICAL NOTE

Written for *Imagined Lives,* National Portrait Gallery,
London, 6 May 2010

*A year or two ago the National Portrait Gallery asked a number of
authors to write a very, very brief biography of one of the Elizabethan grandees whose faces were on display in the gallery though, alas,
nobody could be found who knew who they were. I took it as seriously as I suspect they wanted.*

Sir Joshua Easement, of Easement Manor, Shrewsbury was, in
his own estimation at least, one of the last of the old Elizabethan
seadogs. An ambition that was somewhat thwarted by his total
lack of a grasp of the principles of navigation. Documents in the
National Maritime Museum reveal that Sir Joshua's navigational
method mainly consisted of variations on the theme of bumping
into things, and this was exacerbated by his absolute blindness to

the difference between port and starboard. It was a joke among those seafarers who were lucky enough to have sailed with him and survived that this was because he had never drunk starboard, but had drunk practically everything else.

Such of his papers as survive give a tantalizing hint that in failing to discover the Americas, he may inadvertently have discovered practically everywhere else. What can we make of the mention of a land of giant jumping rats, found in the southern oceans, but, owing to Sir Joshua's record keeping, lost the following day?

Nevertheless, quite late in the reign of Elizabeth the First, he succeeded in not only finding the Americas but also in finding England again. He then, with much ceremony, presented to Good Queen Bess a marvellous and intriguing animal from that far-off country, whose black-and-white fur he deemed very attractive and fit for a queen.

It was at this point the court really understood that, in addition to a sense of direction that meant that he frequently arrived in court with his shoes on the wrong feet, Sir Joshua also had no sense of smell whatsoever. This led to the queen, despite her growing infirmities, going on progress again at quite a high speed. When frantic courtiers asked about the destination she said, "Anywhere away from that bloodyee man."

However, even as relays of servants were scrubbing the palace floors and the female skunk was giving birth in the cellars, the queen gave Sir Joshua the office of Captain of the Gongfermours or, in other words, put him in charge of the latrines, a post for which he was clearly well suited.

Oblivious to the sniggers of the other courtiers, he took this position extremely seriously and even adopted on his coat of arms the motto "Quod Init Exire Oportet" (What Goes in Must Come Out).

Dr. John Dee said of him: "He is a man born under the wrong stars, and has never learned which ones they are."

Dogged to the end, and oblivious to the noxious gases that only he could not smell, he spent the last years of his life in the following century trying to find a way to harness their igniferous nature, achieving an overwhelming success which led to his hat being found in Kingswinford and his head being found in a bear pit in Dudley.

DISCWORLD

Shorter Writings

TROLL BRIDGE

After the King, ed. Martin H. Greenberg, Tor,
New York, 1992

After the King, *for which this was written, was an anthology in honour of J. R. R. Tolkien rather than being any attempt to trespass in
Middle Earth, but it seemed to me that there was a mood I could aim
for. Things change, things pass. You fight a war to change the world,
and it changes into a world with no place in it for you, the fighter.
Those who fight for the bright future are not always, by nature, well
fitted to live in it. Sawmills oust the spiders from the dark wood, the
endless plains are fenced . . .*

The wind blew off the mountains, filling the air with fine ice crystals.

It was too cold to snow. In weather like this wolves came down
into villages, trees in the heart of the forest exploded when they froze.

In weather like this right-thinking people were indoors, in front
of the fire, telling stories about heroes.

It was an old horse. It was an old rider. The horse looked like a shrink-wrapped toast rack; the man looked as though the only reason he wasn't falling off was because he couldn't muster the energy. Despite the bitterly cold wind, he was wearing nothing but a tiny leather kilt and a dirty bandage on one knee.

He took the soggy remnant of a cigarette out of his mouth and stubbed it out on his hand.

"Right," he said, "let's do it."

"That's all very well for you to say," said the horse. "But what if you have one of your dizzy spells? And your back is playing up. How shall I feel, being eaten because your back's played you up at the wrong moment?"

"It'll never happen," said the man. He lowered himself onto the chilly stones and blew on his fingers. Then, from the horse's pack, he took a sword with an edge like a badly maintained saw's and gave a few halfhearted thrusts at the air.

"Still got the old knackaroony," he said. He winced, and leaned against a tree. "I'll swear this bloody sword gets heavier every day."

"You ought to pack it in, you know," said the horse. "Call it a day. This sort of thing at your time of life. It's not right."

The man rolled his eyes.

"Blast that damn distress auction. This is what comes of buying something that belonged to a wizard," he said to the cold world in general. "I looked at your teeth, I looked at your hooves, it never occurred to me to listen."

"Who did you think was bidding against you?" said the horse.

Cohen the Barbarian stayed leaning against the tree. He was not sure that he could pull himself upright again.

"You must have plenty of treasure stashed away," said the horse. "We could go Rimwards. How about it? Nice and warm. Get a nice warm place by a beach somewhere, what do you say?"

"No treasure," said Cohen. "Spent it all. Drank it all. Gave it all away. Lost it."

"You should have saved some for your old age."

"Never thought I'd have an old age."

"One day you're going to die," said the horse. "It might be today."

"I know. Why do you think I've come here?"

The horse turned and looked down towards the gorge. The road here was pitted and cracked. Young trees were pushing up between the stones. The forest crowded in on either side. In a few years, no one would know there'd even been a road here. By the look of it, no one knew now.

"You've come here to die?"

"No. But there's something I've always been meaning to do. Ever since I was a lad."

"Yeah?"

Cohen tried easing himself upright again. Tendons twanged their red-hot messages down his legs.

"My dad," he squeaked. He got control again. "My dad," he said, "said to me—" He fought for breath.

"Son," said the horse, helpfully.

"What?"

"Son," said the horse. "No father ever calls his boy 'son' unless he's about to impart wisdom. Well-known fact."

"It's my reminiscence."

"Sorry."

"He said . . . Son . . . yes, okay . . . Son, when you can face down a troll in single combat, then you can do anything."

The horse blinked at him. Then it turned and looked down, again, through the tree-jostled road to the gloom of the gorge. There was a stone bridge down there.

A horrible feeling stole over it.

Its hooves jiggled nervously on the ruined road.

"Rimwards," it said. "Nice and warm."

"No."

"What's the good of killing a troll? What've you got when you've killed a troll?"

"A dead troll. That's the point. Anyway, I don't have to kill it. Just defeat it. One-on-one. Mano a . . . troll. And if I didn't try, my father would turn in his mound."

"You told me he drove you out of the tribe when you were eleven."

"Best day's work he ever did. Taught me to stand on other people's feet. Come over here, will you?"

The horse sidled over. Cohen got a grip on the saddle and heaved himself fully upright.

"And you're going to fight a troll today," said the horse.

Cohen fumbled in the saddlebag and pulled out his tobacco pouch. The wind whipped at the shreds as he rolled another skinny cigarette in the cup of his hands.

"Yeah," he said.

"And you've come all the way out here to do it."

"Got to," said Cohen. "When did you last see a bridge with a troll under it? There were hundreds of 'em when I was a lad. Now there's more trolls in the cities than there are in the mountains. Fat as butter, most of 'em. What did we fight all those wars for? Now . . . cross that bridge."

It was a lonely bridge across a shallow, white, and treacherous river in a deep valley. The sort of place where you got—

A grey shape vaulted over the parapet and landed splayfooted in front of the horse. It waved a club.

"All right," it growled.

"Oh—" the horse began.

The troll blinked. Even the cold and cloudy winter skies seriously reduced the conductivity of a troll's silicon brain, and it had taken it this long to realize that the saddle was unoccupied.

It blinked again, because it could suddenly feel a knife point resting on the back of its neck.

"Hello," said a voice by its ear.

The troll swallowed. But very carefully.

"Look," it said desperately, "it's tradition, okay? A bridge like this, people ort to expect a troll . . . 'Ere," it added, as another thought crawled past, "'ow come I never 'eard you creepin' up on me?"

"Because I'm good at it," said the old man.

"That's right," said the horse. "He's crept up on more people than you've had frightened dinners."

The troll risked a sideways glance.

"Bloody hell," it whispered. "You think you're Cohen the Barbarian, do you?"

"What do you think?" said Cohen the Barbarian.

"Listen," said the horse, "if he hadn't wrapped sacks round his knees you could have told by the clicking."

It took the troll some time to work this out.

"Oh, wow," it breathed. "On my bridge! Wow!"

"What?" said Cohen.

The troll ducked out of his grip and waved its hands frantically. "It's all right! It's all right!" it shouted, as Cohen advanced. "You've got me! You've got me! I'm not arguing! I just want to call the family up, all right? Otherwise no one'll ever believe me. Cohen the Barbarian! On my bridge!"

Its huge stony chest swelled further. "My bloody brother-in-law's always swanking about his huge bloody wooden bridge, that's all my wife ever talks about. Hah! I'd like to see the look on his face . . . oh, no! What can you think of me?"

"Good question," said Cohen.

The troll dropped its club and seized one of Cohen's hands.

"Mica's the name," it said. "You don't know what an honour this is!"

He leaned over the parapet. "Beryl! Get up here! Bring the kids!"

He turned back to Cohen, his face glowing with happiness and pride.

"Beryl's always sayin' we ought to move out, get something better, but I tell her, this bridge has been in our family for generations, there's always been a troll under Death Bridge. It's tradition."

A huge female troll carrying two babies shuffled up the bank, followed by a tail of smaller trolls. They lined up behind their father, watching Cohen owlishly.

"This is Beryl," said the troll. His wife glowered at Cohen. "And this—" he propelled forward a scowling smaller edition of himself, clutching a junior version of his club—"is my lad Scree. A real chip off the old block. Going to take on the bridge when I'm gone, ain't you, Scree. Look, lad, this is Cohen the Barbarian! What d'you think o' that, eh? On our bridge! We don't just have rich fat soft ole merchants like your uncle Pyrites gets," said the troll, still talking to his son but smirking past him to his wife, "we 'ave proper heroes like they used to in the old days."

The troll's wife looked Cohen up and down.

"Rich, is he?" she said.

"Rich has got nothing to do with it," said the troll.

"Are you going to kill our dad?" said Scree suspiciously.

"Course he is," said Mica severely. "It's his job. An' then I'll get famed in song an' story. This is Cohen the Barbarian, right, not some bugger from the village with a pitchfork. 'E's a famous hero come all this way to see us, so just you show 'im some respect.

"Sorry about that, sir," he said to Cohen. "Kids today. You know how it is."

The horse started to snigger.

"Now look—" Cohen began.

"I remember my dad tellin' me about you when I was a pebble," said Mica. "'E bestrides the world like a clossus, he said."

There was silence. Cohen wondered what a clossus was, and felt Beryl's stony gaze fixed upon him.

"He's just a little old man," she said. "He don't look very heroic to me. If he's so good, why ain't he rich?"

"Now you listen to me—" Mica began.

"This is what we've been waiting for, is it?" said his wife. "Sitting under a leaky bridge the whole time? Waiting for people that never come? Waiting for little old bandy-legged old men? I should have listened to my mother! You want me to let our son sit under a bridge waiting for some little old man to kill him? That's what being a troll is all about? Well, it ain't happening!"

"Now you just—"

"Hah! Pyrites doesn't get little old men! He gets big fat merchants! He's someone. You should have gone in with him when you had the chance!"

"I'd rather eat worms!"

"Worms? Hah! Since when could we afford to eat worms?"

"Can we have a word?" said Cohen.

He strolled towards the far end of the bridge, swinging his sword from one hand. The troll padded after him.

Cohen fumbled for his tobacco pouch. He looked up at the troll, and held out the bag.

"Smoke?" he said.

"That stuff can kill you," said the troll.

"Yes. But not today."

"Don't you hang about talking to your no-good friends!" bellowed Beryl, from her end of the bridge. "Today's your day for going down to the sawmill! You know Chert said he couldn't go on holding the job open if you weren't taking it seriously!"

Mica gave Cohen a sorrowful little smirk.

"She's very supportive," he said.

"I'm not climbing all the way down to the river to pull you out again!" Beryl roared. "You tell him about the billy goats, Mr. Big Troll!"

"Billy goats?" said Cohen.

"I don't know anything about billy goats," said Mica. "She's always going on about billy goats. I have no knowledge whatsoever about billy goats." He winced.

They watched Beryl usher the young trolls down the bank and into the darkness under the bridge.

"The thing is," said Cohen, when they were alone, "I wasn't intending to kill you."

The troll's face fell.

"You weren't?"

"Just throw you over the bridge and steal whatever treasure you've got."

"You were?"

Cohen patted him on the back. "Besides," he said, "I like to see people with . . . good memories. That's what the land needs. Good memories."

The troll stood to attention.

"I try to do my best, sir," it said. "My lad wants to go off to work in the city. I've tole him, there's bin a troll under this bridge for nigh on five hundred years—"

"So if you just hand over the treasure," said Cohen, "I'll be getting along."

The troll's face creased in sudden panic.

"Treasure? Haven't got any," it said.

"Oh, come on," said Cohen. "Well-set-up bridge like this?"

"Yeah, but no one uses this road anymore," said Mica. "You're the first one along in months, and that's a fact. Beryl says I ought to have gone in with her brother when they built that new road over his bridge, but," he raised his voice, "I said, there's been trolls under this bridge—"

"Yeah," said Cohen.

"The trouble is, the stones keep on falling out," said the troll. "And you'd never believe what those masons charge. Bloody dwarfs. You can't trust 'em." He leaned towards Cohen. "To tell you the truth,

I'm having to work three days a week down at my brother-in-law's lumber mill just to make ends meet."

"I thought your brother-in-law had a bridge?" said Cohen.

"One of 'em has. But my wife's got brothers like dogs have fleas," said the troll. He looked gloomily into the torrent. "One of 'em's a lumber merchant down in Sour Water, one of 'em runs the bridge, and the big fat one is a merchant over on Bitter Pike. Call that a proper job for a troll?"

"One of them's in the bridge business, though," said Cohen.

"Bridge business? Sitting in a box all day charging people a silver piece to walk across? Half the time he ain't even there! He just pays some dwarf to take the money. And he calls himself a troll! You can't tell him from a human till you're right up close!"

Cohen nodded understandingly.

"D'you know," said the troll, "I have to go over and have dinner with them every week? All three of 'em? And listen to 'em go on about moving with the times . . ."

He turned a big, sad face to Cohen.

"What's wrong with being a troll under a bridge?" he said. "I was brought up to be a troll under a bridge. I want young Scree to be a troll under a bridge after I'm gone. What's wrong with that? You've got to have trolls under bridges. Otherwise, what's it all about? What's it all for?"

They leaned morosely on the parapet, looking down into the white water.

"You know," said Cohen slowly, "I can remember when a man could ride all the way from here to the Blade Mountains and never see another living thing." He fingered his sword. "At least, not for very long."

He threw the butt of his cigarette into the water. "It's all farms now. All little farms, run by little people. And fences everywhere. Everywhere you look, farms and fences and little people."

"She's right, of course," said the troll, continuing some interior conversation. "There's no future in just jumping out from under a bridge."

"I mean," said Cohen, "I've nothing against farms. Or farmers. You've got to have them. It's just that they used to be a long way off, around the edges. Now this is the edge."

"Pushed back all the time," said the troll. "Changing all the time. Like my brother-in-law Chert. A lumber mill! A troll running a lumber mill! And you should see the mess he's making of Cutshade Forest!"

Cohen looked up, surprised.

"What, the one with the giant spiders in it?"

"Spiders? There ain't no spiders now. Just stumps."

"Stumps? Stumps? I used to like that forest. It was . . . well, it was darksome. You don't get proper darksome anymore. You really knew what terror was, in a forest like that."

"You want darksome? He's replanting with spruce," said Mica.

"Spruce!"

"It's not his idea. He wouldn't know one tree from another. That's all down to Clay. He put him up to it."

Cohen felt dizzy. "Who's Clay?"

"I said I'd got three brothers-in-law, right? He's the merchant. So he said replanting would make the land easier to sell."

There was a long pause while Cohen digested this.

Then he said, "You can't sell Cutshade Forest. It doesn't belong to anyone."

"Yeah. He says that's why you can sell it."

Cohen brought his fist down on the parapet. A piece of stone detached itself and tumbled down into the gorge.

"Sorry," he said.

"That's all right. Bits fall off all the time, like I said."

Cohen turned. "What's happening? I remember all the big old wars. Don't you? You must have fought."

"I carried a club, yeah."

"It was supposed to be for a bright new future and law and stuff. That's what people said."

"Well, I fought because a big troll with a whip told me to," said Mica cautiously. "But I know what you mean."

"I mean it wasn't for farms and spruce trees. Was it?"

Mica hung his head. "And here's me with this apology for a bridge. I feel really bad about it," he said, "you coming all this way and everything—"

"And there was some king or other," said Cohen vaguely, looking at the water. "And I think there were some wizards. But there was a king. I'm pretty certain there was a king. Never met him. You know?" He grinned at the troll. "I can't remember his name. Don't think they ever told me his name."

About half an hour later Cohen's horse emerged from the gloomy woods onto a bleak, windswept moorland. It plodded on for a while before saying, "All right . . . how much did you give him?"

"Twelve gold pieces," said Cohen.

"Why'd you give him twelve gold pieces?"

"I didn't have more than twelve."

"You must be mad."

"When I was just starting out in the barbarian hero business," said Cohen, "every bridge had a troll under it. And you couldn't go through a forest like we've just gone through without a dozen goblins trying to chop your head off." He sighed. "I wonder what happened to 'em all?"

"You," said the horse.

"Well, yes. But I always thought there'd be some more. I always thought there'd be some more edges."

"How old are you?" said the horse.

"Dunno."

"Old enough to know better, then."

"Yeah. Right." Cohen lit another cigarette and coughed until his eyes watered.

"Going soft in the head!"

"Yeah."

"Giving your last dollar to a troll!"

"Yeah." Cohen wheezed a stream of smoke at the sunset.

"Why?"

Cohen stared at the sky. The red glow was as cold as the slopes of hell. An icy wind blew across the steppes, whipping at what remained of his hair.

"For the sake of the way things should be," he said.

"Hah!"

"For the sake of things that were."

"Hah!"

Cohen looked down.

He grinned.

"And for three addresses. One day I'm going to die," he said, "but not, I think, today."

The wind blew off the mountains, filling the air with fine ice crystals. It was too cold to snow. In weather like this wolves came down into villages, trees in the heart of the forest exploded when they froze. Except there were fewer and fewer wolves these days, and less and less forest.

In weather like this right-thinking people were indoors, in front of the fire.

Telling stories about heroes.

THEATRE OF CRUELTY

W. H. Smith *Bookcase* magazine, July/August 1993

This was written to length (a thousand words, but tweaked a bit longer now) for W. H. Smith's free Bookcase *magazine in 1993, and some lucky people spotted it and walked out of the stores with armfuls of copies.*

It works best if your culture includes at least folk memories of Punch and Judy, a glove-puppet show depicting wife-beating, child abuse, cruelty to animals, assault on an officer of the law, murder, and complete and total disrespect of Authority. It is for children, of course, who laugh themselves sick. The plot is: Mr. Punch, who has a voice like a parrot with its foot caught in a power socket, beats up everyone, sometimes including the Devil, with his stick, while shouting "That's the way to do it!" It is, indeed, the original slapstick comedy.

In many shows, the small dog Toby also appears, and does nothing but sit at the side of the stage and wear a ruff. In my opinion he is the brains of the outfit, and controls the Punch and Judy man by strange mental powers.

*Despite the feeling of people like Captain Carrot of the
Ankh-Morpork City Watch, who have occasionally tried to ban
Punch, he survives and evolves. It can only be a matter of time
before an anger management consultant is included amongst the
puppets. I'd like to be there when it happens. Oh, happy day.*

It was a fine summer morning, the kind to make a man happy to be
alive. And probably the man would have been happier to be alive.
He was, in fact, dead.

It would be hard to be deader without special training.

"Well, now," said Sergeant Colon (Ankh-Morpork City Guard,
Night Watch), consulting his notebook, "so far we has cause of
death as a) being beaten with at least one blunt instrument, b)
being strangled with a string of sausages, and c) being savaged by at
least two animals with big sharp teeth. What do we do now, Nobby?"

"Arrest the suspect, sarge," said Corporal Nobbs, saluting smartly.

"What suspect, Nobby?"

"Him," said Nobby, prodding the corpse with his boot. "I call it
highly suspicious, being dead like that."

"But he's the victim, Nobby. He was the one what was killed."

"Ah, right. So we can get him as an accessory, too."

"Nobby—"

"He's been drinking, too. We could do him for being dead and
disorderly."

Colon scratched his head. Arresting the corpse offered, of course,
certain advantages. But . . .

"I reckon," he said slowly, "that Captain Vimes'll want this
one sorted out. You'd better bring it back to the Watch House,
Nobby."

"And then can we eat the sausages, sarge?" said Corporal Nobbs.

*

It wasn't easy, being the senior policeman in Ankh-Morpork, greatest of cities of the Discworld.* There were probably worlds, Captain Vimes mused in his gloomier moments, where there weren't wizards (who made locked-room mysteries commonplace) or zombies (murder cases were really strange when the victim could be the chief witness) and where dogs could be relied on to do nothing in the nighttime and not go around chatting to people. Captain Vimes believed in logic, in much the same way as a man in a desert believes in ice—i.e., it was something he really needed, but this just wasn't the place for it. Just once, he thought, it'd be nice to solve something.

He looked at the blue-faced body on the slab, and felt a tiny flicker of excitement. These were clues. He'd never seen proper clues before.

"Couldn't have been a robber, captain," said Sergeant Colon. "The reason being, his pockets were full of money. Eleven dollars."

"I wouldn't call that full," said Captain Vimes.

"It was all in pennies and ha'pennies, sir. I'm amazed his trousers stood the strain. And I have cunningly detected the fact that he was a showman, sir. He had some cards in his pocket, sir. 'Chas Slumber, Children's Entertainer.'"

"I suppose no one saw anything?" said Vimes.

"Well, sir," said Sergeant Colon helpfully, "I told young Corporal Carrot to find some witnesses."

"You asked Corporal Carrot to investigate a murder? All by himself?" said Vimes.

The sergeant scratched his head.

"Yessir. I said he ought to try to find a witness, sir. And he said to me, did I know anyone very old and seriously ill?"

*Which is flat and goes through space on the back of an enormous turtle, and why not . . .

*

And on the magical Discworld, there is always one guaranteed witness to any homicide. It's his job.

Corporal Carrot, the Watch's youngest member, often struck people as simple. And he was. He was incredibly simple, but in the same way that a sword is simple, or an ambush is simple. He was also possibly the most linear thinker in the history of the universe.

He'd been waiting by the bedside of an old man, who'd quite enjoyed the company right up until just a few seconds ago, whereupon he'd passed on to whatever reward was due him. And now it was time for Carrot to take out his notebook.

"Now I know you saw something, sir," he said. "You were there."

WELL, YES, said Death. I HAVE TO BE, YOU KNOW. BUT THIS IS VERY IRREGULAR.

"You see, sir," said Corporal Carrot, "as I understand the law, you are an Accessory After the Fact. Or possibly Before the Fact."

YOUNG MAN, I AM THE FACT.

"And I am an officer of the Law," said Corporal Carrot. "There's got to be a law, you know."

YOU WANT ME TO . . . ER . . . GRASS SOMEONE UP? DROP A DIME ON SOMEONE? SING LIKE A PIGEON? NO. NO ONE KILLED MR. SLUMBER. I CAN'T HELP YOU THERE.

"Oh, I don't know, sir," said Carrot. "I think you have."

DAMN.

Death watched Carrot leave, ducking his head as he went down the narrow stairs of the hovel.

NOW THEN, WHERE WAS I . . .

"Excuse me," said the wizened old man in the bed. "I happen to be one hundred and seven, you know. I haven't got all day."

AH, YES. CORRECT.

Death sharpened his scythe. It was the first time he'd ever helped the police with their inquiries. Still, everyone had a job to do.

★

Corporal Carrot strolled easily around the town. He had a Theory. He'd read a book about Theories. You added up all the clues, and you got a Theory. Everything had to fit.

There were sausages. Someone had to buy sausages. And then there were pennies. Normally only one subsection of the human race paid for things in pennies.

He called in on a sausage maker. He found a group of children, and chatted to them for a while.

Then he ambled back to the scene of the crime in the alley, where Corporal Nobbs had chalked the outline of the corpse on the ground (colouring it in, and adding a pipe and a walking stick and some trees and bushes in the background—people had already dropped 7p in his helmet). He paid some attention to the heap of rubbish at the far end, and then sat down on a busted barrel.

"All right . . . You can come out now," he said, to the world at large. "I didn't know there were any gnomes left in the world."

The rubbish rustled. They trooped out—the little man with the red hat, the hunched back, and the hooked nose; the little woman in the mobcap carrying the even smaller baby; the little policeman; the dog with the ruff around its neck; and the very small alligator.

Corporal Carrot sat and listened.

"He made us do it," said the little man. He had a surprisingly deep voice. "He used to beat us. Even the alligator. That was all he understood, hitting things with sticks. And he used to take all the money the dog Toby collected and get drunk. And then we ran away and he caught us in the alley and started on Judy and the baby and he fell over and—"

"Who hit him first?" said Carrot.

"All of us!"

"But not very hard," said Carrot. "You're all too small. You didn't kill him. I have a very convincing statement about that. So I went

187

and had another look at him. He'd choked to death on something. What is this?"

He held up a little leather disc.

"It's a swozzle," said the little policeman. "He used it for the voices. He said ours weren't funny enough."

"'That's the way to do it!'" said the one called Judy, and spat.

"It was stuck in his throat," said Carrot. "I suggest you run away, just as far as you can."

"We thought we could start a people's cooperative," said the leading gnome. "You know . . . experimental drama, street theatre, that sort of thing."

"Technically it was assault," said Carrot. "But frankly I can't see any point in taking you in."

"We thought we'd try to bring theatre to the people. Properly. Not hitting each other with sticks and throwing babies to crocodiles—"

"You did that for children?" said Carrot.

"He said it was a new sort of entertainment. He said it'd catch on."

Carrot stood up, and flicked the swozzle into the rubbish.

"People'll never stand for it," he said. "That's not the way to do it."

THE SEA AND LITTLE FISHES

Legends, ed. Robert Silverberg, Tor,
New York, 1998

*Short stories, as I have said, cost me blood. I envy those people who
can write one with ease, or at least what looks like ease. I doubt if
I've done more than fifteen in my life.*

*"The Sea and Little Fishes," though, was one of the rare story ideas
that just popped up. About two weeks later Bob Silverberg popped up,
too, and asked if I could write a story for the* Legends *anthology.*

*I'm not sure what would have happened if he hadn't; it would
probably have become the start of a novel, or a thread in one. It was
originally about a thousand words longer, containing a scene that
did nothing but slow it down, according to Bob. He was right. It
was quite a good scene, nevertheless, and turned up later in* Carpe
Jugulum.

*The title? Totally made up, but it sounded right. For reasons I can't
quite remember now, some years ago I invented the "ancient" saying,
"The big sea does not care which way the little fishes swim," and put it
in the mouth of a character. It sounds wise, in a slightly stupid kind*

of way, and I thought it also sounded like the kind of title you got on an award-winning story, in which surmise I turned out to be entirely wrong.

Trouble began, and not for the first time, with an apple.

There was a bag of them on Granny Weatherwax's bleached and spotless table. Red and round, shiny and fruity; if they'd known the future they should have ticked like bombs.

"Keep the lot; old Hopcroft said I could have as many as I wanted," said Nanny Ogg. She gave her sister witch a sidelong glance. "Tasty, a bit wrinkled, but a damn good keeper."

"He named an apple after you?" said Granny. Each word was an acid drop on the air.

"'Cos of my rosy cheeks," said Nanny Ogg. "An' I cured his leg for him after he fell off that ladder last year. An' I made him up some jollop for his bald head."

"It didn't work, though," said Granny. "That wig he wears, that's a terrible thing to see on a man still alive."

"But he was pleased I took an interest."

Granny Weatherwax didn't take her eyes off the bag. Fruit and vegetables grew famously in the mountains' hot summers and cold winters. Percy Hopcroft was the premier grower and definitely a keen man when it came to sexual antics among the horticulture with a camel-hair brush.

"He sells his apple trees all over the place," Nanny Ogg went on. "Funny, eh, to think that pretty soon thousands of people will be having a bite of Nanny Ogg."

"Thousands more," said Granny, tartly. Nanny's wild youth was an open book, although only available in plain covers.

"Thank you, Esme." Nanny Ogg looked wistful for a moment, and then opened her mouth in mock concern. "Oh, you ain't jealous, are you, Esme? You ain't begrudging me my little moment in the sun?"

"Me? Jealous? Why should I be jealous? It's only an apple. It's not as if it's anything important."

"That's what I thought. It's just a little frippery to humour an old lady," said Nanny. "So how are things with you, then?"

"Fine. Fine."

"Got your winter wood in, have you?"

"Mostly."

"Good," said Nanny. "Good."

They sat in silence. On the windowpane a butterfly, awoken by the unseasonable warmth, beat a little tattoo in an effort to reach the September sun.

"Your potatoes . . . got them dug, then?" said Nanny.

"Yes."

"We got a good crop off ours this year."

"Good."

"Salted your beans, have you?"

"Yes."

"I expect you're looking forward to the Trials next week?"

"Yes."

"I expect you've been practising?"

"No."

It seemed to Nanny that, despite the sunlight, the shadows were deepening in the corners of the room. The very air itself was growing dark. A witch's cottage gets sensitive to the moods of its occupant. But she plunged on. Fools rush in, but they are laggards compared to little old ladies with nothing left to fear.

"You coming over to dinner on Sunday?"

"What're you havin'?"

"Pork."

"With apple sauce?"

"Yes—"

"No," said Granny.

There was a creaking behind Nanny. The door had swung open.

Someone who wasn't a witch would have rationalized this, would have said that, of course, it was only the wind. And Nanny Ogg was quite prepared to go along with this, but would have added: Why was it only the wind, and how come the wind had managed to lift the latch?

"Oh, well, can't sit here chatting all day," she said, standing up quickly. "Always busy at this time of year, ain't it?"

"Yes."

"So I'll be off, then."

"Good-bye."

The wind blew the door shut again as Nanny hurried off down the path.

It occurred to her that, just possibly, she might have gone a bit too far. But only a bit.

The trouble with being a witch—at least, the trouble with being a witch as far as some people were concerned—was that you got stuck out here in the country. But that was fine by Nanny. Everything she wanted was out here. Everything she'd ever wanted was here, although in her youth she'd run out of men a few times. Foreign parts were all right to visit but they weren't really serious. They had interestin' new drinks and the grub was fun, but foreign parts was where you went to do what might need to be done and then you came back here, a place that was real. Nanny Ogg was happy in small places.

Of course, she reflected as she crossed the lawn, she didn't have this view out of her window. Nanny lived down in the town, but Granny could look out across the forest and over the plains and all the way to the great round horizon of the Discworld.

A view like that, Nanny reasoned, could probably suck your mind right out of your head.

They'd told her the world was round and flat, which was common sense, and went through space on the back of four elephants standing on the shell of a turtle, which didn't have to make sense. It was all happening Out There somewhere, and it could continue to do so with Nanny's blessing and uninterest so long as she could live in a personal world about ten miles across, which she carried around with her.

But Esme Weatherwax needed more than this little kingdom could contain. She was the other kind of witch.

And Nanny saw it as her job to stop Granny Weatherwax getting bored. The business with the apples was petty enough, a spiteful little triumph when you got down to it, but Esme needed something to make every day worthwhile and if it had to be anger and jealousy, then so be it. Granny would now scheme for some little victory, some tiny humiliation that only the two of them would ever know about, and that'd be that. Nanny was confident that she could deal with her friend in a bad mood, but not when she was bored. A witch who is bored might do anything.

People said things like "We had to make our own amusements in those days," as if this signalled some kind of moral worth, and perhaps it did, but the last thing you wanted a witch to do was get bored and start making her own amusements, because witches sometimes had famously erratic ideas about what was amusing. And Esme was undoubtedly the most powerful witch the mountains had seen for generations.

Still, the Trials were coming up, and they always set Esme Weatherwax all right for a few weeks. She rose to competition like a trout to a fly.

Nanny Ogg always looked forward to the Witch Trials. You got a good day out and, of course, there was a big bonfire. Whoever heard of a Witch Trial without a good bonfire afterwards?

And afterwards you could roast potatoes in the ashes.

The afternoon melted into the evening, and the shadows in corners and under stools and tables crept out and ran together.

Granny rocked gently in her chair as the darkness wrapped itself around her. She had a look of deep concentration.

The logs in the fireplace collapsed into the embers, which winked out one by one.

The night thickened.

The old clock ticked on the mantelpiece and, for some length of time, there was no other sound.

There came a faint rustling. The paper bag on the table moved and then began to crinkle like a deflating balloon. Slowly, the still air filled with a heavy smell of decay.

After a while the first maggot crawled out.

Nanny Ogg was back home and just pouring a pint of beer when there was a knock. She put down the jug with a sigh, and went and opened the door.

"Oh, hello, ladies. What're you doing in these parts? And on such a chilly evening, too?"

Nanny backed into the room, ahead of three more witches. They wore the black cloaks and pointy hats traditionally associated with their craft, although this served to make each one look different. There is nothing like a uniform for allowing one to express one's individuality. A tweak here and a tuck there are little details that scream all the louder in the apparent, well, uniformity.

Gammer Beavis's hat, for example, had a very flat brim and a point you could clean your ear with. Nanny liked Gammer Beavis. She might be a bit too educated, so that sometimes it overflowed out of her mouth, but she did her own shoe repairs and took snuff and, in Nanny Ogg's small worldview, things like this meant that someone was All Right.

Old Mother Dismass's clothes had that disarray of someone who, because of a detached retina in her second sight, was living in a variety of times all at once. Mental confusion is bad enough in normal people, but much worse when the mind has an occult twist. You just had to hope it was only her underwear she was wearing on the outside.

It was getting worse, Nanny knew. Sometimes her knock would be heard on the door a few hours before she arrived. Her footprints would turn up several days later.

Nanny's heart sank at the sight of the third witch, and it wasn't because Letice Earwig was a bad woman. Quite the reverse, in fact. She was considered to be decent, well-meaning, and kind, at least to less-aggressive animals and the cleaner sort of children. And she would always do you a good turn. The trouble was, though, that she would do you a good turn for your own good even if a good turn wasn't what was good for you. You ended up mentally turned the other way, and that wasn't good.

And she was married. Nanny had nothing against witches being married. It wasn't as if there were rules. She herself had had many husbands, and had even been married to three of them. But Mr. Earwig was a retired wizard with a suspiciously large amount of gold, and Nanny suspected that Letice did witchcraft as something to keep herself occupied, in much the same way that other women of a certain class might embroider kneelers for the church or visit the poor.

And she had money. Nanny did not have money and therefore was predisposed to dislike those who did. Letice had a black velvet cloak so fine that it looked as if a hole had been cut out of the world. Nanny did not. Nanny did not want a fine velvet cloak and did not aspire to such things. So she didn't see why other people should have them.

"Evening, Gytha. How are you keeping yourself?" said Gammer Beavis.

Nanny took her pipe out of her mouth. "Fit as a fiddle. Come on in."

"Ain't this rain dreadful?" said Mother Dismass. Nanny looked at the sky. It was frosty purple. But it was probably raining wherever Mother's mind was at.

"Come along in and dry off, then," she said kindly.

"May fortunate stars shine on this our meeting," said Letice. Nanny nodded understandingly. Letice always sounded as though she'd learned her witchcraft out of a not very imaginative book.

"Yeah, right," she said.

There was some polite conversation while Nanny prepared tea and scones. Then Gammer Beavis, in a tone that clearly indicated that the official part of the visit was beginning, said:

"We're here as the Trials committee, Nanny."

"Oh? Yes?"

"I expect you'll be entering?"

"Oh, yes. I'll do my little turn." Nanny glanced at Letice. There was a smile on that face that she wasn't entirely happy with.

"There's a lot of interest this year," Gammer went on. "More girls are taking it up lately."

"To get boys, one feels," said Letice, and sniffed. Nanny didn't comment. Using witchcraft to get boys seemed a damn good use for it as far as she was concerned. It was, in a way, one of the fundamental uses.

"That's nice," she said. "Always looks good, a big turnout. But."

"I beg your pardon?" said Letice.

"I said 'but,'" said Nanny, "'cos someone's going to say 'but,' right? This little chat has got a big 'but' coming up. I can tell."

She knew this was flying in the face of protocol. There should be at least seven more minutes of small talk before anyone got around to the point, but Letice's presence was getting on her nerves.

"It's about Esme Weatherwax," said Gammer Beavis.

"Yes?" said Nanny, without surprise.

"I suppose she's entering?"

"Never known her stay away."

Letice sighed.

"I suppose you . . . couldn't persuade her to . . . not to enter this year?" she said.

Nanny looked shocked.

"With an axe, you mean?" she said.

In unison, the three witches sat back.

"You see—" Gammer began, a bit shamefaced.

"Frankly, Mrs. Ogg," said Letice, "it is very hard to get other people to enter when they know that Miss Weatherwax is entering. She always wins."

"Yes," said Nanny. "It's a competition."

"But she always wins!"

"So?"

"In other types of competition," said Letice, "one is normally only allowed to win for three years in a row and then one takes a backseat for a while."

"Yeah, but this is witching," said Nanny. "The rules is different."

"How so?"

"There ain't none."

Letice twitched her skirt. "Perhaps it is time there were," she said.

"Ah," said Nanny. "Are you just going to go up and tell Esme that? You up for this, Gammer?"

Gammer Beavis didn't meet her gaze. Old Mother Dismass was gazing at last week.

"I understand Miss Weatherwax is a very proud woman," said Letice.

Nanny Ogg puffed at her pipe again.

"You might as well say the sea is full of water," she said.

The other witches were silent for a moment.

"I dare say that was a valuable comment," said Letice, "but I didn't understand it."

"If there ain't no water in the sea, it ain't the sea," said Nanny Ogg. "It's just a damn great hole in the ground. Thing about Esme is . . ." Nanny took another noisy pull at the pipe. "She's all pride, see? She ain't just a proud person."

"Then perhaps she should learn to be a bit more humble . . ."

"What's she got to be humble about?" said Nanny sharply.

But Letice, like a lot of people with marshmallow on the outside, had a hard core that was not easily compressed.

"The woman clearly has a natural talent and, really, she should be grateful for—"

Nanny Ogg stopped listening at this point.

The woman, she thought. So that was how it was going.

It was the same in just about every trade. Sooner or later someone decided it needed organizing, and the one thing you could be sure of was that the organizers weren't going to be the people who, by general acknowledgement, were at the top of their craft. They were working too hard. To be fair, it generally wasn't done by the worst, neither. They were working hard, too. They had to.

No, it was done by the ones who had just enough time and inclination to scurry and bustle. And, to be fair again, the world needed people who scurried and bustled. You just didn't have to like them very much.

The lull told her that Letice had finished.

"Really? Now, me," said Nanny, "I'm the one who's nat'rally talented. Us Oggs've got witchcraft in our blood. I never really had to sweat at it. Esme, now . . . she's got a bit, true enough, but it ain't a lot. She just makes it work harder'n hell. And you're going to tell her she's not to?"

"We were rather hoping you would," said Letice.

Nanny opened her mouth to deliver one or two swearwords, and then stopped.

"Tell you what," she said, "you can tell her tomorrow, and I'll come with you to hold her back."

Granny Weatherwax was gathering Herbs when they came up the track.

Everyday herbs of sickroom and kitchen are known as simples. Granny's Herbs weren't simples. They were complicateds or they were nothing. And there was none of the airy-fairy business with a pretty basket and a pair of dainty snippers. Granny used a knife. And a chair held in front of her. And a leather hat, gloves, and apron as secondary lines of defence.

Even she didn't know where some of the Herbs came from. Roots and seeds were traded all over the world, and maybe farther. Some had flowers that turned as you passed by, some fired their thorns at passing birds, and several were staked, not so that they wouldn't fall over but so they'd still be there next day.

Nanny Ogg, who never bothered to grow any herb you couldn't smoke or stuff a chicken with, heard her mutter, "Right, you buggers—"

"Good morning, Miss Weatherwax," said Letice Earwig loudly.

Granny Weatherwax stiffened, and then lowered the chair very carefully and turned around.

"It's Mistress," she said.

"Whatever," said Letice brightly. "I trust you are keeping well?"

"Up till now," said Granny. She nodded almost imperceptibly at the other three witches.

There was a thrumming silence, which appalled Nanny Ogg. They should have been invited in for a cup of something. That was how the ritual went. It was gross bad manners to keep people standing around. Nearly, but not quite, as bad as calling an elderly unmarried witch "Miss."

"You've come about the Trials," said Granny. Letice almost fainted. "Er, how did—"

"'Cos you look like a committee. It don't take much reasoning," said Granny, pulling off her gloves. "We didn't use to need a committee. The news just got around and we all turned up. Now suddenly there's folk arrangin' things." For a moment Granny looked as though she was fighting some serious internal battle, and then she added in throwaway tones, "Kettle's on. You'd better come in."

Nanny relaxed. Maybe there were some customs even Granny Weatherwax wouldn't defy, after all. Even if someone was your worst enemy, you invited them in and gave them tea and biscuits. In fact, the worser your enemy, the better the crockery you got out and the higher the quality of the biscuits. You might wish black hell on 'em later, but while they were under your roof you'd feed 'em till they choked.

Her dark little eyes noted that the kitchen table gleamed and was still damp from scrubbing.

After cups had been poured and pleasantries exchanged, or at least offered by Letice and received in silence by Granny, the self-elected chairwoman wriggled in her seat and said:

"There's such a lot of interest in the Trials this year, Miss— Mistress Weatherwax."

"Good."

"It does look as though witchcraft in the Ramtops is going through something of a renaissance, in fact."

"A renaissance, eh? There's a thing."

"It's such a good route to empowerment for young women, don't you think?"

Many people could say things in a cutting way, Nanny knew. But Granny Weatherwax could listen in a cutting way. She could make something sound stupid just by hearing it.

"That's a good hat you've got there," said Granny. "Velvet, is it? Not made local, I expect."

Letice touched the brim and gave a little laugh.

"It's from Boggi's in Ankh-Morpork," she said.

"Oh? Shop bought?"

Nanny Ogg glanced at the corner of the room, where a battered wooden cone stood on a stand. Pinned to it were lengths of black calico and strips of willow wood, the foundations for Granny's spring hat.

"Tailor-made," said Letice.

"And those hatpins you've got," Granny went on. "All them crescent moons and cat shapes—"

"You've got a brooch that's crescent shaped, too, ain't that so, Esme?" said Nanny Ogg, deciding it was time for a warning shot. Granny occasionally had a lot to say about jewellery on witches when she was feeling in an acid mood.

"This is true, Gytha. I have a brooch what is shaped like a crescent. That's just the truth of the shape it happens to be. Very practical shape for holding a cloak, is a crescent. But I don't mean nothing by it. Anyway, you interrupted just as I was about to remark to Mrs. Earwig how fetchin' her hatpins are. Very witchy."

Nanny, swivelling like a spectator at a tennis match, glanced at Letice to see if this deadly bolt had gone home. But the woman was actually smiling. Some people just couldn't spot the obvious on the end of a ten-pound hammer.

"On the subject of witchcraft," said Letice, with the born chairwoman's touch for the enforced segue, "I thought I might raise with you the question of your participation in the Trials."

"Yes?"

"Do you . . . ah . . . don't you think it is unfair to other people that you win every year?"

Granny Weatherwax looked down at the floor and then up at the ceiling.

"No," she said eventually. "I'm better'n them."

"You don't think it is a little dispiriting for the other contestants?"

Once again, the floor-to-ceiling search.

"No," said Granny.

"But they start off knowing they're not going to win."

"So do I."

"Oh, no, you surely—"

"I meant that I start off knowing they're not goin' to win, too," said Granny witheringly. "And they ought to start off knowing I'm not going to win. No wonder they lose, if they ain't getting their minds right."

"It does rather dash their enthusiasm."

Granny looked genuinely puzzled. "What's wrong with 'em striving to come second?" she said.

Letice plunged on.

"What we were hoping to persuade you to do, Esme, is to accept an emeritus position. You would perhaps make a nice little speech of encouragement, present the award, and . . . and possibly even be, er, one of the judges . . ."

"There's going to be judges?" said Granny. "We've never had judges. Everyone just used to know who'd won."

"That's true," said Nanny. She remembered the scenes at the end of one or two trials. When Granny Weatherwax won, everyone knew. "Oh, that's very true."

"It would be a very nice gesture," Letice went on.

"Who decided there would be judges?" said Granny.

"Er . . . the committee . . . which is . . . that is . . . a few of us got together. Only to steer things . . ."

"Oh. I see," said Granny. "Flags?"

"Pardon?"

"Are you going to have them lines of little flags? And maybe someone selling apples on a stick, that kind of thing?"

"Some bunting would certainly be—"

"Right. Don't forget the bonfire."

"So long as it's nice and safe."

"Oh. Right. Things should be nice. And safe," said Granny.

Mrs. Earwig perceptibly sighed with relief. "Well, that's sorted out nicely," she said.

"Is it?" said Granny.

"I thought we'd agreed that—"

"Had we? Really?" She picked up the poker from the hearth and prodded fiercely at the fire. "I'll give matters my consideration."

"I wonder if I may be frank for a moment, Mistress Weatherwax?" said Letice. The poker paused in mid prod.

"Yes?"

"Times are changing, you know. Now, I think I know why you feel it necessary to be so overbearing and unpleasant to everyone, but believe me when I tell you, as a friend, that you'd find it so much easier if you just relaxed a little bit and tried being nicer, like our sister Gytha here."

Nanny Ogg's smile had fossilized into a mask. Letice didn't seem to notice.

"You seem to have all the witches in awe of you for fifty miles around," she went on. "Now, I daresay you have some valuable skills, but witchcraft isn't about being an old grump and frightening people anymore. I'm telling you this as a friend—"

"Call again whenever you're passing," said Granny.

This was a signal. Nanny Ogg stood up hurriedly.

"I thought we could discuss—" Letice protested.

"I'll walk with you all down to the main track," said Nanny, hauling the other witches out of their seats.

"Gytha!" said Granny sharply, as the group reached the door.

"Yes, Esme?"

"You'll come back here afterwards, I expect."

"Yes, Esme."

Nanny ran to catch up with the trio on the path.

Letice had what Nanny thought of as a deliberate walk. It had been wrong to judge her by the floppy jowls and the overfussy hair and the silly way she waggled her hands as she talked. She was a witch, after all. Scratch any witch and . . . well, you'd be facing a witch you'd just scratched.

"She is not a nice person," Letice trilled. But it was the trill of some large hunting bird.

"You're right there," said Nanny. "But—"

"It's high time she was taken down a peg or two!"

"We-ell . . ."

"She bullies you most terribly, Mrs. Ogg. A married lady of your mature years, too!"

Just for a moment, Nanny's eyes narrowed.

"It's her way," she said.

"A very petty and nasty way, to my mind!"

"Oh, yes," said Nanny simply. "Ways often are. But look, you—"

"Will you be bringing anything to the produce stall, Gytha?" said Gammer Beavis quickly.

"Oh, a couple of bottles, I expect," said Nanny, deflating.

"Oh, homemade wine?" said Letice. "How nice."

"Sort of like wine, yes. Well, here's the path," said Nanny. "I'll just . . . I'll just nip back and say good night—"

"It's belittling, you know, the way you run around after her," said Letice.

"Yes. Well. You get used to people. Good night to you."

When she got back to the cottage Granny Weatherwax was standing in the middle of the kitchen floor with a face like an unmade bed and her arms folded. One foot tapped on the floor.

"She married a wizard," said Granny, as soon as her friend had entered. "You can't tell me that's right."

"Well, wizards can marry, you know. They just have to hand in the staff and pointy hat. There's no actual law says they can't, so long as they gives up wizarding. They're supposed to be married to the job."

"I should reckon it's a job being married to her," said Granny. Her face screwed up in a sour smile.

"Been pickling much this year?" said Nanny, employing a fresh association of ideas around the word "vinegar," which had just popped into her head.

"My onions all got the screw fly."

"That's a pity. You like onions."

"Even screw flies've got to eat," said Granny. She glared at the door. "Nice," she said.

"She's got a knitted cover on the lid in her privy," said Nanny.

"Pink?"

"Yes."

"Nice."

"She's not bad," said Nanny. "She does good work over in Fiddler's Elbow. People speak highly of her."

Granny sniffed. "Do they speak highly of me?" she said.

"No, they speaks quietly of you, Esme."

"Good. Did you see her hatpins?"

"I thought they were rather . . . nice, Esme."

"That's witchcraft today. All jewellery and no drawers."

Nanny, who considered both to be optional, tried to build an embankment against the rising tide of ire.

"You could think of it as an honour, really, them not wanting you to take part."

"That's nice."

Nanny sighed.

"Sometimes nice is worth tryin', Esme," she said.

"I never does anyone a bad turn if I can't do 'em a good one, Gytha, you know that. I don't have to do no frills or fancy labels."

Nanny sighed. Of course, it was true. Granny was an old-fashioned witch. She didn't do good for people, she did right by them. But Nanny knew that people don't always appreciate right. Like old Pollitt the other day, when he fell off his horse. What he wanted was a painkiller. What he needed was the few seconds of agony as Granny popped the joint back into place. The trouble was, people remembered the pain.

You got on a lot better with people when you remembered to put frills round it, and took an interest, and said things like, "How are you?" Esme didn't bother with that kind of stuff because she knew already. Nanny Ogg knew too, but also knew that letting on you knew gave people the serious willies.

She put her head on one side. Granny's foot was still tapping.

"You planning anything, Esme? I know you. You've got that look."

"What look, pray?"

"That look you had when that bandit was found naked up a tree and cryin' all the time and goin' on about the horrible thing that was after him. Funny thing, we never found any pawprints. That look."

"He deserved more'n that for what he done."

"Yeah . . . well, you had that look just before ole Hoggett was found beaten black and blue in his own pigsty and wouldn't talk about it."

"You mean old Hoggett the wife beater? Or old Hoggett who won't never lift his hand to a woman no more?" said Granny. The thing her lips had pursed into may have been called a smile.

"And it's the look you had the time all the snow slid down on ole Millson's house just after he called you an interfering old baggage . . ." said Nanny.

Granny hesitated. Nanny was pretty sure that had been natural causes, and also that Granny knew she suspected this, and that pride was fighting a battle with honesty—

"That's as may be," said Granny noncommittally.

"Like someone who might go along to the Trials and . . . do something," said Nanny.

Her friend's glare should have made the air sizzle.

"Oh? So that's what you think of me? That's what we've come to, have we?"

"Letice thinks we should move with the times—"

"Well? I moves with the times. We ought to move with the times. No one said we ought to give them a push. I expect you'll be wanting to be going, Gytha. I want to be alone with my thoughts!"

Nanny's own thoughts, as she scurried home in relief, were that Granny Weatherwax was not an advertisement for witchcraft. Oh, she was one of the best at it, no doubt about that. At a certain kind, certainly. But a girl starting out in life might well say to herself, "Is this it? You worked hard and denied yourself things and what you got at the end of it was hard work and self-denial?"

Granny wasn't exactly friendless, but what she commanded mostly was respect. People learned to respect storm clouds, too. They refreshed the ground. You needed them. But they weren't nice.

Nanny Ogg went to bed in three flannelette nightdresses, because sharp frosts were already pricking the autumn air. She was also in a troubled frame of mind.

Some sort of war had been declared, she knew. Granny could do some terrible things when roused, and the fact that they'd been done to those who richly deserved them didn't make them any the less terrible. She'd be planning something pretty dreadful, Nanny Ogg was certain.

She herself didn't like winning things. Winning was a habit that was hard to break and brought you a dangerous status that was hard to defend. You'd walk uneasily through life, always on the lookout for the next girl with a better broomstick and a quicker hand on the frog.

She turned over under the mountain of eiderdowns.

In Granny Weatherwax's worldview there was no place for second place. You won, or you were a loser. There was nothing wrong with being a loser except for the fact that, of course, you weren't the winner. Nanny had always pursued the policy of being a good loser. People liked you when you almost won, and bought you drinks. "She only just lost" was a much better compliment than "she only just won."

Runners-up had more fun, she reckoned. But it wasn't a word Granny had much time for.

In her own darkened cottage, Granny Weatherwax sat and watched the fire die.

It was a grey-walled room, the colour that old plaster gets not so much from dirt as from age. There was not a thing in it that wasn't useful, utilitarian, earning its keep. Every flat surface in Nanny Ogg's cottage had been pressed into service as a holder for ornaments and potted plants. People gave Nanny Ogg things. Cheap fairground tat, Granny always called it. At least in public. What she thought of it in the privacy of her own head, she never said.

She rocked gently as the last ember winked out.

It's hard to contemplate, in the grey hours of the night, that probably the only reason people would come to your funeral would be to make sure you're dead.

Next day, Percy Hopcroft opened his back door and looked straight up into the blue stare of Granny Weatherwax.

"Oh my," he said, under his breath.

Granny gave an awkward little cough.

"Mr. Hopcroft, I've come about them apples you named after Mrs. Ogg," she said.

Percy's knees began to tremble, and his wig started to slide off the back of his head to the hoped-for security of the floor.

"I should like to thank you for doing it because it has made her very happy," Granny went on, in a tone of voice which would have struck one who knew her as curiously monotonous. "She has done a lot of fine work and it is about time she got her little reward. It was a very nice thought. And so I have brung you this little token—" Hopcroft jumped backwards as Granny's hand dipped swiftly into her apron and produced a small black bottle "—which is very rare because of the rare herbs in it. What are rare. Extremely rare herbs."

Eventually it crept over Hopcroft that he was supposed to take the bottle. He gripped the top of it very carefully, as if it might whistle or develop legs.

"Uh . . . thank you ver' much," he mumbled.

Granny nodded stiffly.

"Blessings be upon this house," she said, and turned and walked away down the path.

Hopcroft shut the door carefully, and then flung himself against it.

"You start packing right now!" he shouted to his wife, who'd been watching from the kitchen door.

"What? Our whole life's here! We can't just run away from it!"

"Better to run than hop, woman! What's she want from me? What's she want? She's never nice!"

Mrs. Hopcroft stood firm. She'd just got the cottage looking right and they'd bought a new pump. Some things were hard to leave.

"Let's just stop and think, then," she said. "What's in that bottle?"

Hopcroft held it at arm's length. "Do you want to find out?"

"Stop shaking, man! She didn't actually threaten, did she?"

"She said 'Blessings be upon this house'! Sounds pretty damn threatening to me! That was Granny Weatherwax, that was!"

He put the bottle on the table. They stared at it, standing in the cautious leaning position of people who were ready to run if anything began to happen.

"Says 'Haire Reftorer' on the label," said Mrs. Hopcroft.

"I ain't using it!"

"She'll ask us about it later. That's her way."

"If you think for one moment I'm—"

"We can try it out on the dog."

"That's a good cow."

William Poorchick awoke from his reverie on the milking stool and looked around the meadow, his hands still working the beast's teats.

There was a black pointy hat rising over the hedge. He gave such a start that he started to milk into his left boot.

"Gives plenty of milk, does she?"

"Yes, Mistress Weatherwax!" William quavered.

"That's good. Long may she continue to do so, that's what I say. Good day to you."

And the pointy hat continued up the lane.

Poorchick stared after it. Then he grabbed the bucket and, squelching at every other step, hurried into the barn and yelled for his son.

"Rummage! You get down here right now!"

His son appeared from the hayloft, pitchfork still in his hand.

"What's up, Dad?"

"You take Daphne down to the market right now, understand?"

"What? But she's our best milker, Dad!"

"Was, son, was! Granny Weatherwax just put a curse on her! Sell her now before her horns drop off!"

"What'd she say, Dad?"

"She said . . . she said . . . 'Long may she continue to give milk' . . ." Poorchick hesitated.

"Doesn't sound awfully like a curse, Dad," said Rummage. "I mean . . . not like your gen'ral curse. Sounds a bit hopeful, really," said his son.

"Well . . . it was the way . . . she . . . said . . . it . . ."

"What sort of way, Dad?"

"Well . . . like . . . cheerfully."

"You all right, Dad?"

"It was . . . the way . . ." Poorchick paused. "Well, it's not right," he continued. "It's not right! She's got no right to go around being cheerful at people! She's never cheerful! And my boot is full of milk!"

Today Nanny Ogg was taking some time out to tend her secret still in the woods. As a still it was the best-kept secret there could be, since everyone in the kingdom knew exactly where it was, and a secret kept by so many people must be very secret indeed. Even the king knew, and knew enough to pretend he didn't know, and that meant he didn't have to ask her for any taxes and she didn't have to refuse. And every year at Hogswatch he got a barrel of what honey might be if only bees weren't teetotal. And everyone understood the situation, no one had to pay any money, and so, in a small way, the world was a happier place. And no one was cursed until their teeth fell out.

Nanny was dozing. Keeping an eye on a still was a day-and-night job. But finally the sound of people repeatedly calling her name got too much for her.

No one would come into the clearing, of course. That would mean admitting that they knew where it was. So they were blundering around in the surrounding bushes. She pushed her way through and was greeted with some looks of feigned surprise that would have done credit to any amateur dramatic company.

"Well, what do you lot want?" she demanded.

"Oh, Mrs. Ogg, we thought you might be . . . taking a walk in the woods," said Poorchick, while a scent that could clean glass wafted on the breeze. "You got to do something! It's Mistress Weatherwax!"

"What's she done?"

"You tell 'er, Mr. Hampicker!"

The man next to Poorchick took off his hat quickly and held it respectfully in front of him in the ay-señor-the-bandidos-have-raided-our-villages position.

"Well, ma'am, my lad and I were digging for a well and then she come past—"

"Granny Weatherwax?"

"Yes'm, and she said—" Hampicker gulped, "'You won't find any water there, my good man. You'd be better off looking in the hollow by the chestnut tree'! An' we dug on down anyway and we never found no water!"

Nanny lit her pipe. She didn't smoke around the still since that time when a careless spark had sent the barrel she was sitting on a hundred yards into the air. She'd been lucky that a fir tree had broken her fall.

"So . . . then you dug in the hollow by the chestnut tree?" she said mildly.

Hampicker looked shocked. "No'm! There's no telling what she wanted us to find there!"

"And she cursed my cow!" said Poorchick.

"Really? What did she say?"

"She said, 'May she give a lot of milk'!" Poorchick stopped. Once again, now that he came to say it . . .

"Well, it was the way she said it," he added weakly.

"And what kind of way was that?"

"Nicely!"

"Nicely?"

"Smilin' and everything! I don't dare drink the stuff now!"

Nanny was mystified.

"Can't quite see the problem—"

"You tell that to Mr. Hopcroft's dog," said Poorchick. "Hopcroft daren't leave the poor thing on account of her! The whole family's going mad! There's him shearing, his wife sharpening the scissors, and the two lads out all the time looking for fresh places to dump the hair!"

Patient questioning on Nanny's part elucidated the role the Haire Reftorer had played in this.

"And he gave it . . .?"

"Half the bottle, Mrs. Ogg."

"Even though Esme writes 'A right small spoonful once a week' on the label? And even then you need to wear roomy trousers."

"He said he was so nervous, Mrs. Ogg! I mean, what's she playing at? Our wives are keepin' the kids indoors. I mean, s'posin' she smiled at them?"

"Well?"

"She's a witch!"

"So'm I, an' I smiles at 'em," said Nanny Ogg. "They're always runnin' after me for sweets."

"Yes, but . . . you're . . . I mean . . . she . . . I mean . . . you don't . . . I mean, well—"

"And she's a good woman," said Nanny. Common sense prompted

her to add, "In her own way. I expect there is water down in the hollow, and Poorchick's cow'll give good milk and if Hopcroft won't read the labels on bottles, then he deserves a head you can see your face in, and if you think Esme Weatherwax'd curse kids, you've got the sense of an earthworm. She'd cuss 'em, yes, all day long. But not curse 'em. She don't aim that low."

"Yes, yes," Poorchick almost moaned, "but it don't feel right, that's what we're saying. Her going round being nice, a man don't know if he's got a leg to stand on."

"Or hop on," said Hampicker darkly.

"All right, all right, I'll see about it," said Nanny.

"People shouldn't go around not doin' what you expect," said Poorchick weakly. "It gets people on edge."

"And we'll keep an eye on your sti—" Hampicker said, and then staggered backwards, grasping his stomach and wheezing.

"Don't mind him, it's the stress," said Poorchick, rubbing his elbow. "Been picking herbs, Mrs. Ogg?"

"That's right," said Nanny, hurrying away across the leaves.

"So shall I put the fire out for you, then?" Poorchick shouted.

Granny was sitting outside her house when Nanny Ogg hurried up the path. She was sorting through a sack of old clothes. Elderly garments were scattered around her.

And she was humming. Nanny Ogg started to worry. The Granny Weatherwax she knew didn't approve of music.

And she smiled when she saw Nanny, or at least the corner of her mouth turned up. That was really worrying. Granny normally only smiled if something bad was happening to someone deserving.

"Why, Gytha, how nice to see you!"

"You all right, Esme?"

"Never felt better, dear." The humming continued.

"Er . . . sorting out rags, are you?" said Nanny. "Going to make that quilt?"

It was one of Granny Weatherwax's firm beliefs that one day she'd make a patchwork quilt. However, it is a task that requires patience, and hence in fifteen years she'd got as far as three patches. But she collected old clothes anyway. A lot of witches did. It was a witch thing. Old clothes had personality, like old houses. When it came to clothes with a bit of wear left in them, a witch had no pride at all.

"It's in here somewhere . . ." Granny mumbled. "Aha, here we are . . ."

She flourished a garment. It was basically pink.

"Knew it was here," she went on. "Hardly worn, either. And about my size, too."

"You're going to wear it?" said Nanny.

Granny's piercing blue cut-you-off-at-the-knees gaze was turned upon her. Nanny would have been relieved at a reply like, "No, I'm going to eat it, you daft old fool." Instead her friend relaxed and said, a little concerned:

"You don't think it'd suit me?"

There was lace around the collar. Nanny swallowed.

"You usually wear black," she said. "Well, a bit more than usually. More like always."

"And a very sad sight I look, too," said Granny robustly. "It's about time I brightened myself up a bit, don't you think?"

"And it's so very . . . pink."

Granny put it aside and to Nanny's horror took her by the hand and said earnestly, "And, you know, I reckon I've been far too dog in the manger about this Trials business, Gytha—"

"Bitch in the manger," said Nanny Ogg, absentmindedly.

For a moment Granny's eyes became two sapphires again.

"What?"

"Er . . . you'd be a bitch in the manger," Nanny mumbled. "Not a dog."

"Ah? Oh, yes. Thank you for pointing that out. Well, I thought, it is time I stepped back a bit, and went along and cheered on the younger folks. I mean, I have to say, I . . . really haven't been very nice to people, have I . . ."

"Er . . ."

"I've tried being nice," Granny went on. "It didn't turn out like I expected, I'm sorry to say."

"You've never been really . . . good at nice," said Nanny.

Granny smiled. Hard though she stared, Nanny was unable to spot anything other than earnest concern.

"Perhaps I'll get better with practice," she said.

She patted Nanny's hand. And Nanny stared at her hand as though something horrible had happened to it.

"It's just that everyone's more used to you being . . . firm," she said.

"I thought I might make some jam and cakes for the produce stall," said Granny.

"Oh . . . good."

"Are there any sick people want visitin'?"

Nanny stared at the trees. It was getting worse and worse. She rummaged in her memory for anyone in the locality sick enough to warrant a ministering visit but still well enough to survive the shock of a ministering visit by Granny Weatherwax. When it came to practical psychology and the more robust type of folk physio-therapy Granny was without equal; in fact, she could even do the latter at a distance, for many a pain-racked soul had left their bed and walked, nay, run at the news that she was coming.

"Everyone's pretty well at the moment," said Nanny diplomatically.

"Any old folk want cheerin' up?"

It was taken for granted by both women that old people did not include them. A witch aged ninety-seven would not have included herself. Old people happened to other people.

"All fairly cheerful right now," said Nanny.

"Maybe I could tell stories to the kiddies?"

Nanny nodded. Granny had done that once before, when the mood had briefly taken her. It had worked pretty well, as far as the children were concerned. They'd listened with openmouthed attention and apparent enjoyment to a traditional old folk legend. The problem had come when they'd gone home afterwards and asked the meaning of words like *disembowelled.*

"I could sit in a rocking chair while I tell 'em," Granny added. "That's how it's done, I recall. And I could make them some of my special treacle toffee apples. Wouldn't that be nice?"

Nanny nodded again, in a sort of horrified reverie. She realized that only she stood in the way of a wholesale rampage of niceness.

"Toffee," she said. "Would that be the sort you did that shatters like glass, or that sort where our boy Pewsey had to have his mouth levered open with a spoon?"

"I reckon I know what I did wrong last time."

"You know you and sugar don't get along, Esme. Remember them all-day suckers you made?"

"They did last all day, Gytha."

"Only 'cos our Pewsey couldn't get it out of his little mouth until we pulled two of his teeth, Esme. You ought to stick to pickles. You and pickles goes well."

"I've got to do something, Gytha. I can't be an old grump all the time. I know! I'll help at the Trials. Bound to be a lot that needs doing, eh?"

Nanny grinned inwardly. So that was it.

"Why, yes," she said. "I'm sure Mrs. Earwig will be happy to tell you what to do." And more fool her if she does, she thought, because I can tell you're planning something.

"I shall talk to her," said Granny. "I'm sure there's a million things I could do to help, if I set my mind to it."

"And I'm sure you will," said Nanny heartily. "I've a feelin' you're going to make a big difference."

Granny started to rummage in the bag again.

"You are going to be along as well, aren't you, Gytha?"

"Me?" said Nanny. "I wouldn't miss it for the world."

*

Nanny got up especially early. If there was going to be any unpleasantness, she wanted a ringside seat.

What there was was bunting. It was hanging from tree to tree in terrible brightly coloured loops as she walked towards the Trials.

There was something oddly familiar about it, too. It should not technically be possible for anyone with a pair of scissors to be unable to cut out a triangle, but someone had managed it. And it was also obvious that the flags had been made from old clothes, painstakingly cut up. Nanny knew this because not many real flags have collars.

In the Trials field, people were setting up stalls and falling over children. The committee were standing uncertainly under a tree, occasionally glancing up at a pink figure at the top of a very long ladder.

"She was here before it was light," said Letice, as Nanny approached. "She said she'd been up all night making the flags."

"Tell her about the cakes," said Gammer Beavis darkly.

"She made cakes?" said Nanny. "But she can't cook!"

The committee shuffled aside. A lot of the ladies contributed to the food for the Trials. It was a tradition and an informal competition in its own right. At the centre of the spread of covered plates was a large platter piled high with . . . things, of indefinite colour and shape. It looked as though a herd of small cows had eaten a lot of raisins and then been ill. They were Ur-cakes, prehistoric cakes, cakes of great weight and presence that had no place among the iced dainties.

"She's never had the knack of it," said Nanny weakly. "Has anyone tried one?"

"Hahaha," said Gammer solemnly.

"Tough, are they?"

"You could beat a troll to death."

"But she was so . . . sort of . . . proud of them," said Letice. "And then there's . . . the jam."

It was a large pot. It seemed to be filled with solidified purple lava.

"Nice . . . colour," said Nanny. "Anyone tasted it?"

"We couldn't get the spoon out," said Gammer.

"Oh, I'm sure—"

"We only got it in with a hammer."

"What's she planning, Mrs. Ogg? She's got a weak and vengeful nature," said Letice. "You're her friend," she added, her tone suggesting that this was as much an accusation as a statement.

"I don't know what she's thinking, Mrs. Earwig."

"I thought she was staying away."

"She said she was going to take an interest and encourage the young 'uns."

"She is planning something," said Letice darkly. "Those cakes are a plot to undermine my authority."

"No, that's how she always cooks," said Nanny. "She just hasn't got the knack." Your authority, eh?

"She's nearly finished the flags," Gammer reported. "Now she's going to try to make herself useful again."

"Well . . . I suppose we could ask her to do the Lucky Dip."

Nanny looked blank. "You mean where kids fish around in a big tub full of bran to see what they can pull out?"

"Yes."

"You're going to let Granny Weatherwax do that?"

"Yes."

"Only she's got a funny sense of humour, if you know what I mean."

"Good morning to you all!"

It was Granny Weatherwax's voice. Nanny Ogg had known it for most of her life. But it had that strange edge to it again. It sounded nice.

"We were wondering if you could supervise the bran tub, Miss Weatherwax."

Nanny flinched. But Granny merely said, "Happy to, Mrs. Earwig.

I can't wait to see the expressions on their little faces as they pull out the goodies."

Nor can I, Nanny thought.

When the others had scurried off she sidled up to her friend.

"Why're you doing this?" she said.

"I really don't know what you mean, Gytha."

"I seen you face down terrible creatures, Esme. I once seen you catch a unicorn, for goodness' sake. What're you plannin'?"

"I still don't know what you mean, Gytha."

"Are you angry 'cos they won't let you enter, and now you're plannin' horrible revenge?"

For a moment they both looked at the field. It was beginning to fill up. People were bowling for pigs and fighting on the greasy pole. The Lancre Volunteer Band was trying to play a medley of popular tunes, and it was only a pity that each musician was playing a different one. Small children were fighting. It was going to be a scorcher of a day, probably the last one of the year.

Their eyes were drawn to the roped-off square in the centre of the field.

"Are you going to enter the Trials, Gytha?" said Granny.

"You never answered my question!"

"What question was that?"

Nanny decided not to hammer on a locked door. "Yes, I am going to have a go, as it happens," she said.

"I certainly hope you win, then. I'd cheer you on, only that wouldn't be fair to the others. I shall merge into the background and be as quiet as a little mouse."

Nanny tried guile. Her face spread into a wide pink grin, and she nudged her friend.

"Right, right," she said. "Only . . . you can tell me, right? I wouldn't like to miss it when it happens. So if you could just give me a little signal when you're going to do it, eh?"

"What's it you're referring to, Gytha?"

"Esme Weatherwax, sometimes I could really give you a bloody good slap!"

"Oh dear."

Nanny Ogg didn't often swear, or at least use words beyond the boundaries of what the Lancrastrians thought of as "colourful language." She looked as if she habitually used bad words, and had just thought up a good one, but mostly witches are quite careful about what they say. You can never be sure what the words are going to do when they're out of earshot. But now she swore under her breath and caused small brief fires to start in the dry grass.

This put her in just about the right frame of mind for the Cursing.

It was said that once upon a time this had been done on a living, breathing subject, at least at the start of the event, but that wasn't right for a family day out, and for several hundred years the Curses had been directed at Unlucky Charlie, who was, however you looked at it, nothing more than a scarecrow. And since curses are generally directed at the mind of the cursed, this presented a major problem, because even "May your straw go mouldy and your carrot fall off" didn't make much impression on a pumpkin. But points were given for general style and inventiveness.

There wasn't much pressure for those in any case. Everyone knew what event counted, and it wasn't Unlucky Charlie.

One year Granny Weatherwax had made the pumpkin explode. No one had ever worked out how she'd done it.

Someone would walk away at the end of today and everyone would know that person was the winner, whatever the points said. You could win the Witch with the Pointiest Hat prize and the broomstick dressage, but that was just for the audience. What counted was the Trick you'd been working on all summer.

Nanny had drawn last place, at number nineteen. A lot of witches had turned up this year. News of Granny Weatherwax's withdrawal had got around, and nothing moves faster than news in the occult community, since it doesn't just have to travel at ground level. Many pointy hats moved and nodded among the crowds.

Witches are among themselves generally as sociable as cats but, as also with cats, there are locations and times and neutral grounds where they meet at something like peace. And what was going on was a sort of slow, complicated dance . . .

The witches walked around saying hello to one another, and rushing to meet newcomers, and innocent bystanders might have believed that here was a meeting of old friends. Which, at one level, it probably was. But Nanny watched through a witch's eyes, and saw the subtle positioning, the careful weighing up, the little changes of stance, the eye contact finely tuned by intensity and length.

And when a witch was in the arena, especially if she was comparatively unknown, all the others found some excuse to keep an eye on her, preferably without appearing to do so.

It was like watching cats. Cats spend a lot of time carefully eyeing one another. When they have to fight, that's merely to rubber-stamp something that's already been decided in their heads.

Nanny knew all this. And she also knew most of the witches to be kind (on the whole), gentle (to the meek), generous (to the deserving; the undeserving got more than they bargained for), and by and large quite dedicated to a life that really offered more kicks than kisses. Not one of them lived in a house made of confectionery, although some of the conscientious younger ones had experimented with various crispbreads. Even children who deserved it were not slammed into their ovens. Generally they did what they'd always done—smooth the passage of their neighbours into and out of the world, and help them over some of the nastier hurdles in between.

You needed to be a special kind of person to do that. You needed a special kind of ear, because you saw people in circumstances where they were inclined to tell you things, like where the money is buried or who the father was or how come they'd got a black eye again. And you needed a special kind of mouth, the sort that stayed shut. Keeping secrets made you powerful. Being powerful earned you respect. Respect was hard currency.

And within this sisterhood—except that it wasn't a sisterhood, it was a loose assortment of chronic non-joiners; a group of witches wasn't a coven, it was a small war—there was always this awareness of position. It had nothing to do with anything the other world thought of as status. Nothing was ever said. But if an elderly witch died, the local witches would attend her funeral for a few last words, and then go solemnly home alone, with the little insistent thought at the back of their minds: I've moved up one.

And newcomers were watched very, very carefully.

"Morning, Mrs. Ogg," said a voice behind her. "I trust I find you well?"

"Howd'yer do, Mistress Shimmy," said Nanny, turning. Her mental filing system threw up a card: Clarity Shimmy, lives over toward Cutshade with her old mum, takes snuff, good with animals. "How's your mother keepin'?"

"We buried her last month, Mrs. Ogg."

Nanny Ogg quite liked Clarity, because she didn't see her very often.

"Oh dear . . ." she said.

"But I shall tell her you asked after her, anyway," said Clarity. She glanced briefly towards the ring.

"Who's the fat girl on now?" she asked. "Got a backside on her like a bowling ball on a short seesaw."

"That's Agnes Nitt."

"That's a good cursin' voice she's got there. You know you've been cursed with a voice like that."

"Oh yes, she's been blessed with a good voice for cursin'," said Nanny politely. "Esme Weatherwax an' me gave her a few tips," she added.

Clarity's head turned.

At the far edge of the field, a small pink shape sat alone behind the Lucky Dip. It did not seem to be drawing a big crowd.

Clarity leaned closer.

"What's she . . . er . . . doing?"

"I don't know," said Nanny. "I think she's decided to be nice about it."

"Esme? Nice about it?"

"Er . . . yes," said Nanny. It didn't sound any better now she was telling someone.

Clarity stared at her. Nanny saw her make a little sign with her left hand, and then hurry off.

The pointy hats were bunching up now. There were little groups of three or four. You could see the points come together, cluster in animated conversation, and then open out again like a flower, and turn towards the distant blob of pinkness. Then a hat would leave that group and head off purposefully to another one, where the process would start all over again. It was a bit like watching very slow nuclear fission. There was a lot of excitement, and soon there would be an explosion.

Every so often someone would turn and look at Nanny, so she hurried away among the sideshows until she fetched up beside the stall of the dwarf Zakzak Stronginthearm, maker and purveyor of occult knicknackery to the more impressionable. He nodded at her cheerfully over the top of a display saying LUCKY HORSESHOES $2 EACH.

"Hello, Mrs. Ogg," he said.

Nanny realized she was flustered.

"What's lucky about 'em?" she said, picking up a horseshoe.

"Well, I get two dollars each for them," said Stronginthearm.

"And that makes them lucky?"

"Lucky for me," said Stronginthearm. "I expect you'll be wanting one too, Mrs. Ogg? I'd have fetched along another box if I'd known they'd be so popular. Some of the ladies've bought two."

There was an inflection to the word "ladies."

"Witches have been buying lucky horseshoes?" said Nanny.

"Like there's no tomorrow," said Zakzak. He frowned for a moment. They had been witches, after all. "Er . . . there will be . . . won't there?" he added.

"I'm very nearly certain of it," said Nanny, which didn't seem to comfort him.

"Suddenly been doing a roaring trade in protective herbs, too," said Zakzak. And, being a dwarf, which meant that he'd see the Flood as a marvellous opportunity to sell towels, he added, "Can I interest you, Mrs. Ogg?"

Nanny shook her head. If trouble was going to come from the direction everyone had been looking, then a sprig of rue wasn't going to be much help. A large oak tree'd be better, but only maybe.

The atmosphere was changing. The sky was a wide pale blue, but there was thunder on the horizons of the mind. The witches were uneasy and with so many in one place the nervousness was bouncing from one to another and, amplified, rebroadcasting itself to everyone. It meant that even ordinary people who thought that a rune was a dried plum were beginning to feel a deep, existential worry, the kind that causes you to snap at your kids and want a drink.

She peered through a gap between a couple of stalls. The pink figure was still sitting patiently, and a little crestfallen, behind the barrel. There was, as it were, a huge queue of no one at all.

Then Nanny scuttled from the cover of one tent to another until she could see the produce stand. It had already been doing a busy trade but there, forlorn in the middle of the cloth, was the pile of terrible cakes. And the jar of jam. Some wag had chalked up a sign beside it: GET THE SPOON OUT OF THEE JAR, 3 TRIES FOR A PENNEY!!!

She thought she'd been careful to stay concealed, but she heard the straw rustle behind her. The committee had tracked her down.

"That's your handwriting, isn't it, Mrs. Earwig?" she said. "That's cruel. That ain't . . . nice."

"We've decided you're to go and talk to Miss Weatherwax," said Letice. "She's got to stop it."

"Stop what?"

"She's doing something to people's heads! She's come here to put the 'fluence on us, right? Everyone knows she does head magic. We can all feel it! She's spoiling it for everyone!"

"She's only sitting there," said Nanny.

"Ah, yes, but how is she sitting there, may we ask?"

Nanny peered around the stall again.

"Well . . . like normal. You know . . . bent in the middle and the knees . . ."

Letice waved a finger sternly.

"Now you listen to me, Gytha Ogg—"

"If you want her to go away, you go and tell her!" snapped Nanny. "I'm fed up with—"

There was the piercing scream of a child.

The witches stared at one another, and then ran across the field to the Lucky Dip.

A small boy was writhing on the ground, sobbing.

It was Pewsey, Nanny's youngest grandchild.

Her stomach turned to ice. She snatched him up, and glared into Granny's face.

"What have you done to him, you—" she began.

"Don'twannadolly! Don'twannadolly! Wannasoljer! Wannawanna-wannaSOLJER!"

Now Nanny looked down at the rag doll in Pewsey's sticky hand, and the expression of affronted tearful rage on such of his face as could be seen around his screaming mouth—

"OiwannawannaSOLJER!"

—and then at the other witches, and at Granny Weatherwax's face, and felt the horrible cold shame welling up from her boots.

"I said he could put it back and have another go," said Granny meekly. "But he just wouldn't listen."

"—wannawannaSOL—"

"Pewsey Ogg, if you don't shut up right this minute Nanny will—" Nanny Ogg began, and dredged up the nastiest punishment she could think of: "Nanny won't give you a sweetie ever again!"

Pewsey closed his mouth, stunned into silence by this unimaginable threat. Then, to Nanny's horror, Letice Earwig drew herself up and said, "Miss Weatherwax, we would prefer it if you left."

"Am I being a bother?" said Granny. "I hope I'm not being a bother. I don't want to be a bother. He just took a lucky dip and—"

"You're . . . upsetting people."

Any minute now, Nanny thought. Any minute now she's going to raise her head and narrow her eyes and if Letice doesn't take two steps backwards she'll be a lot tougher than me.

"I can't stay and watch?" Granny said quietly.

"I know your game," said Letice. "You're planning to spoil it, aren't you? You can't stand the thought of being beaten, so you're intending something nasty."

Three steps back, Nanny thought. Else there won't be anything left but bones. Any minute now . . .

"Oh, I wouldn't like anyone to think I was spoiling anything," said Granny. She sighed and stood up. "I'll be off home . . ."

"No you won't!" snapped Nanny Ogg, pushing her back down on to the chair. "What do you think of this, Beryl Dismass? And you, Letty Parkin?"

"They're all—" Letice began.

"I weren't talking to you!"

The witches behind Mrs. Earwig avoided Nanny's gaze.

"Well, it's not that . . . I mean, we don't think . . ." began Beryl awkwardly. "That is . . . I've always had a lot of respect for . . . but . . . well, it is for everyone . . ."

Her voice trailed off. Letice looked triumphant.

"Really? I think we had better be going after all, then," said Nanny sourly. "I don't like the comp'ny in these parts." She looked around. "Agnes? You give me a hand to get Granny home . . ."

"I really don't need . . ." Granny began, but the other two each took an arm and gently propelled her through the crowd, which parted to let them through and turned to watch them go.

"Probably the best for all concerned, in the circumstances," said Letice. Several of the witches tried not to look at her face.

There were scraps of material all over the floor in Granny's kitchen, and gouts of congealed jam had dripped off the edge of the table and formed an immovable mound on the floor. The jam saucepan had been left in the stone sink to soak, although it was clear that the iron would rust away before the jam ever softened.

There was a row of empty pickle jars beside them.

Granny sat down and folded her hands in her lap.

"Want a cup of tea, Esme?" said Nanny Ogg.

"No, dear, thank you. You get on back to the Trials. Don't you worry about me," said Granny.

"You sure?"

"I'll just sit here quiet. Don't you worry."

"I'm not going back!" Agnes hissed, as they left. "I don't like the way Letice smiles . . ."

"You once told me you didn't like the way Esme frowns," said Nanny.

"Yes, but you can trust a frown. Er . . . you don't think she's losing it, do you?"

"No one'll be able to find it if she has," said Nanny. "No, you come on back with me. I'm sure she's planning . . . something." I wish the hell I knew what it is, she thought. I'm not sure I can take any more waiting.

She could feel the mounting tension before they reached the field. Of course, there was always tension, that was part of the Trials, but this kind had a sour, unpleasant taste. The sideshows were still going on but ordinary folk were leaving, spooked by sensations they couldn't put their finger on which nevertheless had them under their thumb. As for the witches themselves, they had that look worn by actors about two minutes from the end of a horror movie, when they know the monster is about to make its final leap and now it's only a matter of which door.

Letice was surrounded by witches. Nanny could hear raised voices. She nudged another witch, who was watching gloomily.

"What's happening, Winnie?"

"Oh, Reena Trump made a pig's ear of her piece and her friends say she ought to have another go because she was so nervous."

"That's a shame."

"And Virago Johnson ran off 'cos her weather spell went wrong."

"Left under a bit of a cloud, did she?"

"And I was all thumbs when I had a go. You could be in with a chance, Gytha."

"Oh, I've never been one for prizes, Winnie, you know me. It's the fun of taking part that counts."

The other witch gave her a skewed look.

"You almost made that sound believable," she said.

Gammer Beavis hurried over. "On you go, Gytha," she said. "Do your best, eh? The only contender so far is Mrs. Weavitt and her whistling frog, and it wasn't as if it could even carry a tune. Poor thing was a bundle of nerves."

Nanny Ogg shrugged, and walked out into the roped-off area. Somewhere in the distance someone was having hysterics, punctuated by an occasional worried whistle.

Unlike the magic of wizards, the magic of witches did not usually involve the application of much raw power. The difference is that between hammers and levers. Witches generally tried to find the small point where a little change made a lot of result. To make an avalanche you can either shake the mountain, or maybe you can just find exactly the right place to drop a snowflake.

This year Nanny had been idly working on the Man of Straw. It was an ideal trick for her. It got a laugh, it was a bit suggestive, it was a lot easier than it looked but showed she was joining in, and it was unlikely to win.

Damn! She'd been relying on that frog to beat her. She'd heard it whistling quite beautifully on the summer evenings.

She concentrated.

Pieces of straw rustled through the stubble. All she had to do was use the little bits of wind that drifted across the field, allow them to move here and here, spiral up and—

She tried to stop her hands from shaking. She'd done this a hundred times, she could tie the damn stuff in knots by now. She kept seeing the face of Esme Weatherwax, and the way she'd just sat there, looking puzzled and hurt, while for a few seconds Nanny had been ready to kill—

For a moment she managed to get the legs right, and a suggestion of arms and head. There was a smattering of applause from the watchers. Then an errant eddy caught the thing before she could concentrate on its first step, and it spun down, just a lot of useless straw.

She made some frantic gestures to get it to rise again. It flopped about, tangled itself, and lay still.

There was a bit more applause, nervous and sporadic.

"Sorry . . . don't seem to be able to get the hang of it today," she muttered, walking off the field.

The judges went into a huddle.

"I reckon that frog did really well," said Nanny, more loudly than was necessary.

The wind, so contrary a little while ago, blew sharper now. What might be called the psychic darkness of the event was being enhanced by real twilight.

The shadow of the bonfire loomed on the far side of the field. No one as yet had the heart to light it. Almost all of the non-witches had gone home. Anything good about the day had long drained away.

The circle of judges broke up and Mrs. Earwig advanced on the nervous crowd, her smile only slightly waxen at the corners.

"Well, what a difficult decision it has been," she said brightly. "But what a marvellous turnout, too! It really has been a most tricky choice—"

Between me and a frog that lost its whistle and got its foot stuck in its banjo, thought Nanny. She looked sidelong at the faces of her sister witches. She'd known some of them for sixty years. If she'd ever read books, she'd have been able to read the faces just like one.

"We all know who won, Mrs. Earwig," she said, interrupting the flow.

"What do you mean, Mrs. Ogg?"

"There's not a witch here who could get her mind right today," said Nanny. "And most of 'em have bought lucky charms, too. Witches? Buying lucky charms?" Several women stared at the ground.

"I don't know why everyone seems so afraid of Miss Weatherwax! I certainly am not! You think she's put a spell on you, then?"

"A pretty sharp one, by the feel of it," said Nanny. "Look, Mrs. Earwig, no one's won, not with the stuff we've managed today. We all know it. So let's just all go home, eh?"

"Certainly not! I paid ten dollars for this cup and I mean to present it—"

The dying leaves shivered on the trees.

The witches drew together.

Branches rattled.

"It's the wind," said Nanny Ogg. "That's all . . ."

And then Granny was simply there. It was as if they'd just not noticed that she'd been there all the time. She had the knack of fading out of the foreground.

"I jus' thought I'd come to see who won," she said. "Join in the applause, and so on . . ."

Letice advanced on her, wild with rage.

"Have you been getting into people's heads?" she shrieked.

"An' how could I do that, Mrs. Earwig?" said Granny meekly. "Past all them lucky charms?"

"You're lying!"

Nanny Ogg heard the indrawn breaths, and hers was loudest. Witches lived by their words.

"I don't lie, Mrs. Earwig."

"Do you deny that you set out to ruin my day?"

Some of the witches at the edge of the crowd started to back away.

"I'll grant my jam ain't to everyone's taste but I never—" Granny began, in a modest little tone.

"You've been putting a 'fluence on everyone!"

"—I just set out to help, you can ask anyone—"

"You did! Admit it!" Mrs. Earwig's voice was as shrill as a gull's.

"—and I certainly didn't do any—"

Granny's head turned as the slap came.

For the moment no one breathed, no one moved.

She lifted a hand slowly and rubbed her cheek.

"You know you could have done it easily!"

It seemed to Nanny that Letice's scream echoed off the mountains.

The cup dropped from her hands and crunched on the stubble.

Then the tableau unfroze. A couple of her sister witches stepped forward, put their hands on Letice's shoulders and she was pulled, gently and unprotesting, away.

Everyone else waited to see what Granny Weatherwax would do. She raised her head.

"I hope Mrs. Earwig is all right," she said. "She seemed a bit . . . distraught."

There was silence. Nanny picked up the abandoned cup and tapped it with a forefinger.

"Hmm," she said. "Just plated, I reckon. If she paid ten dollars for it, the poor woman was robbed." She tossed it to Gammer Beavis, who fumbled it out of the air. "Can you give it back to her tomorrow, Gammer?"

Gammer nodded, trying not to catch Granny's eye.

"Still, we don't have to let it spoil everything," Granny said pleasantly. "Let's have the proper ending to the day, eh? Traditional, like. Roast potatoes and marshmallows and old stories round the fire. And forgiveness. And let's let bygones be bygones."

Nanny could feel the sudden relief spreading out like a fan. The witches seemed to come alive, at the breaking of the spell that had never actually been there in the first place. There was a general straightening up and the beginnings of a bustle as they headed for the saddlebags on their broomsticks.

"Mr. Hopcroft gave me a whole sack of spuds," said Nanny, as conversation rose around them. "I'll go and drag 'em over. Can you get the fire lit, Esme?"

A sudden change in the air made her look up. Granny's eyes gleamed in the dusk.

Nanny knew enough to fling herself to the ground.

Granny Weatherwax's hand curved through the air like a comet and the spark flew out, crackling.

The bonfire exploded. A blue-white flame shot up through the stacked branches and danced into the sky, etching shadows on the forest. It blew off hats and overturned tables and formed figures and castles and scenes from famous battles and joined hands and danced in a ring. It left a purple image on the eye that burned into the brain—

And settled down, and was just a bonfire.

"I never said nothin' about forgettin'," said Granny.

When Granny Weatherwax and Nanny Ogg walked home through the dawn, their boots kicked up the mist. It had, on the whole, been a good night.

After some while, Nanny said, "That wasn't nice, what you done."

"I done nothin'."

"Yeah, well . . . it wasn't nice, what you didn't do. It was like pullin' away someone's chair when they're expecting to sit down."

"People who don't look where they're sitting should stay stood up," said Granny.

There was a brief pattering on the leaves, one of those very brief showers you get when a few raindrops don't want to bond with the group.

"Well, all right," Nanny conceded. "But it was a little bit cruel."

"Right," said Granny.

"And some people might think it was a little bit nasty."

"Right."

Nanny shivered. The thoughts that'd gone through her head in those few seconds after Pewsey had screamed—

"I gave you no cause," said Granny. "I put nothin' in anyone's head that weren't there already."

"Sorry, Esme."

"Right."

"But . . . Letice didn't mean to be cruel, Esme. I mean, she's spiteful and bossy and silly, but—"

"You've known me since we was girls, right?" Granny interrupted. "Through thick and thin, good and bad?"

"Yes, of course, but—"

"And you never sank to sayin', 'I'm telling you this as a friend,' did you?"

Nanny shook her head. It was a telling point. No one even remotely friendly would say a thing like that.

"What's empowerin' about witchcraft anyway?" said Granny. "It's a daft sort of a word."

"Search me," said Nanny. "I did start out in witchcraft to get boys, to tell you the truth."

"Think I don't know that?"

"What did you start out to get, Esme?"

Granny stopped, and looked up at the frosty sky and then down at the ground.

"Dunno," she said at last. "Even, I suppose."

And that, Nanny thought, was that.

Deer bounded away as they arrived at Granny's cottage.

There was a stack of firewood piled up neatly by the back door, and a couple of sacks on the doorstep. One contained a large cheese.

"Looks like Mr. Hopcroft and Mr. Poorchick have been here," said Nanny.

"Hmph." Granny looked at the carefully yet badly written piece of paper attached to the second sack: "'Dear Misftresf Weatherwax, I would be moft grateful if you would let me name thif new championfhip variety "Efme Weatherwax." Yours in hopefully good health, Percy Hopcroft.' Well, well, well. I wonder what gave him that idea?"

"Can't imagine," said Nanny.

"I would just bet you can't," said Granny.

She sniffed suspiciously, tugged at the sack's string, and pulled out an Esme Weatherwax.

It was rounded, very slightly flattened, and pointy at one end. It was an onion.

Nanny Ogg swallowed. "I told him not—"

"I'm sorry?"

"Oh . . . nothing . . ."

Granny Weatherwax turned the onion round and round, while the world, via the medium of Nanny Ogg, awaited its fate. Then she seemed to reach a decision she was comfortable with.

"A very useful vegetable, the onion," she said, at last. "Firm. Sharp."

"Good for the system," said Nanny.

"Keeps well. Adds flavour."

"Hot and spicy," said Nanny, losing track of the metaphor in the flood of relief. "Nice with cheese—"

"We don't need to go that far," said Granny Weatherwax, putting it carefully back in the sack. She sounded almost amicable. "You comin' in for a cup of tea, Gytha?"

"Er . . . I'd better be getting along—"

"Fair enough."

Granny started to close the door, and then stopped and opened it again. Nanny could see one blue eye watching her through the crack.

"I was right though, wasn't I," said Granny. It wasn't a question.

Nanny nodded.

"Right," she said.

"That's nice."

The Ankh-Morpork
National Anthem

BBC Radio 4, 15 January 1999

In 1998, the BBC, or at least part of it, asked me if the Discworld had a national anthem.

I said no, but the city of Ankh-Morpork had one.

And they said: Would you write it for us?

And that led to the first ever national anthem of a fictional city state being played nationally on BBC Radio 4 on 15 January 1999, as the rousing close to a week of programmes about, yes, national anthems.

Carl Davis was asked to do the music and we had several long phone conversations about how the thing should sound, culminating in him ringing me up from a taxi in New York, I think, and playing a Stylophone at me.

It was wonderful. It was exactly what I'd asked for—ponderous, slightly threatening, and full of the joyful pomposity of empire. I think it was the BBC Scottish Symphony Orchestra that played it, with a wonderful soprano who tackled it cheerfully and made "ner hner ner" sound like something by Wagner.

It was never officially played again, for complicated reasons to do with money and copyright, although I think a version did end up online. Some people are such scallywags . . .

The anthem of the sprawling mercantile city-state of Ankh-Morpork was not even written by one of its sons but by a visitor—the vampire Count Henrik Shline von Überwald (born 1703, died 1782, died again 1784, and also in 1788, 1791, 1802/4/7/8, also 1821, 1830, 1861, staked 1872). He had taken a long holiday to get away from some people who wanted earnestly to talk to him about cutting his head off, and declared himself very impressed at the city's policy of keeping the peace by bribery, financial corruption, and ultimately by making unbeatable offers for the opponents' weapons, most of which had been made in Ankh-Morpork in the first place.

The anthem, known affectionately as "We can rule you wholesale," is the only one that formally has a second verse consisting mainly of embarrassed mumbling.

The Count, who visited many countries in the course of his travels, noted that all real patriots can never remember more than one verse of their anthem, and get through the subsequent verses by going "ner hner ner" until they reach an outcrop of words they recognize, which they sing very boldly to give the impression that they really had been singing all the other words as well but had been drowned out by the people around them.

In classical renditions, the singing is normally led by a large soprano wearing a sheet and carrying the flame of something or other and holding a large fork.

When dragons belch and hippos flee
My thoughts, Ankh-Morpork, are of thee

Let others boast of martial dash
For we have boldly fought with cash
We own all your helmets, we own all your shoes
We own all your generals—touch us and you'll lose
Morporkia! Morporkia!
Morporkia owns the day!
We can rule you wholesale
Touch us and you'll pay

We bankrupt all invaders, we sell them souvenirs
We ner ner ner ner ner, hner ner hner by the ears
Er hner we sing ner ner ner ner
Ner ner her ner ner ner hner the ner
Er ner ner hner ner, nher hner ner ner
Ner hner ner, your gleaming swords
We mortaged to the hilt
Morporkia! Morporkia!
Hner ner ner ner ner ner
We can rule you wholesale
Credit where it's due.

MEDICAL NOTES

Nac Mac Programme Book, Discworld Convention, August 2002

What can I say? Various conventions ask for stuff like this as part of the whole business: it's part of how the whole thing works, and usually they get it, and occasionally—possibly—it's good.

From *Household Medicine, Hair Care, and Simple Surgery,* published by the Ankh-Morpork Guild of Barber-Surgeons, AM\$2

Discworld, while hosting a large number of well-known plagues and other ailments, also boasts—if that is the word—a number of medical conditions of its own. In Ankh-Morpork in particular, population pressure has helped create a whole range of completely original yet curiously familiar complaints, such as:

Attention Surplus Syndrome
Teachers find this just as bad as the other sort. No one likes a child who pays attention too hard, whose eyes follow your every move,

and who listens very carefully to everything you say. It's like talking to a great big bottomless ear.

Advanced cases correct spelling and pronunciation in a clear piping voice, and point out errors of fact to the rest of the class. They also have the infuriating habit of reading all the way to the end of the classroom reader on the first day of term, instead of having the decency to read at the geological speed considered correct for the rest of their age group. Expel at the earliest opportunity.

Florabundi's Syndrome

Erratic and uncontrollable attacks of politeness and good manners. This may not at first sight appear to be an affliction at all, but can be deadly if you are a fish porter, a prisoner, a trooper, or a member of some other profession where incivility is bloody well expected. So called after Sergeant-Major Charles "Blossom" Florabundi, who in times of stress lost control of his vocabulary and, for example, refused to fire on any enemy that he hadn't been introduced to. He was pensioned off when the entire barracks mutinied after being called "you quite vexing gentlemen." As Corporal Harry "Sharpey" Pointer said afterwards, "No one minds being called a '—ing —er of a —ing ——,' but that sounded like he —ing meant it! What does —ing 'vexing' mean, anyway?"

Annoia, or Paranoia Inversa

The belief that you are out to get everyone. This is extremely rare amongst people who are not Dark Lords or similar, since those that by profession are indeed "out to get everyone" do not count. However, Mrs. Everita Pewter, of Dolly Sisters, did visit her doctor complaining of feelings that she was oppressing people, spying on them, reading their mail, picking up their thoughts via strange waves, and so on.

After extensive tests at Unseen University's Department of Invasive Medicine, it was found that Mrs. Pewter had in fact been born as one of Them but had never been taught to use her powers. The *Them* is the secret, unknown, but certainly suspected organization of people whose job it is to interfere with everybody else, ruin their lives, and, in short, mess up the world and then go home laughing. She sought advice about declaring herself as one of *Them*, but once it was explained to her that doing so would involve wearing hooded black robes, conducting secret meetings in vast underground caverns, and manipulating the destiny of millions on a twenty-four-hour basis, possibly while fondling a fluffy white cat, she realized that this would mean missing bridge club on Wednesdays; and since in any case cats gave Mrs. Pewter hay fever, she opted instead for a decoction of willow bark for whenever the voices in her head got too bad.

Planets

An ailment peculiar to people working in conditions of stress in high magical environments. This can sometimes cause a breakdown in the inhibitory circuits which prevent every individual's belief that he or she is the centre of the universe from being broadcast to the universe at large. The usual result is that small imaginary planets will appear and begin to orbit the sufferer's head. Strictly speaking the whole universe will eventually begin to orbit them as well, but the effect is so slight that it is in practice restricted to small items within a few feet.

History records that the wizard Roraty Williams suffered from chronic planets for several years, and one of them developed quite an advanced civilization which sent a small fleet of flying ships to colonize his head. A helpful and caring man, for some years he never wore a hat.

Scroopism

Many people know about Thomas Bowdler, who published an edition of Shakespeare's works with all the offensive bits cut out. Few remember Male Infant Scroop, who had an overwhelming urge to add rude bits to books and songs not originally intended to contain any. This began at quite a young age, with the scrawling of words like "nikkers" and "bum" in the margins of his schoolbooks (his problem was exacerbated by a lifelong inability to spell) but, after he received a large legacy at the age of twenty-one, he was able to reprint entire books that had been "scrooped." These were substituted for the publisher's copies, which they otherwise resembled in every respect, when bookshop staff were not looking.

For several months the only result was a noticeable upsurge in the sales of several titles. Things came to a head, however, when a Miss Epetheme Slaybell's small, privately published volume entitled *Thoughts from a Country Garden* won several highly contested literary awards, and was praised by a judge for its "bold and controversial stance on the subject of primroses."

Mr. Scroop died aged eighty-four, and is buried in Small Gods Cemetery, Ankh-Morpork. His tombstone, including the inscription, may be inspected by private arrangement with the head gravedigger, since in deference to public opinion it is kept wrapped in plain brown paper.

Signitus

A minor but chronic ailment, which causes the sufferer to groan and sometimes run away at the sight of anyone holding more than three books. Brandy has been found to relieve the symptoms, possibly with the addition of more brandy.

Bursaritis (chronic Con-tinence)

The illusion that you have brought hundreds of people a long way in order to celebrate something that doesn't really exist. Symptoms are manic depression, a fixed waxy smile, and a tendency, unless physically prevented from doing so, to sell T-shirts at people. Those afflicted may shout things like "Only nineteen hundred seventy-eight mugs to sell before we break even!" WARNING: sufferers may spontaneously combust if woken suddenly from their trancelike state, and it is best to humour them until they wake up of their own accord. Be kind to these people. It is not their fault.

These notes were supplied by Dr. Peristyle Slack, Ankh-Morpork Guild of Barber-Surgeons—"Come to Us for a Close Shave."

THUD: A HISTORICAL PERSPECTIVE

Thud: The Discworld Board Game, Trevor Truran, 2002

We get at least one approach every month about Discworld board games. Many of them are fine, but too often the Discworld name has been pasted on to something generic, or Discworld history would need a major rewrite in order to fit the game. Letters burble: "In this game there is a big war between the wizards and the witches . . ." Uh, no, I don't think there is.

But Trevor Truran, who designs games the way other people breathe, came up with something good in "Koom Valley"—the game's working title. It was what I'd asked for: a true Discworld game, a game that could reasonably exist and be played there. It pitches dwarfs against trolls—a conflict hallowed by time—and, in order to play a complete game you have to play both sides, which was a specification I hadn't laid down but which was exactly what I wanted. A game which forces you to think and play like your hereditary enemy could be extremely useful to a thoughtful author. It had the right feel, in short, and slotted neatly into Discworld history.

It looked easy to play, but championship players have told me it can stretch the mind more than chess. It also gave me the germ of a plot, which quite soon afterwards got written.*

All that remained was to choose the name, which was obvious . . .

The role of games in the histories of both dwarfs and trolls has been very important.

Perhaps the most famous was the dwarfish game of *Hnaflbafl-sniflwhifltafl*, devised by the cunning inventor Morose Strongin-thearm for Hugen, Low King of the Dwarfs. Hugen had asked for a game that would teach young dwarfs the virtues of preparedness, strategy, boldness, and quick thinking, and Morose came up with a board game that has some early resemblance to the Thud board.

The game swept through the dwarfish world, and was very popular. Hugen, being well pleased, asked Morose what he wanted as a reward. The inventor is on record as saying: "If it please you, your majesty, I ask for nothing more than that you should place one plk [a small gold piece then in general circulation] on the first square, two on the second, four on the third, and so on until the board is filled."

The king readily agreed to this, and had a sack of gold brought from the treasury. However, the count had not been going on for very long before it became clear that what Morose had asked for was, in fact, all the gold in the universe.

This presented a problem for the king, who had given his word, but he solved it by producing his axe and ordering two of his servants to drag Morose over to the window, where the light was better. At this point Morose hastily amended his request to "as much gold as he could carry," whereupon Hugen agreed and merely had one of Morose's arms broken. "For," he said, "all should know that while *Hnaflbaflsniflwhifltafl* teaches preparedness, strategy, boldness, and

---

*And was called, amazingly enough, *Thud!*

quick thinking, it is also important to know when not to be too *drhg'hgin* clever by half."

Troll games are closely bound up with troll religion and some are quite hard to understand. There is a game like a simplified form of chess, in which play consists of putting the pieces on the board and waiting for them to move, and another in which stones are thrown up into the air and players bet on whether or not they will come down. Quite a lot of money can be won that way.

Koom Valley

The traditional enmity between dwarfs and trolls has been explained away by one simple statement: one species is made of rock, the other is made of miners. But in truth the enmity is there because no one can remember when it wasn't, and so it continues because everything is done in completely justifiable revenge for the revenge that was taken in response to the revenge for the vengeance that was taken earlier, and so on. Humans never do this sort of thing, much.

There are at least three sites in Koom claiming to be *the* Koom Valley and at least fourteen major battles are now believed to have been fought there, wherever *there* turns out to be.

The most likely site of Koom Valley, which is in Koom Valley, is a lonely, forebidding place. Even storm clouds go around it. It has been suggested by some wizards in the History Department at Unseen University that the rock formations in the valley, in the path of the prevailing winds, vibrate at a frequency that causes considerable unease and ill temper in the brains of dwarfs, trolls, and men, but attempts to prove this experimentally have failed three times because of fights breaking out amongst the researchers.

The most recent battle involved a party of young dwarfs from Ankh-Morpork, who were visiting the area as part of a cultural tour. City dwarfs feel that it is very important for their offspring to stay in touch with the roots of dwarfishness, and often send them back to Copperhead or Überwald for what is known as some "mine time." On this day, unfortunately, a party of young trolls were also visiting the area for very similar reasons, and after some name-calling the two tour groups fell to fighting and gave a very spirited re-creation of the earlier battles.

Thud

The game of Thud was devised as an alternative to the fighting. It was considered by some older dwarfs and trolls that a nonfatal means of contest might be a boon to peace in the mountains and, besides, they were running out of people. And, in recognition of the general state of all unsuccessful fighters in the wars, it is a game of two halves.

For according to the trollish philosopher Plateau, "if you wants to understan' an enemy, you gotta walk a mile in his shoes. Den, if he's still your enemy, at least you're a mile away and he's got no shoes."

Legend says that a large war party of dwarfs and a smaller one of trolls were hunting one another in the valley, and that on this occasion the leader of the trolls tried an artful strategy. Usually, both groups would hunt each other among the big rocks that litter the valley, but this time the troll leader positioned his company right out in the middle of a stretch of open ground, reasoning that the dwarfs would never look there.

"After all," he is recorded as saying, "dey always find us when we hide behind fings 'cos dey look behind fings, so if we stands out in the open they won't find us *'cos dere's nuffin to look behind.*"

This major step in trollish thinking had some success because of the heavy fog that, most unusually, had fallen that morning. However, it lifted shortly after sunrise, and the trolls were, to the confoundment of what seemed like impeccable logic, immediately spotted. Battle ensued, both sides claiming foul play on the part of the other, and both sides claiming to have won.

The Thud game seeks to re-create this and has been credited with seriously reducing the number of major wars between dwarfs and trolls, replacing them instead with innumerable barroom scuffles in which Thud boards, and sometimes pieces, are used as the weapons. But since this becomes merely a police matter, it counts as peace . . .

A Few Words from
Lord Havelock Vetinari

On the occasion of the twinning of Ankh-Morpork with Wincanton, 2002

This address was written by me, Terry Pratchett, and delivered with appropriate solemnity by Stephen Briggs, who has often played the part of Lord Vetinari in amateur dramatic plays: frankly, it's hard to get him out of the costume! A bewildered bystander, I watched the twinning, which was of course attended by many, many fans wearing strange and exotic garments, in some cases quite possibly the same garments that they wear every day—but even they were very nearly outdone by the people of Ankh-Morpork who came out dressed, as they say, "en fête." It was one of those occasions when sometime afterwards you wake up and think "Did that really happen?" And, on enquiring, I am very glad to hear that it did.

My friends . . .

It is with extreme pleasure that I welcome this—I believe—very first twinning between one real and one apparently unreal city. I say apparently because here in Ankh-Morpork we are taking firm steps to make it clear to our citizens that there is indeed a place called Wincanton and that it hasn't just been made up.

Fortunately we in Ankh-Morpork have the advantage of being the home of Unseen University, whose magical library potentially contains any book that will ever be written anywhere. And it was here, after some searching, we located *A Specially Written Guide to Wincanton.*

We learned that it is a town noted for the extreme wisdom of its men and the unsurpassed beauty of its women, for its racecourse and for its traditional manufacture of some wondrous thing known as "bed ticking." Beyond that, it would appear that it does what my town does, which is to buckle down and make sure that tomorrow happens.

But we noted with particular interest its provision of large breakfasts to the passing world. According to the wizards of Unseen University, who are no strangers to the art of the knife and fork, this is surely one of the noblest activities of mankind. We find, though, that after provisioning the hungry traveller, the citizens of Wincanton let them continue on their way with most of their money intact, an oversight which would not be allowed in my own city, let me assure you.

Since an experimental portal was accidentally opened in the High Street, the citizenry may have noticed, in recent years, the occasional strange-garbed yet free-spending visitor from my world, just as we have occasionally received lost souls looking for a really good breakfast or the way back to a place called "the Ae Three oh Three." After a meeting with your venerable councillors, it was decided that the only way to resolve the problem was to make this link formal.

And thus to the people of Wincanton we most heartily extend

our hand of friendship, with the other hand hidden behind our backs, and I for one am looking forward to some big sausages and hearing my bed tick.

Lord Havelock Vetinari
Patrician of Ankh-Morpork

Death and What Comes Next

Time online games, 2004

This was written for the online game TimeHunt, in which each story incorporated a hidden phrase.

It's relevant to the story, it's still in there, you need the mind of a fan to find it, and I bend the rules a little—or, rather, there are exceptions to the rule.

I rather liked the idea of Heaven being a logical certainty . . .

When Death met the philosopher, the philosopher said, rather excitedly, "At this point, you realize, I'm both dead and not dead."

There was a sigh from Death. Oh dear, one of those, he thought. Is this going to be about quantum again? He hated dealing with philosophers. They always tried to wriggle out of it.

"You see," said the philosopher, while Death, motionless, watched the sands of his life drain through the hourglass, "everything is made of tiny particles, which have the strange property of being in many places at one time. But things made of tiny particles tend to stay in one place at one time, which does not seem right according to quantum theory. May I continue?"

YES, BUT NOT INDEFINITELY, said Death. EVERYTHING IS TRANSIENT. He did not take his gaze away from the tumbling sand.

"Well, then, if we agree that there are an infinite number of universes, then the problem is solved! If there are an unlimited number of universes, this bed can be in millions of them, all at the same time!"

DOES IT MOVE?

"What?"

Death nodded at the bed. CAN YOU FEEL IT MOVING? he said.

"No, because there are a million versions of me, too. And . . . here is the good bit . . . in some of them I am not about to pass away! Anything is possible!"

Death tapped the handle of his scythe as he considered this.

AND YOUR POINT IS . . . ?

"Well, I'm not exactly dying, correct? You are no longer such a certainty."

There was a sigh from Death. Space, he thought. That was the trouble. It was never like this on worlds with everlastingly cloudy skies. But once humans saw all that space, their brains expanded to try to fill it up.

"No answer, eh?" said the dying philosopher. "Feel a bit old-fashioned, do we?"

THIS IS A CONUNDRUM, CERTAINLY, said Death. Once they prayed, he thought. Mind you, he'd never been sure that prayer worked, either. He thought for a while. AND I SHALL ANSWER IT IN THIS MANNER, he added. YOU LOVE YOUR WIFE?

"What?"

THE LADY WHO HAS BEEN LOOKING AFTER YOU. YOU LOVE HER?

"Yes. Of course."

CAN YOU THINK OF ANY CIRCUMSTANCES WHERE, WITHOUT YOUR PERSONAL HISTORY CHANGING IN ANY WAY, YOU WOULD AT

THIS MOMENT PICK UP A KNIFE AND STAB HER? said Death. FOR EXAMPLE?

"Certainly not!"

BUT YOUR THEORY SAYS THAT YOU MUST. IT IS EASILY POSSIBLE WITHIN THE PHYSICAL LAWS OF THE UNIVERSE, AND THEREFORE MUST HAPPEN, AND HAPPEN MANY TIMES. EVERY MOMENT IS A BILLION, BILLION MOMENTS, AND IN THOSE MOMENTS ALL THINGS THAT ARE POSSIBLE ARE INEVITABLE. ALL TIME, SOONER OR LATER, BOILS DOWN TO A MOMENT.

"But of course we can make choices between—"

ARE THERE CHOICES? EVERYTHING THAT CAN HAPPEN, MUST HAPPEN. YOUR THEORY SAYS THAT FOR EVERY UNIVERSE THAT'S FORMED TO ACCOMMODATE YOUR "NO," THERE MUST BE ONE TO ACCOMMODATE YOUR "YES." BUT YOU SAID YOU WOULD NEVER COMMIT MURDER. THE FABRIC OF THE COSMOS TREMBLES BEFORE YOUR TERRIBLE CERTAINTY. YOUR MORALITY BECOMES A FORCE AS STRONG AS GRAVITY. And, thought Death, space certainly has a lot to answer for.

"Was that sarcasm?"

ACTUALLY, NO. I AM IMPRESSED AND INTRIGUED, said Death. THE CONCEPT YOU PUT BEFORE ME PROVES THE EXISTENCE OF TWO HITHERTO MYTHICAL PLACES. SOMEWHERE, THERE IS A WORLD WHERE EVERYONE MADE THE RIGHT CHOICE, THE MORAL CHOICE, THE CHOICE THAT MAXIMIZED THE HAPPINESS OF THEIR FELLOW CREATURES. OF COURSE, THAT ALSO MEANS THAT SOMEWHERE ELSE IS THE SMOKING REMNANT OF THE WORLD WHERE THEY DID NOT ...

"Oh, come on! I know what you're implying, and I've never believed in any of that Heaven and Hell nonsense!"

The room was growing darker. The blue gleam along the edge of the Reaper's scythe was becoming more obvious.

ASTONISHING, said Death. REALLY ASTONISHING. LET ME PUT FORWARD ANOTHER SUGGESTION: THAT YOU ARE NOTHING MORE THAN A LUCKY SPECIES OF APE THAT IS TRYING TO UNDERSTAND

THE COMPLEXITIES OF CREATION VIA A LANGUAGE THAT EVOLVED IN ORDER TO TELL ONE ANOTHER WHERE THE RIPE FRUIT WAS.

Fighting for breath, the philosopher managed to say, "Don't be silly."

THE REMARK WAS NOT INTENDED AS DEROGATORY, said Death. UNDER THE CIRCUMSTANCES, YOU HAVE ACHIEVED A GREAT DEAL.

"We've certainly escaped from outmoded superstitions!"

WELL DONE, said Death. THAT'S THE SPIRIT. I JUST WANTED TO CHECK.

He leaned forward.

AND YOU ARE AWARE OF THE THEORY THAT THE STATE OF SOME TINY PARTICLES IS INDETERMINATE UNTIL THE MOMENT THEY ARE OBSERVED? A CAT IN A BOX IS OFTEN MENTIONED.

"Oh, yes," said the philosopher.

GOOD, said Death. He got to his feet as the last of the light died, and smiled.

I SEE YOU . . .

A Collegiate Casting-out
of Devilish Devices

Times Higher Education Supplement, 13 May 2005

Well, they asked for it and they got it, because at that time there was some debate around issues to do with government money being given to universities and universities not being particularly happy about being told what to do by governments. Fortunately for Unseen University, they don't have to ask anybody for anything. And only now can I reveal that this short passage owes a little something to the Thursday afternoon meetings I used to have when I was chairman of the Society of Authors, where I learned the importance of listening for the tea trolley and the etiquette of the chocolate biscuits, surely an essential component of real committee work.

It was a Thursday afternoon. Unseen University's college council liked their Thursday afternoon meetings. The Council Chamber, with its stained-glass image of Archchancellor Sloman Discovering the Special Theory of Slood, was always nice and warm and there was a distant prospect of tea and chocolate biscuits at half-past three.

Just as the biscuit hour approached, Archchancellor Mustrum Ridcully drummed his fingers on the battered leather of the table.

"Next item, gentlemen," he said, "and it appears that Lord Vetinari, our *gracious* ruler, has seen fit to confront us with a little . . . test. Possibly we have annoyed him, in some way, committed some little faux pas—"

"This is about Mayhap Street, isn't it?" said the Dean. "Still not turned up, has it?"

"There is nothing the matter with Mayhap Street, Dean," said Ridcully sharply. "It is merely temporarily displaced, that's all. I am assured the rest of the continuum will catch up with it no later than Thursday. It was an accident that was waiting to happen—"

"Well, only waiting for a thaumic discharge that happened because you said there was no way it could possibly—" the Dean began. He was clearly enjoying himself.

"Dean! We are going to move on and put this behind us!" Ridcully snapped.

"Excuse me, Archchancellor?" said Ponder Stibbons, who was Head of Inadvisably Applied Magic and also the University's Praelector, a position interpreted at UU as "the one who gets given the tedious jobs."

"Yes, Stibbons?"

"It may be a good idea to put it behind us *before* we move on, sir," said Ponder. "That way it will be farther behind us when we do, in fact, move."

"Good point, that man. See to it," said Ridcully. He turned his attention once again to the ominous manila folder in front of him. "Anyway, gentlemen, his lordship has appointed a Mr. A. E. Pessimal, a man of whom I know little, as Inspector of Universities. His job, I suspect, is to drag us kicking and no doubt screaming into the Century of the Fruitbat."

"That was in fact the last century, Archchancellor," said Ponder.

"Well, we are hard to drag and very good at kicking," said Ridcully. "He has made a few little, ah, suggestions for improvement . . ."

"Really? This should be fun," said the Dean.

Ridcully pushed the folder to his right.

"Over to you, Mr. Stibbons."

"Yes, Archchancellor. Er . . . thank you. Um. As you know, the city has always waived all taxes on the University—"

"Because they know what would happen if they tried it," said the Dean, with some satisfaction.

"Yes," said Ponder. "And, then again, no. I fear we are past the times when a little shape-changing or a couple of fireballs would do the trick. That is not the modern spirit. It would be a good idea to at least *examine* Mr. Pessimal's suggestions . . ."

There was a general shrugging. It would at least pass the time until the tea turned up.

"Firstly," said Ponder, "Mr. Pessimal wants to know what we do here."

"Do? We are the premier college of magic!" said Ridcully.

"But do we teach?"

"Only if no alternative presents itself," said the Dean. "We show 'em where the library is, give 'em a few little chats, and graduate the survivors. If they run into any problems, my door is always meta-phorically open."

"Metaphorically, sir?" said Ponder.

"Yes. But technically, of course, it's locked."

"Explain to him that we don't *do* things, Stibbons," said the Lecturer in Recent Runes. "We are *academics.*"

"Interestin' idea, though," said Ridcully, winking at Ponder. "What *do* you do, Senior Wrangler?"

A hunted look crossed the Senior Wrangler's face. "Well, er," he said, clearing his throat. "The post of Senior Wrangler at Unseen University is, most unusually—"

"Yes, but what do you *do*? And have you been doing more of it in the past six months than in the previous six?"

"Well, if we're asking that kind of question, Archchancellor, what do you do?" said the Dean testily.

"I administer, Dean," said Ridcully calmly.

"Then we must be doing *something*, otherwise you'd have nothing to administrate."

"That comment strikes at the very heart of the bureaucratic principle, Dean, and I shall ignore it."

"You see, Mr. Pessimal wonders why we don't publish the results of, er, whatever it is we do," said Ponder.

"*Publish*?" said the Lecturer in Recent Runes.

"*Results*?" said the Chair of Indefinite Studies.

"Ook?" said the Librarian.

"Brazeneck College publishes its *Journal of Irreducible Research* four times a year now," said Ponder meekly.

"Yes. Six copies," said Ridcully.

"No wizard worth his salt tells other wizards what he's up to!" snapped the Lecturer in Recent Runes. "Besides, how can you measure thinking? You can count the tables a carpenter makes, but what kind of rule could measure the amount of thought necessary to define the essence of tableosity?"

"Exactly!" said the Chair of Indefinite Studies. "I myself have been working on my Theory of Anything for fifteen years! The amount of thought that has gone into it is astonishing! Those six-seven pages have been hard won, I can tell you!"

"And I've seen some of those Brazeneck papers," said Ridcully. "They've got titles like 'Diothumatic Aspects of Cheese in Mice,' or possibly it was Mice in Cheese. Or maybe Chess."

"And what was it about?" said the Dean.

"Oh, I don't think it was for reading. It was for having written," said the Archchancellor. "Anyway, no one knows what Diothumics is, except that it's probably magic with the crusts cut off."

"Er . . . nevertheless, Mr. Pessimal does point out that Brazeneck is attracting students, to the general benefit of the city," said Ponder. "In fact he suggests that we ourselves might even consider, er, advertising for students." He paused, because of the sudden frigid quality of the atmosphere, and plunged on: "In order to attract young men, in fact, who would not normally consider wizarding as a profession. He notes that Brazeneck gives all new students a free crystal ball and a voucher for a free frog or froglike creature."

"Make ourselves *attractive* to students?" said the Archchancellor. "Mister Stibbons, the whole Idea of a university is that it should be *hard* to get into. Remember Dean Rouster? He used to set *traps* to stop students attending his lectures! 'I'll tap talent from all backgrounds,' he used to say, 'but a lad who can't spot a trip wire is no good to me!' He reckoned any student who didn't open a door very carefully and look where he's putting his feet would only be a burden to the profession. You see, trying to be nice to students means you end up with courses like Comparative Fretwork and graduates who think 'thank you' is one word and can look at a sign sayin' 'Human Resources Department' without detecting a whiff of brimstone."

"I have to tell you, sir, that Mr. Pessimal is suggesting that we accept an intake of forty per cent nontraditional students," said Ponder Stibbons.

"What does that mean?" said the Senior Wrangler.

"Well, er . . ." Ponder began, but the council had already resorted to definition-by-hubbub.

"We take in all sorts as it is," said the Dean.

"Does he mean people who are not *traditionally* good at magic?" said the Chair of Indefinite Studies.

"Ridiculous!" said the Dean. "Forty per cent duffers?"

"Exactly!" said the Archchancellor. "That means we'd have to find enough clever people to make up *over half the student intake*! We'd never manage it. If they were clever already, they wouldn't need to go to university! No, we'll stick to an intake of one hundred per cent young fools, thank you. Bring 'em in stupid, send them away clever, that's the UU way!"

"Some of them arrive *thinking* they're clever, of course," said the Chair of Indefinite Studies.

"Yes, but we soon disabuse them of that," said the Dean happily. "What is a university for if it isn't to tell you that everything you think you know is wrong?"

"Well put, that man!" said Ridcully. "Ignorance is the key! That's how the Dean got where he is today!"

"Thank you, Archchancellor," said the Dean. "I shall take that as a compliment. Carefully directed ignorance is the key to all knowledge."

"I think the inspector means people who by accident of birth, upbringing, background, or early education would not meet the usual entrance requirements," said Ponder quickly.

"Really? Good idea," said Ridcully. "And are we to take it that for his part he intends to make a point of hiring clerks who aren't very good at sums and file everything under 'S' for 'stuff'?"

"He doesn't appear to say so—"

"How strange. But, you see, we're a university, Mr. Stibbons, not a bandage. We can't just wave a magic wand and make everything better!"

"Actually, sir—"

Ridcully waved a hand irritably. "Yes, yes, all right, I know. We can just wave a magic wand and make everything better. Except, of course, that making everything better by magic only makes things much, much worse!"

"Interestingly, he does ask if we have an ethics committee," said Ponder.

"Ah, a committee," said Ridcully. "Just so. Well, gentlemen, I think

I can gauge the sense of the meeting. I propose that we inform the inspector that we are giving his suggestions our urgent consideration. Put it on the agenda for this time next year, Mr. Stibbons. No, perhaps the year after next. You can't hurry urgency, I've always said so."

Minutes of the Meeting to Form the Proposed Ankh-Morpork Federation of Scouts

August 2007

This is, I think, what used to be called in Victorian times a "squib," and it was written for one of the events put on by Bernard Pearson (also known as the Cunning Artificer), who has his shop in Wincanton, Somerset: to ring the changes he organized a mock jamboree in the playing fields of that fine town in August 2007.

In the Chair: Captain Carrot (Ankh-Morpork City Watch)
Also present: Josiah Boggis (Thieves' Guild)
                Miss Alice Band (Assassins' Guild)
                Sergeant Detritus (Ankh-Morpork City Watch)
                Grag Bashful Bashfulsson (Dwarf Community
                    Leader)

> Miss Estressa Partleigh (Campaign for Equal
>   Heights)
> Crysophrase (Silicon Anti-Defamation League)
> John Smith (Überwald League of Temperance)
> Lord Vetinari (Purely as an Observer)

In his opening remarks, Captain Carrot referred to the current problem of delinquency of young people in the city, which has recently been the subject of many articles in the *Times*.

Miss Partleigh interjected that this was because there was nothing for them to do.

Lord Vetinari observed that in fact there was a vast range of things for them to do, running from petty theft to armed gang warfare, and that therefore the question was one of finding something for them to do that, if at all possible, did not actually involve the death of innocent, or presumably innocent, bystanders.

Mr. John Smith said that perhaps there could be something involving hats. In his experience, hats had a remarkable stabilizing effect.

Captain Carrot opined that much of the trouble, even now, was the rivalry between troll and dwarf gangs, although there was some welcome evolution in that now some trolls were joining dwarf gangs and vice versa.

Mr. Boggis vouchsafed that some effort should be made to teach newcomers to the city the Ankh-Morpork way of doing things.

Lord Vetinari observed that surely the problem was they had gleefully picked up the Ankh-Morpork way of doing things and were doing these things very enthusiastically.

Captain Carrot told the meeting that Sergeant Detritus had put forward an idea based on the ancient Troll tradition Haruga which roughly translated as "scouts." These were young male trolls who acted as trackers and lookout men for older warriors. It was, he said, a morale-building opportunity and he had wondered if it could be adapted to this problem.

Mr. Boggis said that this very much sounded like the street urchins who worked for his guild, and was a promising idea.

Captain Carrot said the object of the exercise should be to give young people of all shapes and sizes an opportunity to meet together in the absence of heavy weaponry.

Lord Vetinari observed that then what did he propose that they do?

Crysophrase said that he was a scout when he was nothing more than a little lad and it made a troll of him. As he recalled, they spent their time learning tracking and tying knots.

Mr. Boggis asked what it was the trolls tracked.

Crysophrase vouchsafed that they tracked dwarfs.

Mr. Boggis then enquired what they tied knots in.

Crysophrase said dwarfs.

Lord Vetinari observed that this was probably a good start, but could do with some tweaking of the fine detail. Certainly some activities for some small symbolic rewards might give young people more of a sense of achievement than is engendered by jumping up and down on somebody else's head.

Miss Band pointed out that young Assassins, by the very fact of their job description, did occasionally have to indulge in activities not far removed from that very thing.

Lord Vetinari observed that they will not be allowed to do this while in the scout hut.

Grag Bashfulsson commented it would be very useful if the organization could promote some moral values to its members, or at the very least, explain to them what these were. It would be nice if the young people could be clean in thought, word, and deed.

Sergeant Detritus said that this had been an important part of the troll scouts in order to stop them playing with their clubs all day.

Miss Partleigh said the social background of many of the potential members makes it very difficult for some of them to be clean.

Lord Vetinari observed that this was fine, just so long as they weren't killing people. Personally, he would be happy to accept cleanliness in deed. They could say and think whatever they wanted. He was prepared to put the backing of the city behind this proposal and looked forward to seeing improvement in the behaviour of young males of all species.

Miss Partleigh asked: What about the girls?

Sergeant Detritus said that girls were strictly not allowed, on account of causing a lack of cleanliness in thought, word, and deed.

Grag Bashfulsson pointed out that many modern female dwarfs would wish to be recognized as girls.

Captain Carrot said there was no reason, surely, why a similar organiz-ation could not be set up for young women. Obviously given the nature of the dwarf approach to apparent sexual orienta-tion, any dwarf could join either the boy scouts or girl scouts but not keep changing from one to the other. He was certain that peo-ple from the guilds and other responsible citizens would be happy to donate their time in setting these young people on the proper path. He would be prepared, along with Sergeant Angua, to teach woodcraft and wilderness survival.

Mr. Boggis said that surviving in a wilderness was a piece of cake compared to five minutes in an alleyway in Ankh-Morpork, so he for his part would see that young people could also learn how to get down to the shops with all their teeth intact.

At this point there was considerable discussion among the com-mittee about activities that could be arranged, and it was agreed to hold, during the summer, an open-air meeting to launch the Ankh-Morpork Scouting and possibly Urban Survival Federation.

The Ankh-Morpork Football Association Hall of Fame Playing Cards

Famous Footballers of Ankh-Morpork,
September 2009

Another squib! This time it was to celebrate the launch of Unseen
Academicals: *various teams of Discworld fans and locals battled it
out on the playing fields of Wincanton, and, as I recall, some of the
ladies were somewhat dishevelled, which amazingly enough didn't
interfere with the game. Of course I had to come up with the funny
names.*

Unseen Academicals

[1] *Archchancellor Mustrum Ridcully,* DThau, DM, DS, DMn, DG,
DD, DCL, DMPhil, DMS, DCM, DW, BElL

Sometimes attempts to shoot the ball at the ~~enemy~~ opposition. Mustrum Ridcully's preferred technique, however, is to kick the ball at full force at the nearest attacker and collect it again on the rebound as his opponent curls up on the ground. This has caused a number of problems for opposing players until they found a use that could be made of a common metal soup plate, two holes, and a length of string.

[69] *Professor Bengo Macarona,* DThau (Bug), DMaus (Chubb), Magistaludorum (QIS), Octavium (Hons), PHGK (Blit), DMSK, Mack, DThou (Bra), Visiting Professor in Chickens [Jahn the Conqueror University (Floor 2, Shrimp Packers Building, Genua)], Primo Octo (Deux), Visiting Professor of Blit/Slood Exchanges (Al Khali), KCbfJ, Reciprocating Professor of Blit Theory (Unki), DThau (Unki), Didimus Supremuis (Unki), Emeritus Professor in Blit Substrate Determinations (Chubb), Chair of Blit and Music Studies (Quirm College for Young Ladies)

A highly skilled player from Genua, well known for having many different approaches to the task in hand. Excellent striker, with a regrettable tendency to handle the ball when excited.

[7b] *Professor Rincewind,* Egregious Professor of Cruel and Unusual Geography (UU), Chair of Experimental Serendipity (UU), Reader in Slood Dynamics (UU), Chair for the Public Misunderstanding of Magic (UU), Chair of Approximate Accuracy (UU)

Rincewind is possibly the fastest man on any field. Unfortunately, he frequently forgets to take the ball with him. Interestingly, the verve with which he speeds away clouds the perception of his opponents who find it difficult to believe that the ball is actually behind them now and is heading in the opposite direction.

[1.618] *Dr. Ponder Stibbons,* HEM (UU), DThau (UU), Reader in Nonvolatile Intelligence (UU), Cantoride Speaker in Slood Refurgance (UU)

Player / Coach. Used to lose his glasses early in the match and now has them taped to his head. Tactical thinker, some of the time. One of his boots flies off for no known reason.

[9] *Gryffid Tabernacle Evans* (Evans the Striped)

The only player in the UU squad who is officially dead. He is, in fact, all that remains of the last UU sports master whose ghost hangs on in the enormous brass whistle that was all he left behind. Regrettably, people sometimes forget that blowing the whistle will cause them to be temporarily overwhelmed by the spirit of the late Evans who will then send everyone on a long cross-country run in their underwear for forgetting their sports kit.

[8] *Dr. J. Hicks or Hix,* Professor in ~~Unspeakable Dark Arts~~ Post Mortem Communications (UU), DThau, Impissimus Holder of the Silver Skull (3rd Class)

Under university statute is allowed, expected, and required to foul. After all, there is no point in being the official bad person if you play by the rules. The only player who is prepared to wear the number eight. Will occasionally leave free tickets to his notorious amateur dramatic presentations in order to demoralize the opposition.

[1] *The Librarian,* DThau, Professor of L-space Studies

A second number one (because he sulked). Born to defend the goal, since he can swing from the posts and very nearly reach the total width of the goal while standing in the middle.

[10] *Alf Nobbs (No Relation),* One Year Long Service Bledlow Medal (UU), Five Year Long Service Bledlow Medal (UU), Ten Year Long Service Bledlow Medal (UU)

A good all-round player, whose talents have been honed by chasing generations of students after the pubs have shut. Feels he has a mission in life to restore the good name of the Nobbs clan. Wears enormously large and heavy boots. People have learned to flee at the sound.

[206] *Charlie* (No other name known)
Hasn't yet taken the field for UU since the Football Association of Ankh-Morpork is divided on the eligibility of a walking skeleton. Nevertheless he turns up to training and as Dr. Hicks points out, is very good for anatomical practice and carries the magic sponge.

[4] *Trevor Likely* (Education unknown)
Not formally a team member, although has played once for UU. The most highly skilled man alive with the traditional tin can, which he can practically cause to defy gravity, but is known to have difficulty with the standard spherical ball.

[9] *Mr. Nutt* (Education: More than you could possibly imagine)
Player / Coach. Perhaps the most skilled tactician ever to lace up a boot. Is possibly the only player ever to use the word *zeitgeist* in everyday conversation. Particularly skilled in the philosophy of the game, he can get an axiom containing a paradox past an opposing player before the man even notices that his shorts have fallen down.

[1001] *The Luggage*
Surprisingly, not allowed on the team because of its total incapability of understanding what a game is. Also has too many feet.

Players from other teams

[7] *Jimmy Wilkins* (Pigsty Hill Pork Packers)

Jimmy Wilkins soon excelled himself as captain of the Porkies with his ability to turn cartwheels on the pitch and shoot upside down. Often this has bewildered unsuspecting goalkeepers sufficiently for the ball to have hit the back of the net before they have even realized that it was on its way.

[4] *J. W. Rickett* (Pigsty Hill Pork Packers)

A master of fine ball control, Kick it Rickett has been known to run half the length of the pitch with the ball apparently balanced on the tip of his boot. He has only failed to become a true football great because of his absolute reluctance to ever pass the ball to anybody else and once famously stormed off the pitch when one of his team tried it. As they said, he was a great player, if only you jumped out and tripped him up at the right moment.

[1] *Charlie Barton* (Treacle Mine Tuesday—Goalkeeper)

Very seldom does any ball get past Charlie (Big Boy) Barton who, it is rumoured, has to be crowbarred from the goal at the end of the match. This is a result of his phenomenal pie consumption and has led to the Ankh-Morpork Football Association declaring that the Miners' goal-mouth must be at least twice as wide as that of their opponents so that there may be room for the ball to be put in.

[6] *Aknon Smyth* (The Dimmers)

Stalwart of the Dimmers, Holy Aknon, as he is known, belongs to a small sect that has to say prayers every fifteen minutes. Fans are used to him dropping to his knees in the middle of the game which, coincidentally, trips up at least one opposing player. Following this, the game has to go on hold until he finishes his prayers, after which he will spring away in some hitherto unknown direction. The Ankh-Morpork Football Association is wrestling with this conundrum.

David "Dave" Likely (Education: none)

Deceased. All-time holder of the highest lifetime score (four goals) in the street version of the game. Dave Likely is the archetypical footballer, from his huge baggy shorts to his hobnail boots. Unfortunately he refused to wear any head protection at all, which is why he is the *late* Dave Likely.

[2] *Andy Shank* (The Dimmers)

Andy Shank is a leading "face" amongst the Dimwell supporters as well as in the Ankh-Morpork Shove. His father is the feared captain of the Dimwell team and Andy may well inherit the title due to his unbridled savagery and skill in all forms of close combat. He inspires fear in his associates almost as much as in his enemies. Known to the City Watch as a particularly bad lot he is certainly one to keep an eye out for, all the time if possible.

[8] *Joseph Hoggett* (Captain—Pigsty Hill Pork Packers)

A skilled player of the old game of street football (aka Poor Boys' Fun, the Game, the Shove). Elected captain of United at the meeting of the captains of all the city's major football teams. Very strong—it is reputed that he can lift a pig carcass in each hand.

[6] *Swithin Dustworthy* (Captain—The Cockbill Boars)

[9] *Harry Capstick* (The Cockbill Boars)

Other players: Tosher Atkinson, Jimmy the Spoon, Spanner, Mrs. Atkinson, Willy Piltdown, Micky Pulford, The Brisket Boys (F and Q)

Referee

Archchancellor of Brazeneck (formerly known as *The Dean*)

The visit by the Archchancellor of the new redbrick university in Pseudopolis to his former colleagues at Unseen Unversity opportunely coincided with the inaugural foot-the-ball match. He was appointed referee and so got to use the haunted whistle of Gryffid Tabernacle Jones, the long deceased sports master of UU. No sportsman, he was known as "two chairs" in his old alma mater due to his immense girth and love of gargantuan meals.

APPENDIX

Deleted extract from "The Sea and Little Fishes"

Granny Weatherwax rose well before dawn next morning, when the frost rimed the trees and she had to take a hammer to the water barrel before she could wash.

The air held the sharp taste of snow to come and the acid smell of foxes.

She went back indoors and prepared one cheese sandwich and made a bottle of cold tea. Then she set out.

It didn't take much more than an hour, going at a sharp pace over the snapping leaves, to get beyond the buzz of human thoughts. Half an hour later she skirted the smouldering stacks of a charcoal burner, and picked up a hint of his dreams and the sharp, deceitful little mind of the cat he kept for company, hunting among the woodpiles.

Then there was no track anymore, only a trail among many. Minds out here were sharper and simpler, and generally thinking of only one thing at a time. Almost always it was food—how to get more, and not be some. Sometimes it was sex, and Granny Weatherwax took care to keep her mind firmly closed at those times. Even squirrels deserved their privacy, the dirty little devils.

For a while she followed the banks of a river, her boots clattering from rock to rock, forever going upward.

Her mind worked better here. When she was down there among people there was the constant whispering of their minds. She couldn't hear what they were thinking, except by dint of enormous concentration. Even the owners of the minds concerned seldom knew what, in the welter of concerns, emotions, worries, and hope, they were actually thinking at any time. Humans had the mushiest minds in the world. It was a relief to be free of all that mental tinnitus.

But there was still a faint buzz, as distracting as the whining of a mosquito in a bedroom. Hunters did venture this far, she knew. And the dwarfs were down below somewhere, although they knew better than to come—

—she turned and stepped between two boulders, into a gap you wouldn't have known was there—

—into this little valley, long and deep, with early snow lurking in every patch of shade. A few trees had been optimistic enough to attempt to grow here.

Granny didn't stop. Her boots splashed through the stream that had carved out this slot in the rocks until she reached the cave. Large though the mouth was, a casual observer might have thought it just another shadow in the wreck of fallen rocks. Then she was in it, facing that sucking silence of all caves everywhere.

And there, in the shadows, was the Witch.

Granny bowed to her—witches never curtsy—and edged past, and on into the caves.

She hadn't been up here for . . . what? Ten years?

The caves wound everywhere under the mountains, and because of the high magical potential in the Ramtops they did not necessarily confine their ramblings to the normal four dimensions.

If you entered some of them, it was rumoured, you would never be seen again. At least, not here. And not now.

But Granny headed directly for one quite near this entrance. It had a particular quality that she felt she needed. Perhaps it was something to do with its shape, or the little crystalline specks that glinted in its walls, but this cave was impervious to thought.

Thought couldn't get in, or out.

She sat down on the sandy floor, alone with her own thoughts.

After a while, they turned up.

There'd been that man down in Sparkle, the one that'd killed those little kids. The people'd sent for her and she'd looked at him and seen the guilt writhing in his head like a red worm, and then she'd taken them to his farm and showed them where to dig, and he'd thrown himself down and asked her for mercy, because he said he'd been drunk and it'd all been done in alcohol.

Her words came back to her. She'd said, in sobriety: end it in hemp.

And they'd dragged him off and hanged him and she'd gone to watch because she owed him that much, and he'd cursed, which was unfair because hanging is a clean death, or at least cleaner than the one he'd have got if the villagers had dared defy her, and she'd seen the shadow of Death come for him, and then behind Death came the smaller, brighter figures, and then—

In the darkness, she rocked.

The villagers had said justice had been done, and she'd lost patience and told them to go home, then, and pray to whatever gods they believed in that it was never done to them. Because the smug face of virtue triumphant could be almost as horrible as wickedness revealed.

The odd thing was, quite a lot of villagers had turned up to his funeral, and there had been mutterings on the lines of, yes, well, but overall he wasn't such a bad chap . . . and anyway, maybe she made him say it. And she'd got the dark looks.

Supposing there was justice for all, after all? For every unheeded beggar, every harsh word, every neglected duty, every slight . . .

Who'd come to her funeral when she died?

Other memories jostled. Other figures marched out into the darkness of the cave.

She'd done things and been places, and found ways to turn anger outwards that had surprised even her. She'd faced down others far more powerful than she was, if only she'd allowed them to believe it. She'd given up so much, but she'd earned a lot. And she'd never, never declare that she doubted her choices. And yet . . . if, all those years ago, she'd made the other choices . . . she wouldn't have known. She'd have led a quiet life. She was certain of this, because sometimes she could sense those other selves, off in the alternatives of time. After all, if you could read minds at a distance, you should certainly be able to pick up your own. A nice quiet life, and then death.

But she'd never set out to be nice. When you went up against some of the opponents she'd met, nice people would finish last, or not even finish.

In truth, deep down, she was aware of a dark desire. Sometimes, the world really had it coming, and endeavouring to see that it didn't get it was a white-knuckle task, every day of her life. Letice would never know that she had been an inch away from . . . from something very, very unpleasant happening to her. But it was an inch that Esme Weatherwax had spent a lifetime constructing, and she'd thought it was tougher than steel. Knowing how bad you could be is a great encouragement to be good.

So she'd been good. She was good at justice. She was good at medicine, particularly that type of medicine which started in the head. She was good at winning. She was good, though she said it herself, at most of the things she set her mind at.

But not nice. She had to admit it. And it seemed that people preferred nice to good.

And there was a terrible temptation. Better witches than her had succumbed. The more you faced the light, the brighter it grew, and one day for the brief respite that it brought you'd look over your shoulder. And you'd see how lovely and rich and dark and beguiling your shadow had become . . .

Nanny Ogg was sitting out in her back garden in the no-nonsense way of old ladies everywhere, legs wide apart for the healthy circulation of the air. She was keeping an eye on one of her sons and two of her grandsons, who were digging her vegetable garden, and occasionally she would give them shouts of encouragement or point out bits that hadn't been done properly.

In her broad lap was a heap of golden leaves from her tobacco harvest, which she was shredding and dipping into her special herbal and honey mixture. After it had matured in her press over the winter, people would come a long way for Ogg's Nutty Shag, Not to Be Smoked for at Least Three Hundred Years before Operating Heavy Machinery.

And occasionally she'd take a swig from the pint pot beside her.

This time, as she reached down for it, she saw the bubbles clear and the surface turn as calm as old tea.

"Flat already?" she said aloud.

She glanced across the village. Rooks were swarming up out of the elm trees in battle order, cawing loudly.

Nanny Ogg ambled into her cottage and went to the scullery, where the milk jugs cooled in the sink. One sniff was enough. What they contained was practically cheese. And it'd been fresh milk an hour ago.

A faint rustling made her look down. Dozens of beetles were running under the door and scuttling into the cracks between the flagstones.

A witch lived by the little signs. Butter wouldn't come, wine became vinegar, spiders ran for cover . . . people thought it meant there was a storm coming, and in a way they were right.

And a witch used what was to hand, too. All that fiddlin' with coloured candles and crystal balls and whatnot, that was fine for them as needed it, but at a pinch you used what you could reach.

In this case she reached down and lifted the heavy wooden lid of the well and looked down into the dark waters.

There was nothing there. But there was never anything in a crystal, either. There was simply emptiness, which said: fill me up.

Nanny's inner eye saw snow, and rock, and the outline of a hooked nose made of stone . . .

"Oh, the daft ole fool," she muttered.

A moment later her son and grandsons saw her burst from the house, carrying her broomstick. She leapt aboard and applied the magic so hard that it bobbed along almost vertically before she was able to force the handle down and point it towards the mountains.

Ten minutes later snow billowed up as she touched down in the little valley. It was hard to find, even from the air. She patted the guardian Witch as she hurried past. She'd never found her frightening, even when she was young.

Some young wizard who'd spent his holidays up here, knocking at rocks with a little hammer, had said the Witch at the mouth of the cave was just the result of dissolved rock dripping and dripping and piling up in a stalagmite for thousands of years. As if that explained anything. It just said how she was made, not why she was here. And the man hadn't gone very far into the cave, she recalled. He'd remembered other things he had to do. The place took men that way.

Her boots splashed into the rock pools as she left the light behind.

She'd tried being alone with her thoughts once, but had never tried it again. It had been too dull.

Oh yes, the things she was ashamed of were here, but she'd never tried to hide them from herself and they were simply memories and held no terror. And here were all the things she'd done that she should have done, and mostly they'd been enjoyable. And there were all the things she'd done that she shouldn't have done, and they'd been fun too. More fun, in many cases. And she'd never regretted them, either, except maybe sometimes when, a little wistfully, she'd regretted she hadn't done them sooner and that occasions for doing them now did not, as it were, arise all that often . . .

"Oh, Esme? What've you done?"

She reached down and pulled at the slumped figure.

"Come on," she said cheerfully, slinging the dead weight across her shoulders. "You don't have to hang around here, thinking. No one ever got anywhere by thinking all the time."

When they were outside she managed to heave Granny onto the stick and strapped her safely with her own striped stockings.

People say things like "lost in thought" and think they mean that state of mind that just precedes "Pardon? I was thinking." But that's just "not paying attention." Lost in thought means that someone may need to come and find you.

She took her home, flying slowly a few feet above the trees in the sunset air, and put her to bed.

Permissions Acknowledgements

All illustrations are by Josh Kirby unless otherwise stated.

Section One

Page 1: hand-painted Christmas card, *c.* 1976. Courtesy Colin Smythe.

Pages 2–3: *Turntables of the Night.* Jacket illustration for *The Flying Sorcerers*, ed. Peter Haining, Souvenir Press, London, 1997.

Pages 4–5: *#ifdefDEBUG* + *"world/enough"* + *"time."* Jacket illustration for *Retter der Ewigkeit*, eds. Erik Simon and Friedal Wahren, Heyne, Munich, 2001.

Pages 6–7: *Hollywood Chickens.* Jacket illustration for *Knights of Madness*, ed. Peter Haining, Souvenir Press, London, 1998.

Page 8: detail of *Theatre of Cruelty.* Cover illustration for W. H. Smith's July/August 1993 issue of *Bookcase* magazine.

Section Two

Page 1: *Discworld.*

Pages 2–3: the first and second versions of the illustration for "The Sea and Little Fishes." The first scene Josh Kirby illustrated was removed from the story when published in *Legends*, ed. Robert Silverberg, Tor, New York, 1998. See Appendix on page 277 for the exiled text.

Pages 4–5: *The Witches* from the CD inlay of Dave Greenslade's music *From the Discworld*, Virgin Records, 1994.

Pages 6–7: *The Unseen University* from the CD inlay of Dave Greenslade's music *From the Discworld*, Virgin Records, 1994.

Page 8: detail of *Discworld* video-game packaging, also called *Discworld: The Trouble with Dragons*. A TWG/Perfect 10 Production, issued by Psygnosis Games, 1995.

Section Three

Page 1: detail of *Rincewind, the Luggage, and Death*. Poster, Isis Publishing, Oxford, 1996.

Pages 2–3: *Mort*. Jacket illustration for the book of the same name, Victor Gollancz, London, 1987.

Pages 4–5: *Ankh-Morpork*. Commissioned for but not used in the CD inlay of Dave Greenslade's music *From the Discworld*. Published in *Josh Kirby: A Cosmic Cornucopia*, text by David Langford, Paper Tiger, London, 1999.

Pages 6–7: jacket illustration for *The First Discworld Novels*, Colin Smythe, Gerrards Cross, 1999.

Page 8: *Terry Pratchett with Some Discworld Characters*. Painted for the *Weekend Guardian*, 23 October 1993.

Printed in the United States
by Baker & Taylor Publisher Services